praise for psychics of oracle bay

Not in the Cards

An Exciting Introduction: Amy's books immediately go to the top of my queue when they are released and they never disappoint. This was an exciting introduction to Oracle Bay and I'm looking forward to getting to know the rest of the inhabitants in future books.

Found Another Great Author!: I didn't know what to expect when I went into this book. The premise of the book sounded like something I would enjoy. At first, as I started reading the book, I wasn't sure I was going to like it. However, after a few pages, I was drawn into the book and it never let me go. In fact, by the end of the book, I was so ready to find out what was going to happen next from all the hints that were given, I wanted the next book right then. This book was well-written, had a great plot (both romance and intrigue), and I loved the characters, even the villain who I loved to hate. Can't wait to read more and I highly recommend!

Fantastic: A well written story with great characters and the location of Oracle Bay was inspired. The heroine in this story is a tribute to enduring heartache and finding a new life and love.

* * * * * ★ ★ ★ ★ * * * *

First Hand Knowledge

The author does a bang up job of making this mythical place not only enchanting, but a place I'd want to go. To live, even if I were the only mundane in the lot. She also expands characters from her previous book 'Not in the Cards' and keeps the story arc alive and moving forward. There's something to be said for a series that continues with the lives of all the characters, even when the focus is on only two at a time.

* * * * ★ ★ ★ ★ ★ * * * *

Wing and a Prayer

I have this terrible problem with Amy Cissell's books. I get hooked within the first few sentences, and want to read the whole thing in one sitting. They're addictive, fun, clever stories about people you wish you knew.

* * * * ★ ★ ★ ★ ★ * * *

Belle of the Ball

This is the third book in the series, and I think this series is getting better each book. I love how silly, fun, and interesting this book is. Drew and Bill's romance was great, touching, and romantic. And, the mystery was great, too. Add to that, there were some revelations that were hilarious. There was a also point at the very end of the book that made me laugh out loud because when Drew couldn't see Bill, I thought he'd been turned into a toad. What really happened and why? You'll have to read this and find out. If you love a fun, cozy, romantic mystery, give this book and series a try; you'll love it! Highly recommend! I was provided a copy which I voluntarily reviewed.

Hell and High Water

I throughly enjoyed this book. It touches on so many possibilities of paranormal people. It has a good lead in, full rich characters with quirks and an unexpected ending.

Tempest in a Teapot

The ending got me! I have really enjoyed this series, and I was so darn excited to see another one in the series.I was extremely happy with this book as I couldn't figure out who the villain was. I had ideas, but the author was skillful at red herrings. Then the end hit...I was so darn angry! LOL! Highly recommend.

There are curses and bonds, mystery and mild romance, friends and family-both related and found. I do love Oracle Bay. I'm excited for the next story for Morgana

Psychics of Oracle Bay

Not in the Cards
First Hand Knowledge
Wing and a Prayer
Belle of the Ball
Hell and High Water
Tempest in a Teapot
Elements of Surprise
Dead Giveaway*
Bad to the Bones*
Shoot for the Stars*
Fun and Prophet*

Box Sets (ebook only)
Seeing is Believing in Oracle Bay (Books 1-4)

* forthcoming

first hand knowledge

PSYCHICS OF ORACLE BAY
BOOK 2

AMY CISSELL

FIRST HAND KNOWLEDGE
Amy Cissell

A Broken World Publication
13820 NE Airport Way, Suite K395495
Portland, OR 97251-1158

First Hand Knowledge: A Paranormal Romance with a Mystery and a Magic Goat
Copyright © 2018 by Amy Cissell
ISBN 978-1-949410-10-5 (ebook);
ISBN 978-1-949410-11-2 (paperback)

Cover Design: Cissell Ink
Edited by: Aria Jones
Edited & Proofread by: Cissell Ink

To Mom
You always made me want to be even better
I wouldn't be here without that

one

Misty walked into her shop and smiled fondly at the sign hanging in the window. A stylized palm with the important lines highlighted in red neon, the preferred noble gas of the seer community, and surrounded by the shop name— Mystic's First Hand Knowledge. She wasn't exactly a palm reader, but it was close enough for the walk-ins, and she could fake it with the best of them. She only needed skin to skin contact to see into someone's past, present, or future, and with a specific question in mind, she could point her vision in that direction. She couldn't control her visions, though, which is why she almost never had any bare skin visible below the neck.

She walked in, flipped the sign to open, and sat down at the table that graced the center of the room. Every psychic had a different style in their shops or rooms where they did private readings, and Misty favored an aesthetic she referred to as cozy rockabilly goth. Black, overstuffed chairs crowded the round table covered with a scarlet cloth. Rich black and red carpets softened the hardwood floors, and a red and black fainting couch lined the back wall, which was painted a dark red like the others. Gilt-framed photos of famous seers, both real and fictional, as well as abandoned buildings, shipwrecks, and cemeteries hung on the wall in no discernible fashion. The haphazard arrangement grated on her nerves, but it furthered her persona as an eccentric psychic, which gave her clients what they expected, so she gritted her teeth and resisted the urge to rearrange and straighten them.

She was only open for walk-in hours from ten until two Monday through Thursday, and Mondays were the only day she usually saw a steady stream of customers. She had no expectations of being overly busy today, so she pulled out her laptop. It was just under two months until the event of the year—Oracle Bay's Fall Bazaar. She'd spent the last month planning and organizing and arranging, and things were rapidly coming to a head. Every year, her goal was to have everything set in stone by October first so she could start prepping for the winter tourist season, which included not only the Bazaar but the Oracle Bay Halloween Festival—which began the season—and the Yule Ball—which ended it.

The Bazaar—her biggest and most stressful project every year—was a finely tuned machine that incorporated food and beverage vendors, a craft fair, musical acts, a bake sale, and the biggest draw —the Dessert contest and raffle.

The population of Oracle Bay quadrupled for the two days of the Bazaar, and they made a lot of money for the county domestic violence shelter and related programs. The Sleeping Inn—Oracle Bay's upscale hotel had been booked solid since April, and the smaller motels on the outskirts of towns, and even most of the hotels in Long Beach, were also completely sold out.

Misty had single-handedly run the entire thing the last three years when her co-chair retired to enjoy her sunset years somewhere warmer. She knew she should find someone else to bring on board, but that would be more effort than it was worth. She usually appointed an honorary chair so the spotlight could stay off her and she could remain behind the scenes, but she didn't have one this year. Yet.

She sighed, rubbed her sternum to relieve the stress, and opened her email. She deleted the first few emails and then her mouse hand froze when she saw the email that'd come in overnight. The email, with the subject line "Bizarrely can't bazaar this year" was from Joseph McEwen, her childhood crush and the town crank. He and his family had been in Oracle Bay almost as long as her family had, and he'd been a grade above her in school. In elementary school, she, Joseph, and their other best friend Bill had been inseparable, but they grew apart in middle school, and by high school, Misty was left crushing on Joseph from afar while he ignored her and dated every other girl in school.

Besides her unrequited crush from over a decade ago, he was also responsible for the second biggest draw at the Bazaar—his artisan cheeses always sold out and for way more than he'd ever charge for them. He donated the cheeses every year, as his father had before him, but every year he found a way to make her life miserable in the process. She'd been expecting him to attempt to withdraw again this year only to cave under very little pressure. He always came through —he just did it with the maximum amount of jerkiness.

Two years ago, he'd left her a voice mail in mid-October claiming he was too upset about the state of the country to make cheese. She'd called him, listened to a political rant, and agreed with him politely until he backed down and agreed to donate the cheese. Last year, he'd tried to back out at the end of September claiming that he'd developed an inexplicable fear of getting rained on. He didn't answer any of her calls, so she tucked herself in the back corner of Bill's coffee shop, Caffiend Dreams, and waited until he'd shown up, drenched from the rain, to confront him.

If he wanted to stop participating, all he had to do was say, "Hey, I can't make it this year. I'm so sorry for backing out at the last minute. Hit me up next year." The prevarication was ridiculous.

She took a deep breath and clicked on his email.

"Mystic—" she glared at the screen. She hated her first name, and he knew it. "Can't donate this year. I know I said that the last two years, but this time I mean it. Dark forces and personal reasons conspire to make my time less available, and I'd rather let you know now than later. Don't bother calling—I won't answer and let you talk me into it. I'll also be forgoing Bill's until after the Bazaar. You won't trap me there two years in a row. Take care. Best of luck with the shindig. Joseph.

"PS - Bet you didn't see this one coming."

Misty prided herself on being a fairly even tempered person. She did not lose her temper. She didn't rage. She was serene. Unless Joseph the Jerk was involved.

She snapped her laptop shut. She'd give him until two o'clock to recant, and then she'd call him out on his ridiculous excuse. She had had enough.

⋅ ⋅ ⋆ ★ ★ ★ ★ ★ ⋆ ⋅ ⋅

EXACTLY FORTY-FIVE MINUTES AFTER CLOSING HER SHOP—LONG ENOUGH TO change clothes and drive out to the farm—Misty stormed up the long drive, wishing she'd parked a little closer to the house. When she'd pulled into the driveway, she'd parked at the first convenient spot, positive that his house was just beyond the hedge and not wanting to be too close in case she changed her mind before knocking on his door. Now, more than ten minutes later, the house and the rest of the farm buildings were finally in view. She balled up her hands and could almost feel the smoke coming out of her ears. When she finally got to the front door of the picturesque farmhouse of Joseph McEwen's "Get Your Goat" farm, she was breathing heavily from a combination of exertion and anger. Sweat beaded on her brow; she bent over, placed her hands on her knees, and blew out forcefully trying to get her pulse to slow down before knocking.

The door opened, and Joseph stood in the doorway. His startled expression was quickly replaced with annoyance. "What do you want, Mystic?"

Misty rose to her full height. "For starters, I want you to stop calling me that. You know I prefer to be called Misty."

"You didn't...run?...all the way out to the farm to rag on my use of your name. Why are you here, and where's your car?"

"I parked at the end of the drive. It's deceptively long and entirely uphill. I'm here because I got your email about backing out of the Fall Bazaar. It's less than two months away. You can't back out now, not after you've already committed. This is the third year in a row that you've pulled this stunt, and you always have the uncanny ability to try to back out the day after I firm up all the table arrangements."

"I can do anything I damn well please," Joseph said. "I didn't sign a contract. I'm having a rough year, and I don't need one more thing on my plate."

"Your cheeses are one of our biggest sellers, and you know how much money we make for the Women's Shelter."

"The world doesn't revolve around you and your Bazaar. Other people have things going on in their lives, too. Things that are more important than donating cheese."

"I'd care more if we didn't do the same song and dance every year. You say you're overcommitted and can't do the bazaar. I tell you you're being an idiot, and you back down. I suspect you do this purely to mess with me."

"It's different this year. This year, I really don't have the energy to make your damn cheeses. I'll still make sure Bill gets the milk and cream he needs for the bake sale and contest."

"You can back out next year," Misty said, arms akimbo. The flush that had started in her cheeks spread to her neck, and the fact she was visibly angry over something that really mattered very little made her even madder. Tears formed in the corner of her eyes and a lump grew in her throat. "Damnit," she muttered, repeatedly swallowing in an attempt to stave off her angry cry until she got back to the car. At no point would she examine exactly why Joseph's reasonable reason for withdrawing upset her to the verge of a tantrum.

"What's wrong with you?" Joseph asked. "Why does it matter so much that you'd come out here and yell at me? You don't like me; why not send a harshly worded email like usual?"

Misty shrugged and swallowed the lump in her throat. "You're one of the biggest jerks I've ever met, but I've also seen you do things that no real asshole would ever do. I'm the property manager for most of Main Street and I know which people are struggling to make rent, and I know when it gets paid and who pays it. You are a generous man. Plus, Bill likes you, and he's an excellent judge of character, even if he's nearly as pig-headed as you."

"Most of the time," Joseph said. "He's made some missteps."

"If you're referring to Drew…"

Joseph held up his hand. "I don't have the time or the energy to fight right now, not even about the breakup of our best friends. Do you want to come in?"

"Come in? To your house?" Misty was confused. She didn't know anyone who'd ever been in Joseph's house except Bill. It was a running joke in town—there was wild speculation about what horrors the town crank might have hidden in his house. Current popular speculation was leaning towards a horrifying yet awe-inspiring collection of erotic art.

"Yes, into my house. But please don't tell anyone about the naked sculptures. I like to keep the mystery alive."

A smile cracked Misty's face for a second before she remembered how angry she was and that she still hadn't gotten him to agree to give her cheeses for the Bazaar. She forced her expression back into stern grimness and followed him into the house.

"Do you want something to drink? I've got water, soda, beer, and of course milk. If you'd rather have something hot, I could make you coffee or tea."

"Water would be great."

Joseph smiled at her. Misty shot him some side eye. "Water it is. I hope you don't mind if I have a beer? I have a growler of pilsner from The Pour House that I don't want to go off. Can I tempt you?"

Misty attempted a polite smile. "Fine. I'll have a beer. She followed him into the kitchen, looking around. Despite his earlier claim, there were no naked statues anywhere. It was a bit disappointing. In fact, the whole farmhouse—as far as she could see—was about as normal as possible. Nothing weird jumped out at her, either literally or figuratively.

The kitchen was huge, full of natural light, and exuded a sense of peace and calm.

"This is a great kitchen! The white cabinets and yellow accents are perfect."

"Thank you."

There was a large country table near a bay window that had a distant view of the ocean. She sat and angled her chair so she could look out over the pasture dotted with sheep and beyond to the coastline. "What an amazing view."

"The views are the best things about living in Oracle Bay," Joseph affirmed. "Thinking about relocating is gut-wrenching."

"You've lived here your whole life," Misty protested. "Why are you thinking about leaving?"

He shrugged. "Sometimes, the choices are made for you, rather than the other way around."

"Is it financial?" She clapped her hands over her mouth. "I am so sorry. It's none of my business, and that was a rude question to ask. I've been rude since you opened the door. I'm sorry."

"It's okay. I bring out the best in people. As for the relocation, it's not something I want to talk about in detail." He held out a glass of beer. "But there are some difficulties with the farm. That's why I pulled out of the bazaar."

"Is there something I can do to help? The McEwen's have been here for well over a hundred years, and it'd be a loss for the town if your farm—and you—were gone."

Misty stood up to take the beer, then realized she was standing closer than was considered normal in polite society. She tilted her head back to look at him, then tilted it back a bit further.

"That's really generous, Misty, but I don't know how you could help at this point."

"We were friends once, even if it was a long time ago. I can keep your secrets again." The longing that returned every time she spent more than a few minutes in his presence flushed her cheeks and desire bloomed low in her abdomen. She grabbed the glass, her fingers brushing against his. He didn't let go. She licked her lips nervously and felt her heart rate kick up when his eyes tracked the movement of her tongue.

"What?" he asked. His free hand reached up and tucked a strand of hair behind her ear. He leaned down, keeping eye contact, and slowly brushed his lips against hers.

Misty's pulse beat out an erratic staccato. Raising up on her tiptoes, she returned the kiss. Her hand slipped on the glass and beer splashed out over both their hands, breaking the mood. They both stepped back at the same time, and each let go of the glass. It hit the tile floor with a crash and shattered, leaving a spreading pool of beer and a sparkling circle of broken glass in its wake.

"I'm sorry," Misty started. She looked down and noticed that in addition to the mud she'd picked up on her hike to the house, the hems of her jeans were soaked with beer.

"No, that was my fault," Joseph said. "I shouldn't have kissed you."

"That's not why the glass broke."

"I'll clean up this mess, and I'll donate the damn cheeses to the bazaar this year. Can you see yourself out? I'm sure you want to get home and out of your clothes."

Misty stared at him for a minute, dumbfounded that he was willing to leave it like this. She turned and stalked out of his house, back down the mile-long drive, and drove home.

· · · · ★ ★ ★ ★ · · · ·

MISTY GLARED AT HER GLASS OF WATER. SHE'D GOTTEN EVERYTHING SHE wanted; why was she still so angry? It couldn't be because they'd kissed and she'd liked it. Or that it seemed like he didn't. Surely her ego wasn't that fragile, was it?

"That arrogant, mangy goat farmer!" she fumed. "Who does he think he is?"

"Was that a no-go on the cheese and a yes go on memorizing insults you heard on BBC?" Ceri asked.

Misty whirled around, hand at her throat. A pale, willowy woman with long, red hair and a knowing twinkle in her blue eyes stood in front of her. "What the hell, Ceri! Why are you here?"

"You asked me to stop by this afternoon to talk about the new tenant in Alexandra's shop. You weren't here when I arrived, so I let myself in. That's why I have a key, right?"

Misty felt some of the tension drain out of her body. "I'm sorry. I'm in a crappy mood, and you surprised me."

"Clearly. Sorry you had to deal with that jerk. Next time, send someone else."

"No, it's fine." Misty opened her mouth to tell Ceri about the kiss, then decided against it. She was usually an open book, but she didn't really have anything to share. It was just a tiny kiss and had only lasted a couple seconds. She closed her mouth again and sighed. "He's going to do the cheeses as usual. It was just a weird visit."

"Did you actually get to cross the threshold into his lair?" Ceri asked.

Misty narrowed her eyes. "Why do you ask?"

Ceri shrugged and affected a casual demeanor. "No reason." She flipped her hair over her right shoulder.

Misty huffed. Keeping secrets was hard enough for her. When all her best friends were psychics, it made it next to impossible. "What do you know?" She didn't mean to, but her question came out as a growl.

Ceri's eyebrows shot up into her hairline. "Not as much as I thought, apparently. Just that he invited you in."

Misty pursed her lips and regarded her friend. Ceri was a scryer, which meant that any reflective liquid could give her glimpses of the future. It was almost never more than a glimpse, though, unless she was scrying on purpose. "He invited me in and seemed almost like a normal person for a bit. He was funny, he offered me a beer, and tried to convince me to leave him alone. Then, there was a mix-up with the beer handoff, it dropped and broke, and he reverted to the Joseph the Jerk McEwen that we all know. He told me he'd donate the damn cheeses then told me to leave."

Ceri canted her head to one side and regarded Misty. She forced herself to meet her friend's gaze and used every last bit of self-control to keep from blushing. There was no way anyone needed to know she'd kissed the Jerk and then been humiliated.

"I'm sorry he was rude," Ceri finally said. "Wanna talk about the new kid on the block? Morgana is chomping at the bit to test her ability with the tarot cards. Do you think she's the real deal?"

"She literally moved in this morning," Misty said. "It's gonna take her some time to get situated. Plus, she's coming from a difficult divorce, and I don't want to push her."

"You shook hands?"

"I did. I wanted to make sure she was tenant material," Misty confirmed. "She's definitely a gen-u-ine—" Misty stretched out all three syllables of the word until she almost twanged "—oracle. Not sure why Morgana still wants to test her; I'm never wrong."

"You've met Morgana," Ceri laughed. "The term control freak was coined to describe her."

Misty laughed, allowing more tension to drain away and her shoulders to distance themselves from her ears. "Not only is she the real deal, she's also gonna save the town."

"From what?"

"No idea. She doesn't know, either. Not about saving the town, and not about her powers. She's on the run and thought this would be a good place to stop. When I showed her the shop with the sign in the window, she laughed and said maybe the cards she'd bought when she was in college would come in handy for more than beer money."

"What's she running from? Does she need help?"

"She left a bad marriage and an ex-husband in Portland. I didn't see anything that would suggest she needed anything other than what we've already given her--a place to live and a chance to use her god-given talents."

"I wonder which god she has to thank for her mystical oracular powers," Ceri said. "This town heavily favors descendants of the seers from the western pantheons—which seems exceptionally colonizer-esque, if you ask me."

"Her name is Cassandra. It'd make a lot of sense if she had a little Zeus back in the line—he was one of the original gods who chose this place to hide from his responsibilities and the consequences of his latest actions. If what we believe about the history of this town is true, he definitely had a hand in its founding and with the imbuing of mystical seer powers."

"I'm honestly surprised there aren't more Zeus descendants showing up. He wasn't a good person. His character is suspect, and he had more kids than you can shake a stick at."

"He wasn't a person at all, you know," Misty said.

Ceri whacked her on the shoulder. "Do you have enough wine for tonight? It's your turn to host, and they'll all be here soon."

Misty opened the door to the pantry and revealed a built-in wine rack. "I think we'll be okay unless Paska goes on a bender. I do not want to see what happens when that man loses control. Not only is reading the future in burned bones exceptionally creepy, he exudes age like no one else—not even Morgana."

"He advertises his services as rune-reading, not bone reading."

"Have you ever seen his runestones? They're made from bone. He won't tell me what kind, but I have my suspicions. And they are old. He won't let me touch them, and he never lets me touch him. Someday I'd like to find out what he's hiding."

"And someday, in the not too distant future, we will. Are you feeling better? More centered?"

"Yes. Thank you. Maybe I should make the new girl the chair of the Bazaar Committee so she has to deal with all the recalcitrant donors every year. I've about had it."

"Let me pour you a glass of wine. Why don't you go get changed? You look disheveled, and you know the others will ask a million questions if you don't look as put together as usual."

"Ugh, you're right. Clothes first, wine second. You're the best, Ceri."

"I know. It is as I foretold."

Misty rolled her eyes, then headed upstairs to the bedroom that took the entire second floor of her house, and changed into something that wasn't splashed with beer and mud from her visit to the Jerk's house. She pulled on a tight, A-line skirt that skimmed over her butt and hips, a button-down blouse that clung to her generous bosom, and a lime-green cardigan. It was a little more dressed up than she usually was at home, but damnit! sometimes a woman wants to look good.

The doorbell rang as she was headed back downstairs and she heard the door open. She paused, just out of sight, and tried to figure out who was here before they spoke. She'd just decided it was Drew —he was almost always the first to arrive—when Morgana said, "If I don't have a glass of wine in my hand in five minutes, I see a bleak future for everyone here."

Ceri laughed. "I just opened a couple bottles. Drew, do you want the Cab or would you rather have bubbles?"

"If there are bubbles, I will drink them. But first, let's make sure Morgana gets hers. Where's Misty?"

"Right here," she said, walking into the kitchen and snagging the glass Ceri'd already poured for her. "I had to change out of the clothes I wore to the goat rodeo today."

"You went to a goat rodeo?" Morgana asked. She was standing in the middle of the floor, her long, lithe body, pale skin, and dark hair, eyes, and clothes painting the perfect picture of a modern witch. "That sounds...quaint."

Ceri stifled her laughter. "She was visiting Joseph's farm to convince him to continue his annual donation to the Bazaar."

"He is unpleasant," Morgana said.

"He's not that bad," Drew said. "He's just prickly...until you get to know him."

"He hates you," Morgana pointed out.

"He really does," Ceri confirmed.

Drew rolled his eyes. "He doesn't hate me. He's just angry with me. He'll get over it."

"It's been two years," Misty said. "He blames you for breaking his best friend's heart."

"He's a passionate man. I'm sure someday he'll forgive me."

The doorbell rang again, and Paska and Jezebel walked in. Misty poured everyone a glass and led them into the living room.

"First on the agenda today is our newest psychic, Cassandra Franklin," Misty said. "Whose turn is it to give her the official test?"

"Mine," Morgana said.

"It's always your turn," Drew complained. "Let someone else have a turn."

"You scare people, Morgana," Jezebel said. "I almost packed my bags and ran away the night after you tested me."

Misty stifled a giggle and the memory of Jezebel's testing—the last one they'd done—flooded back.

Misty followed Morgana into the new astrologer's shop, somehow hiding her more ample frame behind Morgana's shorter and slighter build. It was easy to be cloaked in darkness when Morgana was around...she oozed shadow. While Morgana marched up to the tall, black woman standing in the center of the shop, hands clasped and wringing in front of her, Misty slipped to the windowed corner and partially concealed herself behind the floor-length drapes.

"I am here for my horoscope," Morgana said, voice ringing out and

echoing against the walls. "I am very particular, have studied the subject extensively, and will not pay you if you're wrong."

Misty winced. The last self-proclaimed psychic to move to Oracle Bay had as much oracular power as your average farm animal, and even though it'd been five years ago, Morgana hadn't yet recovered.

"Okay," the new psychic said. "I don't usually do a star chart for someone who will only pay if they like the outcome, but if that's the way of things in this town, I'll give it a shot."

Morgana's shoulders tensed only enough that you'd have to know her to know what was happening. Misty grinned. It was good to have a little fire if you were going to make it in Oracle Bay.

"If you tell me your birth date, including year, as well as the time and place of your birth, I can get started," Jezebel said. She smiled and pulled out a large sheet of paper.

"June twenty-first, the year isn't important. I was born a minute after midnight in Tintagel in Cornwall, England. I realized that without a year, your chart isn't completely accurate, and I will take that into account when deciding if you deserve payment."

"Uh-huh. Sure thing, ma'am."

"Ma'am?" Morgana asked. "Do I look old enough to be referred to as ma'am?"

"You're old enough you don't want to tell me your age, and I was raised to call every woman ma'am if they were a great deal older." She shrugged. "It'll be just a minute as I draw out your chart. I apologize for the wait. Would you like some tea?"

"Why would you offer me tea?" Morgana leaned forward until she was mere inches from the other woman's face.

The astrologer rolled her chair backwards. "Tea is the only beverage I have except water. Although, based on your tension levels, maybe I should find some whiskey."

"No. Tea is fine."

The woman stood, turned on an electric kettle, and grabbed a cup. "I only have bags right now. Herbal or black?"

The tea made, the woman sat back down, and Misty glared at Morgana, willing her to ask the woman's name. Morgana didn't.

Before Morgana had finished her tea, the woman sat up. "Okay, I'm ready."

"Already?" Morgana asked, setting her tea down hard enough to splash some over the side. "That was less than ten minutes."

"It's not a lot of work if you know what you're doing. Now look here...I put your birth year in as 1952, even though you don't appear to be nearly that old. You're a Cancer, and..."

Misty listened to the horoscope, shifting as quietly as possible from foot to foot and regretting volunteering to come along. She wished she'd at least brought a book or something.

"Here's your copy," the woman said. "I hope that was good enough to get paid for my time."

"How much more detail do you put in if you know you're getting paid?" Morgana asked, standing up and staring down at the chart with a look that even from Misty's hidden spot looked derisive.

"Not a lot more. It's easier with a birth year, but I know when I'm being tested and know I'm good enough to pass without giving it my all. What's the worst you could do? Run me out of town? Because I'm not a good enough psychic?" She laughed loudly; Misty grinned in response to the infectious sound.

"I could, child. I could do things to you that you've not even imagined in your worst nightmares. Don't underestimate me."

"My name is Jezebel. I am not your child, and ancient or not, you have no way of knowing how bad my nightmares can be. Now, why don't you and your friend in the curtain go home and leave me to try to make a living."

Misty shrugged as she walked out into the open. "How long did you know I was there?"

"I saw you walk in. You made zero effort to hide."

"She's not bad," Morgana said. "Let's go back to your place and talk about her."

"Nice to meet you," Misty said. "We'll be in touch."

"Sure thing," Jezebel said with false cheer, adding under her breath in a tone clearly meant to go unheard. "This town is even nuttier than I'd heard."

Morgana shrugged. "You help your own. Besides, how am I scary? I am a tiny, little woman who spends most of her working day drinking tea."

"You exude terrifying power," Jezebel replied. "You might be small—although I wouldn't say tiny—but even people with zero psychic sense cross the street to avoid you."

A smile played on Morgana's lips, and she exchanged a glance with Paska.

"Scary is good," Paska said. "I love watching people cower."

The conversation devolved into light-hearted bickering. Misty leaned back, sipped her wine, and remembered the feel of Joseph's lips on hers. Heat bloomed deep inside, and she tried to squash it down. He'd been a jerk, and she had a rule about men like that. Stay away.

THE OPENING BARS OF MAROON 5'S "FORTUNE TELLER" WOKE MISTY UP too early the next morning. She fumbled for her phone, squinted at it blearily, and answered it, even though she didn't recognize the number. "Hello, this is Misty," she said, aiming for professional and not 'barely awake.' You never knew when it might be a potential client.

"Did I wake you?" a voice growled on the other end. Misty's toes were curling in reaction to his voice even before she woke up enough to recognize it.

"Joseph. Hi. What do you want?"

"I wanted to apologize."

"Okay, go for it."

Silence drug out long enough that Misty's eyes started blinking slower and slower and she had to fight to stay awake.

"I'm sorry?"

"Was that a question? Because I can't answer that for you."

There was a huff on the other end of the line. "You are a difficult woman. I am sorry, Mystic."

"For what?"

"What do you mean, for what? Isn't it obvious?"

"Not in the least. I've known you for years, and you are a difficult man. You have a lot of things to apologize for."

"Like what?" He sounded indignant, which made the growl in his voice even deeper.

Misty was no longer fighting sleep. His image appeared in her mind's eye—tan skin, browned from days spent outside, dark hair and a perpetual five o'clock shadow, and the piercing blue eyes that always seemed to peer right into her soul and then dismiss her. She shivered, then grinned. This might be fun.

"Like the fact that you never call me by my preferred name, Joey Joe. Or the fact that you tried to give me a heart attack by dropping out of the bazaar at the last minute three years in a row. Ooh, what about that time a couple years ago when you stormed into my shop, interrupted me with a client, called me a charlatan, then stormed out again? That was douchetastic. You know what people call you, don't you? Joseph the Jerk."

"People, or just you?"

"Not just me," she replied. "I've shared my name for you with a couple other people."

"Ah, so you and your band of con artists."

"Why are you calling? What could you have done now that would be enough to make you apologize after all this time?"

"I'm sorry about calling you a crook that one time. You're right, that was terrible. I was angry, and I handled it poorly. Drew—"

"I figured out the timing pretty quickly," Misty said. "It doesn't make what you did right. I had nothing to do with what happened. Drew is one of my best friends, but that doesn't change anything. You aren't calling to deliver a two-years-overdue apology."

"I'm not." Misty could picture him rubbing his hand through his hair in frustration. She'd seen him do that more times than she could count. He had an uncanny knack for showing up wherever she was. "Wait a minute, are you stalking me?"

"What? No. Of course not. Why would you ask?"

"You're just always where I am, ten minutes later."

"Aren't you supposed to be the psychic one? Maybe you're pre-stalking me."

She breathed out hard and forced herself to relax her grip on her phone to a more manageable level. "This is getting us nowhere. Can you just tell me why you called so I can go back to bed?"

"Back to bed? I was kidding when I asked if I woke you up. It's eight o'clock in the morning."

"Not all of us have goats to milk. I am not a morning person, and I owe you zero explanations for my sleep schedule."

Joseph growled. "Fine. I stand by my earlier assertion that you're a difficult woman, but since I did call you, I might as well tell you why."

"Don't do me any favors."

"Just let me talk. Please."

Misty smiled to herself and stayed silent.

"I'm sorry I was weird yesterday morning. I wanted to explain why I wasn't sure I could commit to the Bazaar, but then things got... out of hand."

Misty wanted to reply, "the only thing that was out of hand was that glass of beer," but she bit her tongue, then gave herself a literal pat on the back for her restraint, and dropped her phone. "Shit, sorry!" she yelled as she got out of bed and scrambled on the floor until she found it. "Dropped my phone."

"Anyway, I should've been nicer, and I shouldn't have freaked out just because I finally got to kiss you after dreaming about it all these years."

Misty almost dropped her phone again. "What did you say?"

"I'm sorry I wasn't nicer to you and basically threw you out of my house."

"No, the other bit."

"You mean the part where I said I kissed you?"

"I mean the part where you said you'd been dreaming about it for years."

"Oh. That. I was kinda hoping I hadn't said that out loud."

"It's out there now."

"One more thing for me to be sorry for, I guess. But, since I've already stepped in it, I don't suppose you want to have dinner with me tomorrow night?"

He spoke so fast the words almost blended together, and Misty wasn't quite sure she'd heard him correctly. "Did you ask me out on a date?"

The silence was long enough that she'd begun to believe he'd hung up. "I think so. If you're interested? Otherwise definitely not." He was still talking too fast, and his normally smooth, confident voice shook a little with stress.

Misty surprised herself—and probably Joseph—and said, "I'd love to. We'll go to Long Beach and hit up the Jetty Brewery. I've heard the food cart in the parking lot serves a good burger. I'll meet you there."

"Don't want to be seen with me, eh?"

"I don't want to deal with questions because two people decided to have dinner. You know how everyone here is. It's a small town and people talk."

"Andy will kill us if he finds out we cheated on The Pour House with another brewery, but I've been wanting to check them out."

"So, we're set, then? I'll see you tomorrow at seven?"

"It's a date." He hung up without saying goodbye and Misty stared at her phone in a mixture of horror and disbelief. What had she gotten herself into now?

two

Misty was running ridiculously late for her meeting—or her date, whatever—with Joseph. Her last client had gone way late, and the weather had taken a seasonal turn for the worse and soaked her on the shortish walk home; she was definitely behind schedule.

She stripped off the long black skirt and colorful peasant top she'd worn to the shop that day, ran a wet washcloth over her body, reapplied deodorant, and got dressed. She didn't often wear jeans, but she wasn't sure she wanted to dress up for Joseph, so jeans it was. She dug out her favorite pair--they made her ass look fabulous--and paired them with black leather lace-up ankle boots, a white button-up blouse that strained across her more than ample breasts, and a coral cardigan that enhanced rather than concealed her curves.

She ran a brush through her hair, cleaned her glasses, once again cursing the long eyelashes that rendered them almost permanently dirty. She was careful to keep her complaints to herself. No one liked to hear how her eyelashes were too long for comfort.

Misty opened the drawer in her bathroom vanity, looked at the small bag of makeup, then closed it decidedly. She wore makeup for special occasions only—and those occasions were the Fall Bazaar, the Yule Ball, New Year's Eve, and Burns Night. This definitely did not qualify.

"Cute," she told her reflection. "And probably more than he deserves, even if he has been dreaming about your lips for years."

Heat blossomed low in her abdomen at the thought of being someone else's fantasy. She might not have thought of him that way until they'd kissed in his kitchen a couple days ago—at least not for a decade—but if she was being honest with herself, she'd noticed his rugged good looks more than once over the years. Usually in a 'too bad he's such a jerk' way, but she'd still noticed.

"Stop it," she said out loud. "Now is not the time. And stop talking to yourself. People will think you're a weirdo."

She grabbed her umbrella and a cute rain jacket, then dashed through the raindrops out to her car. She knew her Miata wasn't the most practical vehicle - particularly for the rain-soaked Pacific coast - but she'd always wanted a convertible, and as soon as she was able to make her own decisions, that's exactly what she'd gotten. She slammed the door with the help of the wind, started the car, and then stared at her hands on the steering wheel. They were shaking, and it took her a minute to figure out why.

She was nervous.

"Damnit," she muttered. "Pull it together. And, for the love of everything holy, stop talking to yourself."

She backed out of the driveway and headed south. She hoped the food cart had covered seating. This was already not shaping up to be the best first date ever.

When Misty pulled into the parking lot, she was only twenty minutes late. She checked her hair and face in the mirror before girding her metaphorical loins and walking into the bar.

She spotted Joseph immediately. He was sitting in a booth in the back staring morosely into an almost-empty pint. A pang of guilt struck her. She was twenty minutes late and hadn't even bothered to give him a heads up. That was not very nice.

She strode forward, slid into the booth across from him, and said, "I'm sorry."

A smile spread, lighting his face up like a slow, misty dawn. "It's your turn to apologize now, is it?"

"I guess so. Work went late, and that threw off my schedule. I should've called and let you know so you didn't have to wonder if I was gonna show or not."

"Oh, I wasn't wondering if you were going to show up. I had no doubt that you'd be here."

Misty's jaw dropped. The hubris of this man!

A waitress came by and dropped off two pints of beer. "I got you a Pilsner," he said. "I know that's your favorite beer, and they don't have liquor."

Misty regained control of her thoughts and unhinged jaw and asked, "If you knew I was going to show, even though I was almost a half hour late, why'd you look so morose when I walked in?"

"Personal stuff," he said. "It's not the kind of stuff you share on a first date. This is more like morning-after breakfast conversation fodder."

"I guess I'll have to resign myself to never knowing," Misty sniped, still irritated, for no good reason, that he was so confident in her.

"At least not for a while," Joseph confirmed. "I prefer to take things slow. I'm not going to be trying any of my patented seducing techniques on you until well after our third date. I'm not in a hurry."

Misty took a sip of her beer, unable to come up with any kind of response. He was simultaneously infuriating and seductive; he knew how to press every one of her buttons. The mixture of teasing and not-so-subtle innuendo were what did it for her. If he threw in some big-eyed sincerity, she'd be a goner.

"Argh!" she said.

"What?" Joseph's look of casual amusement faded into mild alarm.

"This. You. All of it." She waved her arm to encompass him, the bar, and everything. "This is too much, too soon. It's our first date, and I've spent the last decade trying not to like you too much."

"I know why you're here." His smirk was back.

"Enlighten me, then."

"You're curious. You felt the same sparks I did when we kissed, and you want to know if they were really there or just your imagination. You want to find out if there's more to me than the jerk you know."

Misty started to nod. He was right.

"But mostly, you want to find out if a farmer has what it takes to..." he paused for effect, then grinned in the most open expression she'd ever seen on his face, "...float your goat."

* · * · * · ★ · ★ · ★ · ★ · ★ · * · * · ·

Misty eyed her reflection in the bathroom mirror, thankful she'd decided against makeup. She wasn't sure there was a mascara powerful enough to withstand the tears that had been streaming down her face non-stop for the last hour. She couldn't remember the last time she'd laughed this hard and this much.

She came back from the bathroom to find the largest burger she'd ever seen waiting for her, along with another pint of pilsner. "Oh my god, this is the biggest thing I've ever seen."

"That's what she said," Joseph said.

"I have no other response to my food that won't elicit the exact same comment from you, so I'm just going to be quiet now."

Misty pulled off her gloves, took a bite of her burger, moaned in delight, then washed it all down with a swig of beer. "This place is great," she said.

"I'm glad you like it. Especially since it was your idea."

"I love food, so I'm always paying attention to what's buzzing locally. My enthusiasm for beer and wine are purely recreational, though, so I'm not ever going to be much help there."

"I've got you covered for beer. If I weren't so busy with the goats,

I'd probably be at The Pour House begging Andy to give me a job. The science of brewing is fascinating, although I'm definitely better at the drinking parts than anything else. Wine, though...that's a mystery."

"I'd like to pretend I could contribute to any 'best cocktail bar' list, but other than my affinity for Long Island Ice Teas, I've got nothing there."

"No one ever needs to be an expert on everything. I think it's better to be good at only a few things rather than mediocre at a myriad of things."

"That makes sense. I don't have a lot of talents, but those I do have, I use to their fullest. I am a phenomenal property manager, a fantastic event planner, and an excellent seer."

"Two out of three marketable talents aren't bad. I'm only good at goat-related stuff."

Misty tried not to let the hurt overwhelm her. She knew he wasn't a believer, even though he'd grown up in this town, but she didn't think he'd be so dismissive, regardless of his actions when he was angry on his friend's behalf. She should've guessed, though. That was the same issue that broke up Drew and Bill, and it looked like it was going to end this impossible romance before it even got started. She took another bite of her burger. She might be mentally checking out of this date, but she was going to finish her burger.

"I put my foot in it, didn't I?" Joseph asked after Misty polished off her burger and took a drink of her beer. "I didn't mean to imply your psychic powers weren't a marketable talent. You do a great job of bringing in tourists who want to spend a little vacation cash on a fun few minutes."

"If you don't believe in what I do, and you know very well that I take my work very seriously, why are we here, Joseph?"

"I've had a crush on you from the moment you took on our history teacher for his blatantly sexist and racist revisionist history of the American Revolution. You made me think beyond my own family for the first time, and you're the reason I double majored in animal science and history. I never dreamed that there'd be a time when you'd look at me with anything but dismissive disdain, but when we kissed…it made me think that maybe I could have something I never thought I'd be worthy of."

"Even though you think I'm a con artist?"

"I didn't say that," he protested.

"You kinda did. Don't play semantics with me. You think I'm dishonest—either with my customers or with myself." She wiped her hands and put her gloves back on.

"I don't think you're being dishonest to your customers. I think they believe just as I do, that you're very good at the role you play. You have excellent intuition that helps you tell a story."

"What if I said I didn't think you made your own cheese? Or your own soaps?"

"That's different. I can prove I do those things."

A wicked gleam shone in Misty's eyes. "And you think I can't prove likewise?"

"It's all a lot of simple tricks and nonsense."

"Did you seriously just quote Star Wars at me to disprove my far-reaching psychic powers?"

"You recognized the movie from that? Nice."

"Never doubt my nerd cred. If it's all simple tricks, there's no harm in me reading your palm, then, is there? The ethics of fortune-telling are in such a weird, gray area. I can get glimpses of anyone with simple skin contact—hence my gloves. I don't ever take them off unless I'm alone, I'm with a paying client, or, on a very rare occasion, in desperate need of information from someone unlikely to believe in my powers. But I don't go digging into the psyches of friends and long-time acquaintances. Most of us wouldn't violate someone like that—at least not without an excellent reason."

"Okay. I consent. Do it." Joseph held out his hand. Misty pulled off her glove, threw back the rest of her beer to fortify herself, and grabbed his hand.

Like always, she was at first overwhelmed with images. Without a specific question to focus on, she got a rush of past and future, all mixed up. This rush was why she'd taught herself the rudiments of palm reading—it gave her something to focus on while everything came in and swirled around uncomfortably.

"Your lifeline is exceptionally long," she started, the same thing she always said. Like a meditation, it calmed her and allowed her to start homing in on the things that would prove she was the real deal. She was surprised to see that his lifeline was actually exceptionally long. The images flashing in front of her eyes were slowing now. She paused them, flipped them backwards, and found what she needed. She gasped. "It was you! You're the one who tied Mr. Beasley's shoelaces to the lab table in our Junior Year chemistry class. That almost burned down the whole school! Holy crap. I feel like I should turn you in and get my detention stricken from my permanent record."

Joseph gaped at her. "How long have you known?"

"Are you paying attention here? About thirty seconds."

"You must've found out in high school. I can't believe you didn't turn me in."

"Have you even met me? If I'd known, I absolutely would've turned you in. The rest of us got in trouble because no one would confess."

"Fine, then. Bill told you, and you've been sitting on that information." He tried to pull his hand out of hers, but she gripped tighter.

"You want more? I'll give you more. I'll find something I couldn't possibly know." She flipped through the Joseph pages, looking for something light-hearted enough that it wouldn't hurt him, but far removed enough that she wouldn't know from other sources. "You went to Oregon State University, which everyone knows. What no one knows is that you almost dropped out your sophomore year to live with..." Misty's eyes were closed, but she squinted anyway. "...Moonbeam?" Misty opened her eyes. "Holy crap, Joseph, you were going to join a cult? What? Why?"

It was Joseph's turn to have his jaw unhinge. "There is no way you could know that. I've never told anyone, not even Bill. Even when I talked about Moonbeam, I called her by her public name, which was Peggy."

"Why didn't you go with her?" Misty asked.

"You tell me." He was sarcastic and hard, and Misty knew she'd have to tread carefully. She hadn't meant to grab a memory that would hurt.

She closed her eyes again and followed the memory thread to its end. "Wait a minute. You broke it off because you found out that once you were in the cult, all the men were celibate except the leader? You didn't join a cult, not because it was a weirdo creepy religious cult, but because you wouldn't be getting any?"

Misty tried to suppress the giggles that were threatening to erupt but wasn't doing a very good job. She sheepishly met Joseph's eyes. "I'm sorry. I didn't mean to delve into something painful. I was looking for something tucked away that would prove to you I am who I say I am."

"That was pretty convincing. I don't know how you'd know about Moonbeam if you weren't... Wait a minute. I thought you were a palm reader. Other than telling me about my lifeline, you didn't even look at my hand. I don't think real palm readers can pull up ten-year-old memories."

"Real palm readers? Suddenly there's a standard of palm reader skills that you're an expert on? You didn't believe it was anything but nonsense a few minutes ago."

Joseph took a huge swig of his beer and didn't quite meet her eyes. He pulled his hand away, and this time she let him.

She replaced her glove, contemplated her empty pint glass, and said, "Do you believe me now?"

"I'm definitely a lot closer to belief than I was a few minutes ago. Can you do the future, too?"

"Yes. That's usually what people want. It's easier to focus with a question, though. Otherwise, I see too much to sort through. People want to know if their investments or relationships or jobs will work out. I can see a lot of potential futures and the actions that lead to them. It's easier to start with the here and now, hear a question, and then follow it to its end. It's not as clear-cut as reading tarot cards or reading tea leaves or drawing a star chart. It's similar to what Drew and Ceri do, but what they do with a reflective surface, I do with a touch. Ceri has more power than I do, but I have more control."

"And Drew? He's the real deal, too?"

"As real as me."

Joseph ran his fingers through his hair. "Do I tell Bill? Do I even believe this at all?"

"It's up to you what you do with this information."

"I don't want to dismiss any of this," he said. "It's a lot to take in, though."

"I know. How about I buy us another round, then we go for a walk—it looks like the weather's cleared."

"That sounds like a capital idea."

· · ⋆ ★ ★ ★ ★ ⋆ · ·

Misty leaned against the jetty rail, closed her eyes, and let the salt spray hit her face. There was a break in the weather, and the moon was shining through the clouds. A smile played across her lips.

"You are beautiful, you know."

"No, I'm not. I'm cute. I'm vivacious. I'm 'not bad.' On a good day, I'm pretty. But I'm not beautiful."

"Whoever told you that was a liar, and that's a damn shame. You are beautiful. You've got the most gorgeous mahogany hair, green eyes that see too much and make me want to fall on my knees before you, and your nose is a thing of perfection. I never knew I was a nose guy until I saw yours."

"Stop it, you." Misty blushed.

"I will not. Your beauty pales in comparison to what else you've got going on, though."

"Yeah, yeah. I've got a nice rack. I've heard that before."

"I meant your brains, woman. You are so smart. You read more books than anyone I've ever met. You could probably outthink Einstein, and you still find a way to be kind and compassionate to every dunderhead you meet."

"Every dunderhead but you," she said.

"Is that what you think of me?"

Misty opened her eyes and turned towards him. He was holding his breath waiting for her answer.

"No," she said softly, reaching up to touch his face. "I don't. You infuriate me; you always have. Part of it is you were the only one who ever beat me in school, and part of it is you went out with every girl but me."

"You scared me."

She scoffed. "I'm not scary."

"You're intense and intelligent, and you never took shit from anyone."

"What was I supposed to do? Fawn all over you and tell you how dreamy I thought you were?"

"That would've made things easier."

"I'm not very good at making things easy," Misty confessed.

"Me, neither. I'd like to kiss you again."

"Neither of us are holding a glass right now, so I think it's safe." She took a half step towards him and tilted her head up to look into his eyes. Their lips touched, and need flared between them. A wave crashed loudly, sending up more spray than the previous, smaller waves. Misty took a deep breath, wrapped her arms around his neck, and closed her eyes.

She heard him groan deep in her throat and the sound pulled an answering moan from her.

"You taste better than I could've ever imagined," he said. "Like chocolate and sea salt."

"The sea salt is because we're standing over the ocean, you know," Misty said.

"Explain the chocolate, then."

"I can't. No one's ever said that to me before. I think you may be a tiny bit delusional. How much did you have to drink?"

"You were there. I'm not intoxicated. Wait, that's not true. I'm intoxicated by you."

Misty rolled her eyes. "Don't get all flowery and romantic on me now. That's not your style, and it sure isn't mine."

"How do you know it's not my style? We've barely spoken in the last ten years."

Misty leaned away from him and rested her back on the damp rail of the pier. "I could be wrong. We haven't been close since we were in middle school. Tell me, Joseph, should I expect flowery speeches and romance from you?"

"Romance, certainly. I will one hundred percent show up on your doorstep with flowers on every one of your special days. I will buy you cards with cheesy puns to express my feelings."

"But will you write me love poems and read them to me under the light of the full moon?"

"Do you want that?" Joseph tried to hide his grimace.

Misty laughed. "No. Please, god, no. If we're going to make a go at this—and to be honest, I'm still not sure what this is that we're maybe making a go of—I don't need poems and long walks on the beach or even flowers. I need someone I can confide in, someone who will back me, and someone who won't think I'm crazy." Misty mulled over her list, then amended it somewhat. "Someone who won't treat me like I'm irreparably crazy. I am a psychic. It's all real, and I need a partner who can not only accept that I believe in it, but a partner who believes in it themselves. The rest of my crazy is up for mockery."

"I would never mock you. The psychic stuff is weird. I'm not going to lie, it's hard to absorb, much less accept. I don't know why I can't believe…it's not the weirdest thing that's ever happened to me. But I promise you that I believe in you and that I'll get there. If you don't want fancy speeches and fancier flowers, I'm your guy."

"What are we doing, Joseph? Two weeks ago, if anyone had suggested I'd be here with you discussing our romantic future, I would've laughed in their face. Yet, here we are. Moonlit walk, long pier, ocean spray, and kisses. How did we get here so fast?"

"For my part, it's been a long, slow journey. Years of longing and irritation mixed together that culminated in your visit to berate me. When I saw you in my doorway, I knew I couldn't continue being unrequited. I'm toying with leaving Oracle Bay; this might be my last chance. It was do or die time."

"I desperately wanted to go out with you in high school. You were so smart and so arrogantly cool. But you never noticed me, and when I went to college—the same one as you, by the way—and you never even spoke to me once, I gave up. There were plenty of men who were interested in me, so I put away my attraction to you. When we both ended up back in Oracle Bay, and you were rude—not just to me, but to everyone—it just reaffirmed what I'd already decided. Joseph McEwen really was Joseph the Jerk."

"I'm not good at people. I never have been. They confound me."

"Do I confound you?" Misty asked.

"You more than anyone. I've despaired of ever getting to know you, much less understand you. The fact that I'm here with you right now gives me so much joy and hope...I can't even describe it. With all the shit that's going on in my life right now, it's weird that something started to go right."

Misty looked up at him. "I don't know what's happening, and it's a little nerve-wracking. I don't want to take two steps back, but we've been antagonists for so long that I don't want to jump in full throttle, either."

"That's fair. I am a jerk. I don't try hard enough to make people happy. I don't know how. My life is my farm. My goats, my cheeses and soaps, and my very few friends. I'd like to count you among their number, if nothing else."

Misty pursed her lips and considered him. "I think we can friends, but I need two things before we shake on it."

"You want an agreement that I will donate cheeses to your bazaar for the rest of my life?"

Misty grinned. "That's a great idea, and one I wish I would've thought of first, but no. I want an agreement that we will take this slow. Glacially slow. I can't go all in with you right away."

"I'll agree to that if you tell me why."

"You and I have lived in Oracle Bay for almost thirty years. Your parents lived here even longer, before retiring to Seattle. We went to school together. We know all the same people. I cannot lose myself to someone I'll have to see almost every day for the rest of my life if it doesn't work out."

"So, if I was a stranger?"

"Full speed ahead. If it didn't work out, that stranger would be gone and I wouldn't be reminded of my heartbreak every time I grabbed a drink at The Pour House."

"Fair enough. Does that mean we're going to continue secret dating?"

"It's kinda like a sexy adventure if no one else knows, right?"

"We can call it that if you want. I will agree to two months of secret dating, and then you will be my not-secret date to the Yule Ball."

Misty inhaled, held it, then exhaled slowly. "That's fair."

"What's your second condition?"

"Kisses."

"Kisses?"

"Yes. Several. Now."

Joseph grinned and pulled her towards him. "That is a condition I look forward to satisfying over and over again." His lips descended to meet hers, and she melted into him.

three

Misty had regrets. To begin with, she wasn't a morning person; she hadn't crawled into bed until after three that morning, but in a surfeit of optimism earlier that week, she'd scheduled a nine o'clock appointment that morning. She'd said goodbye to Joseph at the perfectly reasonable time of ten-thirty, gotten home by eleven, but then decided she needed a movie or two to unwind and squash all the feelings she was having. Neither comedy had relaxed her enough to erase the feeling she was making a terrible mistake or cool the flames ignited by Joseph's kisses along her jawline. Only the threat of her early-morning client had been enough to send her to the bedroom to toss and turn a good portion of the—could she even call it night?

She yawned, wished she had a servant solely in charge of bringing her coffee, and rolled her head around to work out the kinks that came with restless sleep.

The door opened, jostling the tiny silver bell that Misty was unable to remove, no matter how hard she tried, how many tools she employed, and how many sledgehammers she'd taken to the damned thing. She took a fortifying gulp of water, widened her eyes in an effort to look both awake and alert, and plastered a smile on her face. "Hi!" she said as brightly as she could muster. "Welcome to First Hand Knowledge. I'm Misty, and I'll help guide your path."

"I do not shake hands," the woman announced.

"Neither do I. Would you like to have a seat?"

The woman looked around the interior of the small shop, nose tilted slightly up with an expression of mild disdain on her face. "I suppose that would be agreeable." Misty couldn't place her accent. It was almost Italian, but not as smooth and musical. It was harder and more clipped and completely unidentifiable.

Misty ushered her to an overstuffed chair next to a small, round table. "Would you care for any tea or water?"

"No, let's get on with this nonsense."

Misty bit her tongue to avoid saying what she really wanted to, reminded herself of the sizable deposit that had already been made, and sat down in the other chair, grinning broadly. "Tell me, please, what brings you here? I don't need to know in order to give you a glimpse into the future, but it helps if I know which way to direct my thoughts."

The woman, whose previous communications had specified she was to remain anonymous—the fees were paid from a business account with no names attached—looked down her nose at Misty and considered the question.

While she waited, Misty looked over her reticent client. She had light brown skin, a long, regal nose that flared slightly at the nostrils, and eyes so dark the pupil was barely visible. Her hair was hidden under a variety of colorful scarves, and her nails, tapping the small table while she thought, were blood red. She was terrifyingly beautiful, Misty thought, suddenly anxious to get this show on the road and have the client leave as soon as possible.

"Ma'am?" she prompted. "Do you want me to look in a certain direction, or just see where your palm takes me?"

"I was told you were the most powerful psychic in this...town."

Her lip curled slightly, and it took every bit of self-control for Misty to not roll her eyes.

"I'm not the most powerful. I am, however, the most reliably powerful person you're likely to get an appointment with. The other two that take appointments are scryers, and although they're both very powerful, their power isn't as consistent as mine."

"What of your card witch?"

Misty tilted her head to one side in confusion for a moment before she figured it out. "Oh, the tarot card reader? The one that was here previously has moved on, and our new reader is not yet accepting clients. Her power levels are unknown." Misty stopped abruptly when she realized that not only was she babbling, she was sharing more information than she typically would with a stranger. "Again, how would you like me to proceed?" She was starting to get impatient and desperately trying not to show it.

"I will tell you my conundrum and see if you can help solve it," the woman said. "First, I must tell you who I am."

"You don't have to if you don't want to."

"It is important. I once was a seer like yourself, but as the years went by, my powers waned. My acolytes disappeared, and my family is nowhere to be found. I was drawn here for reasons unknown, but in the months I've been here, I have found the why."

"You've been in Oracle Bay for months? That's impossible. I would've noticed you."

"I am good at blending in when I want to. My dilemma is how to get what I want to help restore my people and my family. Is that enough detail?"

"It is." Misty removed the glove on her right hand. "Please, let me take your hand."

The woman extended her hand outwards, and Misty reached forward. When she grasped the woman's hand, a jolt shot through her, like a super-charged frisson of static electricity, eliciting a gasp of surprise. She turned the palm upwards, as she always did, and squinted at the hand. "You have a very long life line," she said, then looked at it again. "Very long. I've never seen anything quite like this."

"I am unique, I think. Go on."

Misty concentrated on the feel of the woman's skin in her hand. The longer she held on, the hotter it burned. She knew it wasn't scorching her, but it was hard to maintain the reality of the situation over the sensation of heat. Images flashed in front of her eyes, and she concentrated on the woman's quest through the pain.

"You need to regain your true calling, look into your future. Once you claim your power, your path will be made clear. The way home, the way back to your..." Misty reared back in her chair and almost let go of her mystery client's hand. "Your family? That looks like Zeus."

"Zeus? Don't be ridiculous. He's no relation of mine."

Misty shook her head. The adamancy of her statement should've sounded more ridiculous than it did. "You said you used to be an oracle, a fortune-teller—"

"Nothing so crass as all that," the woman said, haughtiness dripping from every word. "You think I'm some common gy—"

"There will be no racial slurs in my shop," Misty interrupted. "I don't care who you are and how much you agreed to pay me."

The woman tilted her head and studied Misty. Her gaze seemed to bore past the surface and brush her inner thoughts. "I am sorry. I did not mean to use a word that is offensive. It's been long and long again since I interacted with others and I did not know it had fallen out of favor. Please accept my apology and, if you can find the grace in your heart to forgive me, bestow that blessing on me."

This woman was weird and more than a little erratic, but she did apologize. "Your apology is accepted, and there are no hard feelings. May I continue?"

"If you would be so kind."

Misty closed her eyes, concentrated on the space she'd been in when the image of what looked like a classical Zeus had thrown her off and pulled herself back in. "Your power lies dormant, waiting for the right catalyst. The answer will be found when you embrace the old ways and look to your future through...haruspicy? What is that?"

"Are you sure?" the woman asked, leaning forward eagerly and grabbing Misty with her free arm. "Haruspicy?"

"Does that mean something to you, because I've no idea what that is."

"I was once the mother of haruspices, but the practice fell out of favor long ago. I know I'm in the right place, but I haven't been trying the right methods."

Misty had a distinctly unsettled feeling forming in her gut, and she couldn't tell if it was a lack of sleep or her current client causing the upset.

"Is there aught else to tell me?" the woman asked. Her dark eyes were sparkling in excitement, and she appeared to be about one more piece of obscure good news away from bouncing up and down in her chair.

Misty smiled tightly and concentrated. "All I see are goats, for some reason," she confessed, bewildered. "It's almost as if something is blocking me from looking deeper."

"Goats?" the woman asked. "I would've expected sheep, or chickens on a bad day." Her speech shifted into a more modern parlance; Misty noticed, but didn't say anything. There was no reason to point out the change, but there was every reason to remember it.

Misty didn't know how to respond to that, so she kept her mouth closed and tried to disengage her hand. The woman held on tightly.

"Are there goats around here? I feel like I've seen something about the creatures."

"There are goats. A local farm sells goat cheese, milk, and soap."

"Give me directions to the farm."

Misty opened her mouth to do just that, but then stopped herself. Why on earth would she tell anyone—particularly an outsider—where Joseph lived. She pulled her hand away. "I'm sorry, I can't tell you that."

"You don't know?"

"Unless there's something else..." Misty pulled out her phone with the square reader attached.

The woman pierced Misty with a gimlet stare before pulling a black credit card out of her pocket and handing it over. "This will work?"

Misty glanced down at Minnie Toscano's black American Express. "Absolutely." After running the woman's card and ushering her out of the shop, Misty closed and locked the door, then leaned against it. The situation was weird enough that it warranted discussing with someone else. Once again, she gave thanks that no one anywhere had ever brought up the idea of psychic-client privilege. She grabbed her phone and sent out a group text.

* * * ★ ★ ★ ★ ★ ★ ★ * * *

"It has been four days since our last gathering," Morgana pointed out. "Why are we here again?"

"I missed you," Misty said, acid dripping from her tongue.

"You're not usually mean," Ceri said. "Something's happened."

"As soon as the others get here, I'll share. I wish Russell would admit he was one of us and come to the meetings. He can pretend he's nothing more than a bartender who wandered into town, but his energy reads 'oracle,' even if he denies it. I wish I'd felt comfortable shaking his hand when I'd first met him. Now it's too late; I never read anyone I know without consent."

"You just want him to make you those abominable drinks," Morgana sniffed.

Misty was spared defending herself when the doorbell rang again, and Drew, Jezebel, and Paska walked in. She handed them drinks—a glass of red for Jezebel, a glass of Prosecco for Drew, and a Scotch, neat for Paska. She led the way from the kitchen to the living room and sat down in her overstuffed chair. As soon as everyone else was situated, she said, "I had the weirdest client today. Something was off."

That got everyone's attention, but Jezebel was the only one who leaned forward. "Was she dark—well, not as dark as me, but darker than the lot of you, with a broad nose, and long, black hair?"

"I don't know about her hair; it was covered with scarves, but she was a medium-brown with almost black eyes, a wider nose, and blood-red nails. Did she stop by to see you today?"

"Yes. She quizzed me on the rest of the psychics in town, spending a particular amount of time on you and the new woman, and then wanted a reading. I couldn't do a complete star chart for her, because she claimed to not know the year of her birth."

"What now?" Drew asked. "How do you not know when you were born?"

"It's more likely that she didn't want to say and used not knowing as an excuse," Paska said. "That's what I do all the time. Well that, or I lie."

"Lying is much less conspicuous," Morgana said. "I always recommend making something up."

"Some people aren't good at lying on their feet," Paska pointed out.

"You're supposed to lie on your back," Jezebel said. "Much easier."

"Your ability to amuse knows no bounds," Paska retorted.

"I try."

"It matters not why she wouldn't give the year of her birth," Morgana said. "What matters is that she didn't and still expected a star chart. How did she expect accuracy?"

"I don't know if she did," Jezebel said. "Most people don't. She couldn't have known that unlike most astrologers one finds on the internet, I'm the real deal. A birth year and time help, but they aren't essential. All I need is a month and a day as a jumping off place, and I can tell a great deal about a person."

"And what were you able to tell about our mysterious visitor?" Morgana asked.

"She's old," Jezebel said.

"Super old," Misty agreed. "Her life line is the longest I've ever seen."

"She's a Pisces, probably," Jezebel said. "She's right on the cusp of that and Aries, but adjusting for age...I'm going with Pisces. It's the sign of wisdom and intuition, and those fit."

"She said she used to be an oracle and was looking to find her way back to her powers and her family, but needed something to get there."

"She's at the end of a self-destructive run and is just learning how many other things were destroyed when she went on her pity-bender. She paid cash, tipped well, and left my shop before I could register what'd happened. Did you get a name?" Jezebel asked.

"She paid with a black Amex card under the name Minnie Toscano, but my Google-fu didn't turn up anyone who looked like the client."

The rest of the psychics were looking back and forth between Misty and Jezebel like they were watching a particularly exciting tennis match.

"I told her too much," Misty admitted. "I couldn't stop myself. Between her questions about all of you and her curiosity about Joseph's farm after I mentioned haru...haru...damnit! I can't remember the word."

"Was it haruspicy?" Paska asked.

"Yes! That's it. I meant to google it but completely forgot."

"Someone needs to warn Joseph," Paska said.

"What is it?" Misty asked.

"Fortune telling through the internal organs of an animal. Sheep and chickens are more common, but a goat would work."

"Wait, what now?"

"It's an ancient and time-honored practice," Paska said. "Many believe it to be the most effective form of divination—better than watching the patterns of birds in flight, better than casting wands, better even than scrying."

"It is much like tasseography," Morgana said. "Reading patterns in what is left over."

Misty felt herself pale and grow green around the edges. "I didn't tell her where Joseph lived. I stopped myself."

"She will find out, though," Morgana pointed out. "It is not a large town, and almost everyone here would have that information."

"That is why someone needs to warn him," Paska said. "As I said before."

"I'll do it," Misty volunteered, too quickly. "I told her she was looking for goats. It's my responsibility."

"He will laugh at you," Morgana said. "He believes that we are all confidence artists, taking money from people by performing tricks."

"Regardless, I will tell him. He may not believe me, but at least he will listen to me. We have reached a truce after my visit there the other morning."

"I wish we had true witches," Paska groused. "It would be good to set a ward of protection around his farm. I know not what this old woman is, but I am not convinced we want her to regain her powers and awaken her family."

"Maybe they're vampires!" Ceri suggested.

Paska gave her a withering look. "There is no such thing as vampires."

"Maybe you just haven't seen one yet." She stuck her tongue out at him.

"If they existed, I would have come across one by now. And if I hadn't, Morgana would have. She is almost as old as me."

"Change of subject," Drew said. He'd been unusually quiet throughout the discussion, and Misty shot him a sharp look. He was up to something.

"Yes?" Misty asked, trying to suss out what it was he was doing.

"Now that the new psychic's been plying her trade for a couple days, should we test her? It'll be nice to have a new oracle with actual power in town. Not that Alexandra lacked...but..."

"I will stop by early next week," Morgana announced. "That will give her some time to get used to what she's doing and start to feel comfortable before we spring one over on her." She cackled and rubbed her hands together.

"Sometimes, you and Paska do great with the modern talk, and sometimes you utterly fail," Drew observed. "I love it."

MISTY DIALED JOSEPH THE NEXT MORNING AS SHE WAS GETTING READY FOR work. He answered on the first ring. "Hey, Mystic," he said in his gravelly voice. "Miss me already?"

"It's only been thirty-six hours," Misty responded primly. "And don't call me Mystic."

"You didn't answer the question," he observed. "And I like your name. If you really don't want me to use it anymore, though, I'll stop. I like teasing you, but I don't want to actually upset you."

A slow grin spread across Misty's face. "You never cease to surprise me," she said.

"Another question unanswered. You're two for two."

"You can call me Mystic if you promise to try not to do it in public. I'd be forced to kill you if it caught on in town."

"Since we're still sneaking around all surreptitious-like, that's an easy promise to make for now."

"Habits are hard to break, though."

"I have raised my right hand, even though you can't see it, and I will solemnly swear that I will do my utmost to avoid calling you Mystic where anyone can hear me. I'll save that kind of talk for the bedroom."

Misty flushed and swallowed twice in order to make her next words not sound breathless. "I actually called to pass along a warning," she said.

"What kind of warning?"

Misty took a deep breath. "This is going to sound weird, and you don't have to believe everything, but I had a strange client yesterday, and we—"

"We? Who's we?"

Misty sighed loudly. "Who do you think, Joe? The psychic's union, of course. Anyway, this client was weird enough that we had a meeting about her last night, and it turns out she'd also visited Jezebel. She is very interested in you and your goats."

"Baby, everyone's interested in me and my goats. We're the number one draw in Oracle Bay. I've had people contact me asking for a tour of the farm. They've offered me money."

"Did you say yes?"

"Of course not. There's not enough money in the world for me to play nice with people who've probably never set foot on a farm in their lives. They'll complain about the smell, probably step in something that upsets them, and then want to pet the goats. And there's no way I'm letting anyone into the cheese kitchen when they don't understand the basics of sanitation. Why would I do that to myself?"

"I guess it's good you're well known as the town crank. No one will think your refusal odd."

"No one warned the lady who called me yesterday, though. She did not want to take no for an answer, and I finally had to hang up on her."

"Yesterday? What time?" Misty's voice got louder with alarm.

"It was later—must've been about eight or eight-thirty. I'd just separated the kids from the does and gotten everyone fed and bedded down for the evening. She was different than the others. Most requests come through on my landline that I publish with all my business stuff. This call was on my cell. Almost no one has that number."

"I do, and I've had it for years," Misty pointed out.

"How many people have you shared it with?"

Misty thought about it. "No one. I've only used it a handful of times before this week. There was never a reason to give it out. If I was mad at you, I preferred yelling at you myself."

"The only other people who have my number are my parents, my siblings, Andy, Bill, and Drew."

"What, no women? How'd you communicate with the women you dated?"

"In case you haven't noticed, I don't date. When's the last time you saw me out with someone besides Bill?"

"Just because I didn't notice doesn't mean it wasn't happening."

"Really?" Joseph sounded skeptical. "You wouldn't have noticed?"

Misty didn't have an answer—at least not one she wanted to give —so she stayed silent.

"Was there more to your warning than you had a weird client and the other diviners agreed?" Joseph prompted, a note of teasing in his voice.

She slapped her forehead in exasperation. "Yes! We got side-tracked by your insistence that all the ladies were interested in you. She claimed to be an oracle who preferred haruspicy."

"Haru what now?"

"Divination using entrails. I think—and the others agree—that she wants to use your goats' guts to divine the location of her missing family and learn how to get her power back."

"What power?"

"I'm not sure, but it's probably not the power of positive thinking."

Misty heard a muffled gasp on the other end and then silence. "Joseph? Are you okay?"

A few seconds later he replied. "Yes, sorry. Just had something in my throat."

"Are you laughing at me?"

"Of course not, Mystic. I would never."

"You're a terrible liar."

"You like me anyway."

"Don't change the subject. What are you going to do to keep you and the goats safe?"

"I'm going to continue living my life. It's not like I can put the goats under house arrest. Have you met my goats? They do not belong in the house. They're already secured every night. It's a farm, not Fort Knox. I don't want a dog, cameras are expensive, and I've never met another person who's had a livestock-related crime. There's not a lot else I can do. I'm not sure there are any goat security guards for hire."

"You're not taking me seriously."

"What do you want me to do? If you have a legitimate suggestion, I'll listen. I might not be taking this as seriously as you want me to, but I'm never going to dismiss you out of hand. So, tell me what you'd have me do."

"I don't know," she said, frustration straining her voice. "I need you to be safe."

"I thought this was about the goats," he teased.

"Yes, of course. Without the goats, the Bazaar won't be as successful. You're only important in relation to the goats. If they were self-milking goats, we'd be fine."

"I promise I'll think about it. And, if it makes you feel better, I'll start locking up in the evening—both for the goats' security and my own. I recently had locks installed on the outbuildings and changed all the locks on the house. I'll give you a spare set of keys, so that if anything ever happens to me, you'll be able to get in and take care of the goats."

"I don't want to take care of your animals. I am not a farm girl."

"You just haven't met *my* goats yet. You'll love them all."

"Sure," Misty snorted. "That sounds likely." A sudden thought hit her. "When I came over that day, you said you were having a rough year. What's going on?"

"Not now. Not yet. There are things I'm not ready to share with you."

"But what if it's important? What if it's related to all of this?"

"My personal problems are not related to a weirdo wanna-be psychic who likes to play with the guts of farm animals. I barely even believe in all of this."

"Okay, I didn't mean to pry. I should probably let you go before we argue."

She heard him sigh, then after a long pause, he said, "That's probably a good idea. Do you want to get a drink tonight?"

"Where?"

"Meet me at my place at seven. I'll lock up the girls a little early. I've got a great idea."

four

J oseph surveyed the clean, bright interior of Bill's coffee shop, Caffiend Dreams. All the tables were vacant, there wasn't a line, and Bill was nowhere to be seen. "Hey, jackass!" he called. "Where the hell are you?"

"In the back. Where else would I be?" He didn't say 'dumbass,' but it was implied.

"Can I come back?"

"Can I hang out in your cheese kitchen next time you're working in there?"

Joseph harrumphed loudly. "Fine, I'll wait."

"I'll be out in a minute. Do you want anything to eat or drink, or did you just come in to hassle me?"

"Yes."

"I'm rolling my eyes at you right now, even though you can't see me. If you want drip, help yourself. You can go behind the counter and grab what you want out of the case, too. Just don't use your bare hands. I don't want eau de goat on my sausage."

"Wouldn't be the worst thing that's touched your sausage, and you know it."

"Are you ever going to grow up?"

"I certainly hope not." Joseph poured himself a cup of drip coffee, found the chilled goat cream to top it off, then perused the baked goods. He settled on a ham and chèvre croissant, popped it in the warming oven, and tapped his foot.

"What are you doing back there that's so important."

"Kneading bread. You're not so important that I'm going to screw up tomorrow's sandwiches."

The microwave dinged, and Joseph grabbed a seat near the window. He shoved the croissant in his mouth and washed the bite down with a gulp of coffee. A couple minutes later, Bill appeared in the shop, drying his hands on a towel. "Why are you here?"

"Can't a guy just want to get coffee and food and shoot the shit with his BFF?"

"I don't think guys use that term; it's reserved for teenage girls."

"You called me immature a couple minutes ago. Why wouldn't I talk like a teenage girl?"

"Excellent question. However, the answer to your earlier one is no. No, you can't just show up for no reason. Not in the middle of the day. You're not spontaneous. You don't knock off work early to hang out."

"You're my best friend. I wanted to hang out," Joseph said, more than a little defensively.

"Dude. I'm about all out of patience today. Stop beating around the bush and tell me why you're here."

"I did something spontaneous a few days ago."

"I'm almost afraid to ask, but did this spontaneous action have anything to do with our resident palm reader?"

Joseph ran his hand through his hair, then took a big gulp of coffee. "Maybe."

Bill sat down across from him and leaned his chin in his left hand. "Spill." He made a 'gimme' gesture with his right hand.

"Now who's the teenage girl?"

"You wouldn't be here if you didn't want to talk about it."

"She showed up to yell at me for backing out of the Bazaar—"

"You can't back out," Bill said. "How am I going to win the contest without you?"

"Make something new? I should suggest to Misty that they instate a new rule that the same item can't be entered two years in a row if it places in the top three. It'll keep you creative. You're stagnating, man. I mean, prosecco mousse three years in a row? I get that it's so good atheists consider converting, but you need to branch out. People will start to believe you're a one-trick pony."

"You have an annoying habit of changing the subject and rambling on about nothing when you're avoiding something uncomfortable. What happened when Misty showed up?"

She'd parked at the bottom of the drive and walked up to the house." Joseph enjoyed the look of horrified surprise on Bill's face. "By the time she got to my front door, she was red-faced and even angrier than she'd probably been when she started. I wasn't in a good mood, either. Someone is trying to blackmail me—well, my dad, really, but they don't seem to know he's retired."

Joseph gave him the CliffsNotes of the rest of Misty's visit while carefully not meeting Bill's eyes.

"Back it up. You kissed her? When did all this happen? It better have been this morning, or we will be having words, immediately followed by me giving you the silent treatment."

"Tuesday."

"Things have changed the last few years. There was a time when you would've downplayed the blackmail—that I definitely want to hear more about, you told me it was a teenage prank—or waited this long to tell me you'd kissed the woman you've been crushing on since sixth grade. Tell me we're still besties, do better, and maybe I'll forgive you."

"I didn't want you involved. You're my friend."

"I'm your friend. I'm already involved."

"It's a secret?" Joseph said, too much question on his statement to be dismissed.

"Which part?"

"All of it."

Bill heaved a dramatic sigh. "If you're going to continue to hold my number one BFF spot, you have to share these oh-so-important life details with me. Have you apologized to her yet?"

"I called her the next day to apologize. We went out on a secret date. There was more kissing."

"Just kissing?" Bill looked skeptical. "I know you, and I know how long it's been."

"I told her I wanted to take it slow."

"You did? That doesn't seem very characteristic."

"I've wanted this for a long time, and I don't want to screw it up. She wants to keep this a secret for a bit. She's worried about getting her heart publicly broken, especially in a small town where we both know everyone."

"I guess that makes sense. It isn't fun when everyone pops in to ask how you're holding up." Bitterness tinged Bill's words. "It's been years, and people still want to know if things have changed with me and Drew. It's not a good place to find yourself."

"There's more, though. And I need you to suspend both your disbelief and your distaste for the subject."

"I am not talking about him."

"It's not about him; it's about *them*. All of them. They think that the goats and I are in danger. There's a weird woman in town asking about me—"

"Tall, dark-skinned, striking, and with an odd accent?"

"I don't know what she looks like. Hold on a minute." He pulled his phone out of his pocket and texted Misty. "*Hey, baby—what did the goat gut lady look like?*"

The answer came almost immediately. "*Tall, dark skin, dark eyes. Red nails. Couldn't place the accent. Very ambiguous. Why?*"

"*Bill was asking. See you later. ;)*"

Joseph relayed the information to Bill and ignored the notification that he'd received another text. "She was in yesterday afternoon right before closing. She was asking about you. Said her name was…you know, I don't remember. Anyway, she was charming, so I gave her your number."

"You gave her my cell number, didn't you?"

"I was trying to set you up!"

"You know the rules about the number. Never, ever give anyone that number."

Bill shook his head. "I know. I'm sorry. I don't know why I did it. She wasn't even your type."

"And what's my type?"

"Small town palm-reader who dresses like a pin-up librarian."

"That's a very specific type.

"Tell me I'm wrong," Bill challenged. "When are you seeing her again?"

"Tonight."

"Not if you don't answer your texts, you aren't."

Joseph swore under his breath and pulled out his phone. "She's not like that. She wouldn't punish me for being slow to answer a message."

The notification on his screen showed twenty new messages. Bill glanced over and whistled. "Are you sure? That's a lot of texts in less than five minutes. Maybe she's not as solid as she seems."

Joseph tapped the screen. Nineteen of the twenty messages were from an unknown number. He read the one from Misty first—a simple confirmation of tonight's plans—then trepidatiously switched to the others. He opened the first one. *"I know where you live. Your secrets will be revealed unless I get what I want. Guard yourself carefully, mortal."*

"Mortal?" Bill asked.

"This is weird," Joseph agreed. He scrolled through the remaining twenty messages—two more appeared while he was reading them. They were variations on the same. "It has to be the woman you gave my number to. She called me last night."

"What secrets do you have that you'd need to guard?"

"Nothing that would be anything more than mildly embarrassing or slightly inconvenient."

"What about the blackmail?"

Joseph tapped his phone against his chin, considering. "I need to talk to my dad; it's his secret rather than mine. I'm not even sure it's legitimate. It sounds pretty far-fetched, but I'd rather know for sure than completely disregard it. Road trip tomorrow?"

"I haven't seen Jonathan and Ann in too long. I'd love to come with you...unless you'd rather take your new girlfriend."

Joseph punched Bill in the shoulder a little harder than was necessary. I'll pick you up at eight-thirty. You'd better be ready, or I'll leave your sorry ass behind."

· · · · · ★ ★ ★ ★ ★ · · ·

Joseph stood in front of the mirror and smoothed down his hair. He didn't know why he was so nervous. He already knew she liked him. It was a second date, and the first one had ended with kissing. He heard a car in the driveway and swore to himself. She was right on time, not that he'd expected anything different. He spared himself one last glimpse, then headed to the front door. He grabbed his jacket from the coat tree and opened the door.

Misty was on the doorstep, hand poised to knock. She was wearing a navy blue dress with tiny white polka-dots scattered over it and a red crinoline poking out underneath. The bodice showed every curve of her breasts and scooped down low enough to show some cleavage. Her hair was pinned back, but a few errant curls had escaped and were framing her face. "You didn't walk up the driveway this time," he said. And then mentally kicked himself. *Nice one.*

She smiled at him. "These shoes are definitely not made for that kind of hike—especially in the dark." She turned her leg to show off the red stiletto, and he swallowed hard when he caught sight of her fishnet stockings.

"You look really nice," he said. "I'm...wow."

"Thank you. You look fantastic, too." Her eyes roved over his body. "New jeans? I don't think I've ever seen you in something so tight."

"You spend a lot of time checking out how tight my pants are?" he asked. His equilibrium was starting to come back, and he was regaining his sense of humor. As long as he kept his eyes firmly away from her cleavage…

"I was just always so happy to see you leaving," she quipped. "Your backside walking away from me was my favorite view of you."

"And now?"

She pursed her lips at him, looked him up and down again, then made a spinning motion with her hand. "Let's see what we have to work with."

He held his arms out and turned slowly in place. When he'd gone one hundred and eighty degrees, he paused for a beat before turning the rest of the way around. "Well?"

"Whoever made these jeans should get an award for how well they frame your backside, but I'm going to have to pick the front as my favorite view now."

He waggled his eyebrows at her. "What part of my front."

She rolled her eyes. "Men. I was looking at that face, and those lips."

He reached out and slid one hand down to rest on her hip, then tugged her forward. "What would you like my lips to be doing right about now?"

Her arms snaked their way around his neck, and she pressed her body against his for long enough to steal a kiss before stepping back out of his arms. "Where are we going tonight, Joseph?"

"How do you feel about karaoke?"

"Karaoke? Like singing a song poorly in front of strangers?"

"You don't have to sing poorly. That is not a prerequisite."

"Where are we going to do karaoke? Despite my best efforts, I haven't yet convinced Andy he needs to add that feature. In fact, I think his exact words were, 'Over my dead body.'"

"Even if Andy had karaoke, we wouldn't be headed there. We're still keeping things on the DL, right?"

"The DL? Who talks like that in real life?"

"Everyone today is criticizing my speech patterns. What's wrong with the way I talk?"

Misty reached up and brushed her thumb along his jawline. "Nothing. I'm sorry. Where are we going for karaoke, then?"

"The Columbia Bar down by the river."

"The Columbia Bar? Are you serious? That place looks divey."

"It is a dive bar. A dive bar with the best karaoke in the state."

"In the whole state? That's a bold claim, Mr. McEwen."

"Think you're up for it?"

"Do they serve cocktails?"

"You can have as many Long Island Ice Teas as you want. I'm buying, and I'm driving."

"You've talked me into it. Let's go."

Joseph led the way out to his car—a black Ford pickup with enough wear to look like a working truck, but enough shine to be fit to be seen in public. "Do you need a hand up? I don't have running boards."

Misty eyed the distance between the ground and the interior of the pickup, then said, "A hand to steady me while I hop up would be nice. If I were wearing different shoes, I'd be more confident, but the heels are pointy, and the ground is just soft enough that I'm worried putting all my weight on one leg might make me sink."

Joseph held out his hand, and she held on while climbing in. Her skirt flared up as she pulled her second leg in after her, and he caught a tantalizing glimpse of thigh. After making sure she and her dress were both in the car, he walked around the truck slowly, taking extra time to slow his racing pulse. He felt like a schoolboy on his first serious date. He needed to pull himself together, or he was going to make a fool of himself.

Thirty minutes and some light conversation later, he pulled into the parking lot of the Columbia Bar Roadhouse. At least fifty percent of the lot was taken up by motorcycles, and the rest of the vehicles were mostly pickups. Misty looked around. "Too bad we didn't bring the Miata. Would've made it much easier to find after."

He grinned and helped her out of the truck, letting his fingers linger at her waist. "We could just go back to my place," he heard himself say.

"But would there be singing?" she asked,

He tugged her a little bit closer and leaned down to brush his lips against her throat. She gasped, and he smiled against her skin. "I supposed I could sing to you."

"We're here, now. We might as well check it out." She caught his face in her hands and kissed him hard three times. "There's plenty of time later for staying in. Let's get to know each other a little better."

"How is karaoke going to result in us knowing each other better?" he demanded, knowing he sounded like he was sulking.

"I'm gonna find out what you like to sing and vice versa. I mean, do you sing country? Punk? Power ballads? Let's go in. I'm ready for that Long Island Ice Tea and a little bit of rock and roll."

"Rock and roll? What kind of rock and roll?"

She winked at him and strode towards the front door, throwing one last look at him over her shoulder before she disappeared around the corner.

Joseph and Misty were at a high table tucked in the back of the bar. She was drinking a Long Island Ice Tea while he was sipped a Rainier. The bar might have a great atmosphere, but it balanced that out with a poor beer selection. Misty was flipping through the song-book and making notes on one of the tiny scraps of paper. He grabbed a scrap, wrote his name and the song name down, then went to turn his in along with a dollar bill.

Misty followed suit a couple minutes later, then rejoined Joseph at the table. "Why'd you ask about that woman earlier?" she asked.

Joseph started a bit. "I'd almost forgotten. Bill thought he'd seen her—and I think he was right. He's the one who handed out my number. She called last night and has been texting me today. I had to turn off my phone notifications."

Misty laughed. "I guess that's why you didn't respond to my text."

Joseph pulled his phone out of his pocket. One hundred and fifteen unread texts. He showed Misty the screen. Her mouth formed an 'O' of surprise. "That is ridiculous! Can't you block her number?"

"I blocked the first few, but they kept coming in, each one from a different number. I gave up and silenced it after the first fifty or so." He opened up his messages and saw the text from Misty. *"Jeans or dress?"*

"Sorry I didn't answer," he said. "But just so you know for the future, I am always, always going to vote dress."

"I might be a little overdressed for the venue, though."

"Better overdressed than underdressed. Besides, you look gorgeous. I wouldn't change a thing."

"Next up is Joseph," the KJ boomed into the microphone. "Gotta say this is one of my favorites of his. Y'all are in for a rare treat."

Misty raised an eyebrow at him. "Come here often?" she asked.

"Be right back. Gotta go sing."

The music started up, and her jaw dropped. *This* is what he was going to sing? He grabbed the microphone, found her in the crowd, and said, "This one goes out to my special lady over there."

Misty stared, flabbergasted, as he started singing." He was really singing Whitney Houston. And he was nailing it. People in the bar were dancing between tables, and all she could do was stare and sip her drink while he finished up with "I Wanna Dance with Somebody."

He returned to their table amidst thunderous applause, red-faced and sweating, and took a bow towards the rest of the bar before sliding in beside her. "What'd you think?" he asked, suddenly nervous. The noise of the applause behind him faded as all his focus went to her response.

"That was...amazing. I don't even have words. Completely unexpected and so, so good. I didn't know you could do that!"

"Years of practice." He buffed his nails on his shirt.

"What made you decide to practice that one?"

"A college dare. I used to karaoke every week with a bunch of friends, and someone dared me to sing some Whitney. I picked this song, and although it was painful and pretty bad, it wasn't as bad as it could've been. I started practicing to avoid classes and to show my friends I could do it...and now? Why waste all those hours I spent honing my Whitney skills when I should've been studying for my Agronomy final?"

"You are a constant surprise."

He leaned in for a kiss. "You're gonna be up next, I think."

"I'm glad I wasn't right after you. There's no way I could've followed that act."

The KJ's voice boomed out as the last strains of "Sweet Caroline" died away. "Up next is Misty. It's her first time here, so let's be gentle, folks! She's going to be gracing us with 'Whole Lotta Love.'"

"You're going with Led Zeppelin? Bold."

Misty winked at him. "Bold is my middle name." She strode towards the front, shimmying a little extra.

Desire suffused Joseph's body, and he was grateful the table blocked him from the waist down. He couldn't let her have the last word, though. "No, it isn't! Your middle name is River!" The glare she shot at him over her shoulder was worth it, and he leaned back in his chair and hoped she didn't butcher the song.

By the time she was halfway through the song, the entire bar was quiet and hanging on the next note. No one was even singing along, trying to cover up her voice. She was not only hitting every note, she was knocking it out of the park. He was afraid his jaw would hit the table. He wanted to walk the line between impressed and unsurprised. He'd known she had a voice—they'd been in the same high school choir, after all—but he hadn't known she had more in her than the alto with a decent voice who never got the solos.

By the time the song ended, everyone in the bar was on their feet, and Misty received no fewer than seven high fives on her way back to the table. "Was that okay?" she asked.

"More than okay, although now I'm rethinking my second song choice."

"Why?" She took a sip of beer and peered up at him through her ridiculously long eyelashes.

"I was going to do a Led Zeppelin song, too, but I don't want anyone to think I'm trying to coast on your glory."

She laughed, stole a kiss, and grabbed a slip of paper. "You should absolutely do Led Zeppelin, but I am absolutely not doing Whitney Houston."

He leaned over the table trying to see what she was writing. She covered up her paper, glared at him, and scribbled hastily behind her hand. "Stop! It's a surprise!" She pulled another dollar out of her wallet and bounded up to the front of the room to hand in her slip. Someone was singing Free Bird to the accompaniment of background chatter and large groups of people heading out for smoke breaks. Joseph took his slip of paper to the KJ and grabbed a couple more beers.

As the night went on, the bar filled up, and Joseph and Misty both switched to water and crossed their fingers that they'd get to sing their second songs. Joseph glanced at Misty. She was singing along loudly and with great enthusiasm to "Goodbye Earl," and he couldn't keep the grin from his face. He'd finally gotten what he'd wanted since junior high, but now he wasn't sure if it was fair. He still had his secrets, and she deserved better than a man who couldn't open himself completely, who, by necessity, had to close himself off. He opened his mouth to suggest that they leave. He could drive them back to his place, explain that he'd made a mistake, then go back to being surly at her. They were only a few days in. Neither of them would suffer for it. Pain shot through his heart when he leaned forward to get her attention. Before he could assess the source, she was sliding off the bar stool and heading up to the front of the room.

She grabbed the mic, smiled mischievously, and the music started. Joan Jett's "I Hate Myself for Loving You" poured out over the room, and he found himself tapping his foot in rhythm. The longer she sang, the less certain he was that he could end things with her, even if it was the right thing to do. The stabbing pain twisting its way through his internal organs slowly dissipating, replaced by a different ache. She was everything he'd ever wanted, and the reality was even better than the fantasy.

He didn't get a chance to congratulate her personally before his name was called. He took a deep breath. The song he was singing wasn't new to his karaoke repertoire, but he'd never sung it for a woman before. Never sung it when a woman was there with him. Butterflies took flight in his stomach and distracted him from all the other various feelings still warring inside.

He poured his heart into "Thank You," and kept his eyes on Misty the whole time. Her gaze didn't leave his for the nearly five minute song, and when he finished and walked back to the table, she blushed.

"I think I need a cigarette after that," she said, fanning herself.

Joseph allowed himself a moment of smugness while holding back what he really wanted to say. Telling a woman on a second date that he'd envisioned that as their song was going a little faster than was prudent. Instead, he said, "That has always been one of my favorite Led Zeppelin songs."

She arched an eyebrow at him. "Always?"

"Maybe just for the last ten years, or so. I didn't really know anything besides Stairway to Heaven before that."

She gasped, hand on her chest. "I am *shocked*, Joseph McEwen. Shocked, I tell you."

The spell was broken, and he was grateful. "Wanna get out of here?"

"Yeah. You must be exhausted, this far past your bedtime." She slid off the stool and grabbed his elbow, letting him lead her out of the bar."

When they got to the car, he looked down at her. "Mystic?"

She reached up on her tiptoes and silenced him with a kiss. "I'm tired, Joe. Let's go."

He opened the door for her, then walked around the car and slid behind the wheel. She hadn't even corrected him when he didn't call her Misty.

· · · · ★ ★ ★ ★ ★ · · ·

"WHY ARE YOU DOING THIS?" MISTY ASKED.

Joseph parked in front of his garage, turned off the truck, and unfastened his seatbelt before answering. "Doing what?"

"Damnit, Joseph! We were having such a good time, and now you're picking fights?"

"How is asking legitimate questions picking a fight? It's not like we were discussing anything important."

Misty heaved a sigh. "Asking me what my favorite shows and movies and bands are is a great way to get to know me better. Criticizing everything I like is not a good way to follow that up. There's no need to find the worst thing about everything I enjoy. I don't particularly like sports, but I'm not going to make snide comments comparing Adam Sandler to Burt Reynolds and the inappropriateness of him playing the lead in the remake of The Longest Yard."

"You don't like sports movies? Why would you dismiss an entire movie genre like that?"

"The only acceptable sports movie is A League of Their Own. Everything else is a testosterone-driven mess."

Joseph opened his mouth then clicked it shut and took a deep breath. He had picked at everything she'd said. He'd made snide comments about everything she liked, starting with her cocktail of choice and ending with her devotion to nerd shows. He was the ass women tweeted about. The click of the door handle forced his eyes open. Misty was halfway out of the car before he could think of anything to say.

"I'm sorry," he said. "You're right. I was being rude."

"I'm going home. You'll have to apologize again later, but thanks for admitting it now." She closed the door, walked to her car, and drove away.

five

Joseph smiled as he woke, kept his eyes closed, and rolled over, reaching for Misty. His hand closed on empty space. He frowned and opened his eyes. She wasn't next to him, and there was no evidence that she'd ever been there. He sat up and looked around the room. His shoulder slumped. She wasn't there—hadn't ever been there. It'd been a dream.

He heaved an overly dramatic sigh and got out of bed, shoving his feet into the slippers waiting for him. The aroma of coffee was wafting from the kitchen, and he followed it almost blindly.

Two cups of coffee later, and he was ready to kick himself as the memory of last night came back. The conversation on the way home had been antagonistic. It was his own fault, he knew. He couldn't stop going back and forth between his desire to be with her, to realize his dreams, and his knowledge that he needed to end things before they went too far. He rested his face in his hands and shook his head. He'd be lucky if she ever spoke to him again. There were too many secrets that he couldn't share. Even Bill didn't know them all, and he was the only person besides his parents and his siblings that he'd even begun to trust.

His family, the McEwens, were not like other families. It was a secret they'd guarded for as long as family lore went back, and he was afraid that someone had finally found out. Between the weirdly nonspecific blackmail attempts and the phone calls from the mysterious and overly persistent woman, something was off, and he couldn't think of anything else that would cause so many strangers to be so interested in him.

Self-recrimination and near-crippling regret weren't enough to keep him inside, though. The goats needed to be fed, watered, and milked.

Joseph filled a thermos with more coffee, dosed liberally with goat's cream, and grabbed a blueberry muffin from the basket on the counter. He didn't think the basket had been there yesterday, which meant Bill had let himself in either last night or early this morning to leave the offering. He had a habit of doing that. Bill said it was the only way he could ensure that Joseph was eating, but Joseph privately suspected that Bill was hoping to catch him with a woman so he'd have new fodder for the ribbing. He took a huge bite of the muffin and chased it with a swig of coffee, ditched the slippers for his work boots while humming the Mr. Rogers theme song, then stepped out of the house and into a...mess.

There was no other word to describe the scene that awaited him. After he'd watched Misty drive off last night, he'd done a last walk-through of all the barns, while willing himself to believe he'd made the right decision in letting her go with nothing more than a perfunctory peck. Everything had been in order. The dirt and gravel driveway had looked like any other driveway. The barns were in order, and all the animals were properly bedded down for the night.

Now, the driveway was torn up, like a very heavy vehicle had driven through with brakes on, and every barn door was wide open.

He dropped the muffin and the thermos and sprinted towards the barn. A hasty check of the first barn—the boys' barn—revealed that all was in order. There were two cranky bucks and three wethers, and the only reaction they had to seeing him was to bleat loudly and rattle their food troughs.

"I'll be right back, boys," Joseph said. Goatzilla turned around and kicked the door to his pen then gave Joseph some stink-eye. "I know you're hungry, but I have to check on the ladies. You and Vincent van Goat are in charge here. Keep an eye on the others, and I'll be back as soon as I can."

Goatzilla snorted but stopped kicking. Joseph double-checked all the doors to make sure no one could make a break for it, then headed next door. The inside of the barn was chaos. Every door was open, and goats were milling about. Joseph turned over a milk crate, stood on top, and clapped his hands loudly. "Ladies, home!" he commanded.

There was sudden order to the chaos, and the does trotted around the barn until each of them had found their pen. He had eight does, and each had a kid—except Billie Holiday—she always had twins. When the goats stopped running around and settled down, each pen had a doe, and there were eight kids bleating like mad.

Joseph counted, then counted again. One was missing. "Find your mamas!" he said. "Find your babies!"

The does bleated softly, and the kids ran to the right pens. Both of Billie's kids were accounted for. He breathed a sigh of relief. He'd never say it out loud, but she was his favorite, and her kids always followed in her extraordinary footsteps.

He walked up and down the pens, making sure the doors were closed, and everyone was unharmed. The only doe without a kid was Goatie Hawn. She was pacing up and down in her pen, bleating softly, and looking around. She tossed the straw in the corner up over her head, then turned and looked at Joseph.

It was probably his imagination, but she looked accusatory. "I don't know, Goatie," he said. "Tell me what happened." She opened her mouth, and for a brief, surreal second, he thought she was going to do just that. Instead, she bared her teeth at him, snorted, and continued pacing.

Joseph went through his regular morning routine. He led the ladies, one at a time, into the milking barn, then made sure everyone had fresh food and clean water. He got less milk than usual—and almost none from Goatie—and he chalked it up to stress. When everyone was taken care of, including the barn cats that he'd not adopted but who'd showed up one day to keep the dairy rodent-free, he went back inside, poured himself another cup of coffee, and called the police.

· · ★ ★ ★ ★ ★ ★ ★ ★ · ·

"What the hell, Joseph!" Bill exclaimed. They were about twenty minutes into their road trip to Seattle, and Joseph had finally finished the goat-crime story. "What did the cops say?"

"Not a lot. Apparently, a kidnapping isn't that big of a deal when it's not a human."

"But your property was clearly broken into, right?"

"Open barn doors and a torn up driveway are 'not evidence of a crime,'" Joseph said taking both hands off the wheel for his over-exaggerated air quotes. "And since I carelessly left all my barn doors open, it's no wonder one of my herd wandered off."

"Do they really believe this crap?" Bill asked. "They know you. Everyone in town knows you. You are the most meticulous person in Oracle Bay. There's no way you'd forget to close your pen doors and the barn doors after doing doughnuts in your own driveway."

A bitter laugh escaped Joseph. "They asked what time I got home last night and if I'd been out to the barns then. I said I'd gotten home a little after midnight, after an evening of karaoke at the Columbia Bar, then implied I'd been intoxicated and careless."

"Were you?" Bill asked bluntly.

"No. You know me. I am never out of control. I do not get drunk. I certainly do not get drunk and then drive. And I would never get drunk and drive someone else home."

"Someone else? Did you have another date with Misty?"

Joseph didn't respond. His hands gripped the steering wheel a little tighter, and he stared stonily ahead.

"That's a yes, then. You took her to karaoke? Bold move for a second date."

Joseph flicked on the windshield wipers and turned on the radio.

"Didn't go well, then? Wasn't she into it? Was she bad? Were *you* bad?"

"Of course I wasn't bad," Joseph snapped. "We've done karaoke a hundred times. You know I'm amazing."

Bill grinned. "So, it was her, then. I don't remember her being a terrible singer, but karaoke is a different beast."

"She was amazing. Brought the house down."

"Then what's the problem? How'd you screw it up?"

"Why would you assume I screwed it up? It's equally likely that it was her."

Bill reached over and patted Joseph's leg. "Joey Joe, we have known each other since second grade. You know all my secrets, and while I don't know any of yours because you are an untrusting bitch, I do know you. You decided that you had too many secrets and couldn't risk breaking her heart or yours, and certainly can't do the responsible adult thing and share your burdens with those who care about you, so you got cold, didn't you?"

"Don't call me that. I hate it when you call me that. And you know most of my secrets. At least eighty-five percent of them."

Bill grinned. "I don't know the good stuff, though. You keep things so close to the vest. But, since you've always been there for me, through everything that's ever gone right or wrong, I guess I'll continue this one-sided friendship a bit longer.

"How many times did you call our girl Mystic, knowing she hates it?"

"Not the point," Joseph ground out.

"Then what is? You finally got the woman of your dreams to go out with you, and I don't understand what dark witchcraft you used to talk her into that, and now you're going to cold-shoulder her until she goes away? What the hell is wrong with you? This is a once-in-a-lifetime opportunity. You have worked for so long to cultivate your Captain Jerkface persona—quite successfully, I might add—and still managed to land Misty Greene after being an ass to her all these years."

Joseph sighed loudly and looked at the road ahead of him. "It's none of your business," he ground out after a too-long silence.

"You know I love you like the obnoxious brother I never wanted—"

"You have three brothers," Joseph said.

"And they are universally dickbags," Bill said. "Stop interrupting. As I was saying, you are my best friend. I would do anything for you, you know that, right? If I saw someone hurting you, I would punch them right in the face. Because you're driving, I'm gonna hold off for now, but you deserve a black eye for the way you're treating yourself and Misty."

"She thinks all the psychic woo stuff is real," Joseph reminded him, doing his best to ignore the fact that there was a lot more evidence for it to be real than against. This was probably not the hill he should die on

"So what? Are you trying to convince yourself or hurt me? Either way, it's not going to work. I made mistakes in the past. They may be irreparable, but that doesn't mean it's okay for you to make the same mistakes right now—not while you can still do something about it."

"What do I do? There are things I can't tell her, for the same reason I can't tell you, and eventually, she'll figure out I'm keeping things from her. I've seen that movie. It never ends well for the intrepid romantic male lead."

"Please. You are the comic relief sidekick at best."

"Really? No one's ever accused me of being the comic relief."

"Good point," Bill conceded. "You are the cranky sidekick who everyone hates."

Joseph tried to force out a laugh, but couldn't mask his bitterness. "That sounds about right."

"It doesn't have to be this way. You had two great dates with Misty. Based solely on your account, it sounds like she had a good time—at least until you freaked out last night. Am I right?"

"We had a good time. But it doesn't matter. In the long run, she's going to want to know things that I can't share, and that—"

"Why?"

"Why what?" Joseph asked, confusion lacing his voice.

"Why can't you share? None of your reasons have ever made that much sense, but I chose not to push you. You said that movie where the romantic leads keep secrets from each other ends badly but have you followed that path to its logical conclusion?"

"What do you mean?"

"Do you want Misty to be your Meg Ryan?"

"What kind of dated reference is that?"

"Just stick with me, here. Do you want Misty to be your romantic comedy lead?"

Joseph rolled his eyes. "Yes, I guess so."

"Do you look into the future and see getting married, doing goat stuff together, maybe starting a bridge league?"

"Well, all but the last one, I guess. I don't need to know anything about bridge. Where are you going with this?"

"If you want the fairytale ending, you're gonna have to make some sacrifices. I suppose there might be a woman out there who'd put up with your grumpy exterior, obsession with goats, unwillingness to leave Oracle Bay, and multiple secrets. But you and I both know that Misty Greene is not going to put up with the secrets. So— and I know this is going to be the most outrageous suggestion anyone could make under these circumstances—what if you told her your secrets?" Bill leaned back into the car seat, interlaced his fingers, and rested his chin on them.

Joseph glanced over at him, and Bill batted his eyelashes.

"I can't. I've told you…"

"Why not, though? What happens if you tell her? Worst case scenario?"

"You don't understand. It's not some dumb secret like the time I almost joined a cult; it's a family secret—one that's been handed down for generations."

"Back up a minute. You almost joined a cult? When? Why? How? I don't even have all the right questions for this revelation."

"You didn't know?" Joseph flicked his eyes towards his friend. "Misty knew, and someone had to have told her; I assumed it was you."

"When?" Bill demanded.

"College. I was dating someone, and it seemed like a good idea at the time. It wasn't you?"

"Sweetie, if I'd known, I would've been teasing you constantly since I found out. That's not something I would've found out and never mentioned. I am too good a friend to let a tidbit like that fade into the background. How did Misty say she found out?"

"She read my palm."

"Do you believe her?"

Joseph shook his head and flexed his fingers on the steering wheel. "I don't know what to believe. Something weird is happening in Oracle Bay."

· · · · · ★ · ★ · ★ · ★ · ★ · · · · ·

JOSEPH PULLED INTO HIS PARENTS' DRIVEWAY AND HONKED ONCE AS AN announcement. He and Bill weren't even out of the car before the front door opened and his mom was bustling out, flour decorating her t-shirt and blue jeans, and a worn dish towel in one hand. "Joey, Billy! It's so good to see both my boys. Why do you have to wait so long between visits?" She enveloped Joseph in a hug, squeezing him hard enough to make his ribs creak, and tipping her face back to look up at him.

"Hi, Mom," he said, dropping a kiss on her forehead. "Did you make pie?"

She swatted him in the butt with her towel, then turned her attention to Bill. "You are taller every time I see you. If I could figure out what was causing it, I'd take some myself. It might be nice to reach the cupboards without a footstool."

"And you look younger every time I see you, Mrs. McEwen."

"Billy?" Her voice held a note of warning so sharp that both Joseph and Bill flinched.

"Sorry, ma'am. I mean Ann. Your timeless beauty just gets me all twitterpated."

"Go on, you," she said, giving him a swat that matched Joseph's. "I made that pie you like."

"You're like the mother I never had," he said, wrapping an arm around her and squeezing her close.

"And you're the son I always wanted," Ann McEwen said.

"I am standing right here," Joseph said. "I'm telling Thomas next time I talk to him, too."

Ann clucked her tongue. "You boys are such a handful. I don't know why we put up with you."

"Because we're adorable," they chorused in unison.

Ann snorted. "Hrmph. That hasn't been true since you were six." They grinned at each other. It was so easy to fall back into the same patterns they'd been following since they were children.

"Hey, Dad," Joseph called as he stepped into the entryway and toed off his shoes.

"In the kitchen," a gravelly voice answered. "If you don't get your butt in here immediately, you're going to miss out on all the pie."

"Nooo," Bill cried, racing past Joseph towards the kitchen. "That's my pie!"

Joseph followed his friend and walked in on a standoff. John

McEwen was sitting at the country-style kitchen table, arms around a pie plate, and hunched over to defend it. Bill was threatening him with a fork, making rapid jabs towards any hole in the pie defense he could find. "Bill, please don't stab my dad."

"It'd be justifiable," Bill said. "He's a pie hoarder."

"What are you going to give me for the pie? You can't just show up empty-handed and expect a slice of peach pie. This is America! You have to pay for your pie!"

Bill grinned, grabbed the bag he'd surreptitiously set down, and reached in. "Chocolate croissants, cranberry orange scones, and a dozen dark chocolate and sea salt cookies with caramel glaze. Will that be enough payment?"

John leaned back, keeping his hands on the pie plate, and thought about it. "It'll do, although I don't know why Ann has to make pie every time you come up when you can just do it yourself."

Bill wasted no time dishing himself a slice of pie and digging in. "Her crusts are amazing—so much better than anything I've ever managed—and she won't give me her recipes."

"A lady needs to keep a few secrets," she said. She went to the stove, peeked under a couple lids, and then turned around to survey the table. "That was supposed to be dessert," she admonished.

"John took the first bite," Bill said.

"I haven't even had any yet," Joseph said. "I was waiting, as is proper."

"He was waiting because I haven't yet decided if he can have any," John said. "He didn't bring payment."

"Bill brought you enough sweets to last for a week!"

"So, he can have your share of pie. What'd you bring? Don't tell me you're going to bring dishonor on the family by trying to claim pie you didn't earn!"

Joseph's smile started to slip from his face, and he tried to hold it in place and laugh at the banter which was a repeat of almost every trip he'd made in the ten years since his dad had retired and moved to Seattle. Something must have shone on his face, because his dad shoved the pie towards him, handed him a fork and a plate, and said, "I guess you can pay double next time. Bill, when you're done with your pie, could you help Ann in the kitchen for a minute?"

Bill rolled his eyes, making sure Joseph and his dad both saw, and got up.

"Sure thing, John. Want me to bring you anything back?"

"You're a good boy, Bill. We sure are glad our Joey has a friend like you to keep him in line."

The exasperation on Bill's face faded somewhat. "You all were the best surrogate family a guy could have. It was easy being Joe's friend; his family was the icing on the cake."

"Get out of here you," John said. "Bring me back a glass of wine."

Once they were alone, John looked at Joseph and held his gaze. "This is about the family legacy, isn't it?"

Joseph nodded. He squirmed in his chair trying to dislodge the discomfort that had settled in when his dad made it possible to talk.

"Is Billie okay?"

"She's fine, Dad, but something's going on."

"More than just Billie? Does it involve the…" he looked around as if to ensure that Ann and Bill were both out of earshot. His voice dropped half an octave and was practically a whisper when he continued. "Trunk? Is it secret? Is it safe?"

"You've been watching too much Lord of the Rings," Joseph said.

John reached out and jabbed his son in the chest with a finger just beginning to gnarl with age. "No such thing, and I am ashamed you said that."

"Did you ever tell mom?"

John didn't even blink at the abrupt subject change. "Of course I told your mother, you daft arse. Did you think all these years I was carrying all this in secret and never sharing with the woman I love?"

Joseph felt his jaw drop as he lost track of why he was there, what he'd come to say. "I thought it was a secret! The family secret!"

"And so it is. I didn't tell every lass who wandered through my bed, now, did I? But when I found one who'd stick around for this side of forever, why would I dishonor her by keeping secrets and telling lies."

"You never said..." Joseph's voice trailed off as he recalled his father's words, spoken in his occasional Irish accent that was a product of several years living abroad before he came home to take over the farm, and repeated many times over the years, "This is something we keep in the family, lad, and no mistake. You can't be telling your mates at school nor using our family secrets to lift a young lass's skirt. This is for family."

"You didn't say I couldn't tell anyone, you just said I couldn't tell anyone who wasn't family," Joseph said. Heat suffused his neck and cheeks.

"That's right, lad. Did you hear my talk so many times and neglect to remember that my Ann, your mother, was family? Don't let her hear you talk that way, or you'll see the wrong side of her wooden spoon. She's been holding back her whole life, and you don't want to be the one she breaks her no violence rules on."

Joseph leaned back in his chair and hung his head back, looking at the ceiling. "I could've told Bill. He's as much family as anyone I've met."

"Do you want to? I could call them back in. They're probably listening at the doorway."

Joseph straightened up and tipped forward in the chair. "Might as well. The more minds working on this, the better."

Bill and Ann were back in the room before Joseph's chair legs hit the floor.

"Tell me everything," Bill said. "I want to know all your dark secrets."

Joseph looked at his dad, down at the table, then reached for the pie. "Billie Holliday is a magical goat." He took a big bite of pie directly from the dish, which earned him a swat on the knuckles from his mom.

"What now?" Bill asked, a glass of juice halfway to his mouth.

Joseph sighed while John and Ann stifled grins. "Billie is at least a hundred years old—she came here with a great great grandmother from Italy. She always has twins. She won't take a buck—I guess they're immaculately conceived—and she can help us make good farm decisions."

"You have a Virgin Mary goat?" Bill asked. He looked at Ann and John for confirmation, and they nodded.

"As far as we can tell. Unless she has a secret lover somewhere," John said.

"And she helps you make farm decisions?"

"Yeah," Joseph said. "Like good areas to graze, which days to expect kidding to happen, and, with only marginal success, which stocks to invest in."

"You have a magic goat. One that can tell the future."

Joseph nodded and finally met his friend's eyes. "I don't know if it's so much telling the future..."

"Of course it is," Ann said. "That's how the stock market and the calendars work. She's a psychic goat."

"Oh." Joseph sat on that word for a moment. He had made a very, very big mistake. "I never thought of it like that before."

Bill said, "Are you guys pranking me? Because this is...weird."

"Not a prank. And that's the blackmail. Someone's been harassing me for a couple years, threatening to expose my 'unnatural relationship' with my goat. I assumed he was either a pervert on a phishing expedition, someone who'd seen me asking Billie to look at a calendar, or just a random weirdo with a grudge. But the threats have increased lately. I'm to wait for instructions, then drop the cash in unmarked bills. I never get a location or an amount or proof of what I'm being blackmailed for, but in the last few days, things have definitely been on an uptick."

"This is a lot," Bill said. "And this makes me rethink a lot of life decisions."

"Yeah," Joseph said. "We might be even bigger idiots than we thought."

"I could've told you boys that," John said. "Now give me back my pie."

M isty stepped out of the shower and cocked her head. There was definitely someone knocking on the door. She grabbed her robe, checked the hall clock and confirmed it was still before ten o'clock in the morning. Her friends knew better, her family no longer lived in town, and her clients weren't supposed to know where she lived. That didn't leave a lot of possibilities.

She marched down the hall to let Joseph in. Just before she yanked open the door, she paused. *What if it's Jehovah's Witnesses?*

Whoever it was deserved a piece of her mind.

She flung open the door, two greetings ready to fling at whoever was violating her Monday morning. "You can take your stuck-up, jerk-face Watchtower and shove it..." she trailed off.

Joseph stood on her front steps, shuffling his feet and holding a bouquet of peonies.

Misty's gaze bounced back and forth between Joseph, who was assiduously refusing to make eye contact, and the peonies which ranged in color from white to deep purple. "Where did you find peonies at this time of year?" she asked at the same time he said, "Jerkface Watchtower? What does that even mean?"

"You first," Misty said, crossing her arms over her chest and ensuring her robe didn't gape.

"I have a lot. Can I come in?"

Misty looked him up and down. He was uncharacteristically rumpled; he had on worn blue jeans with mud—at least she hoped it was mud—staining the cuffs and a wrinkled flannel shirt open at the neck. His hair looked simultaneously slept on and finger tousled.

A car started down the street, deciding the issue. Misty stepped back. "Come in."

Joseph crossed the threshold and looked around with interest. "I've never been here before. It's nice."

Misty stalked towards the stairs. "I'm going to get dressed. Feel free to make me a pot of coffee while you wait."

Misty stood in her bedroom after shedding her robe and glared at her door. She opened her closet and grabbed the outfit in front that she'd picked out the night before. The ruby red calf-length skirt, pearl gray button-down blouse, and black cardigan were pretty and perfect for a day of running errands in town and checking in on her tenants. It was not perfect for telling off a man who wasn't even supposed to be here. She hung up the outfit and grabbed the jeans at the top of her hamper. He didn't deserve her nice clothes. After completing her dressed down look with a ratty, stained t-shirt and slipping on a pair of house shoes, she finger-combed her hair and braided it.

When she walked back downstairs, the aroma of freshly brewed coffee hit her a second before the spattering sound of something frying.

"Are you making me breakfast?" she demanded.

"You told me to."

"I suggested coffee. I didn't suggest invading my kitchen, going through my cupboards, and ransacking my fridge."

Joseph ignored her and plated bacon and eggs just as the toast popped out of the toaster. "Breakfast?"

Misty grabbed the plate, poured herself a cup of coffee, and glared. "Why are you here?" She added creamer to her coffee and stirred.

"I wanted to apologize."

"Then get it over with," Misty said. "Or, maybe just call like you did last time."

Joseph winced. "I do find myself having to apologize to you more often than seems prudent, don't I? I need to spend a lot more time than I thought working on myself to break my habit of jerk first, ask questions later."

Misty suppressed a giggle at his accidental innuendo and blew a long breath through her nose. "It is morning. I hate morning. You are interrupting my routine and disturbing my calm. If you want me to listen to your damn apology, then spit it out and leave. Otherwise, you can skip straight to the part where you get out of my house, and we go back to trading barbed insults when we're forced to interact and ignoring each other the rest of the time."

"Is that what you want?" He sounded completely taken aback, and Misty frowned at him.

"No, jerkwad, I want you to get to the point."

"I was a jerk Saturday night. I have an excuse, although it's a poor one. I have a family secret—a secret I've never told anyone, not even Bill. And it's coming back to bite me in the ass right now. I didn't know how I could continue to be in a relationship with you while also keeping my family secret and protecting everyone."

"Had you considered sharing your secret? I mean, sure, not right away. If it's a big family thing, you don't want to share with just any woman you date, but real relationships mean sharing parts of each other, even the scary parts."

"Until yesterday, it'd never crossed my mind," Joseph admitted.

"What happened yesterday?"

"Bill and I drove up to Seattle to visit Mom and Dad."

Misty's face lit up. "How are Ann and John? I haven't seen them in ages!"

"Doing well and thoroughly enjoying retirement. I don't know how my dad is staying so trim, though. My mom is on a pie baking spree."

"Please continue."

"I'm sorry I tried to ungracefully extricate myself from whatever it is we've got going on solely because I didn't want to hurt either of us by being forced to lie to you regarding the secret that apparently I could've told you."

"That's a lot of words, but do you really mean them?"

"Yes. I spent so much time agonizing about lying to you for the rest of our lives because when I watched you sing Saturday night, I couldn't imagine not spending the rest of my life with you."

"Whoa, there. Back it up about a hundred paces. You are moving way too fast. We've been out twice."

"Sometimes, when you know, you know." Joseph shrugged and plated his own breakfast. "Your eggs are probably cold."

Misty took a bite and chewed slowly. "Are you saying you'd like to keep dating?"

"Yes. I'd like to continue our secret dating relationship, which will culminate in going public at the Yule Ball, at which point we will take our relationship public. Then, at some point in the future, when you're ready, and we're both comfortable, I envision things going even further. It is fast, but I've known you for twenty years. We have some catching up to do on what's changed since middle school, but we know the important things. We know each other's friends and family and careers. It's just the small things that need to be learned. Favorite colors and books and positions." He winked.

"You may need to grovel a little bit more. You were pretty rude Saturday."

"Are you considering forgiving me?"

"Considering... Despite what a jerk you were, this is a plausible explanation, based on what I know about you. It also explains your whole jerk persona. You've been keeping everyone at a distance all these years so that no one will notice you have a secret and you won't have to lie to anyone. I'll give you one more chance, but if you are anything but kind and gracious to me, there won't be any more chances."

"Third time's the charm?" he asked.

"It'd better be because I won't put up with someone who thinks they can apologize their way out of every incidence of terrible human being that they come down with. I am so much better than that."

"Deal," Joseph said. "Wanna know the secret?"

"Yes. Of course. But not yet. You might see forever when you look at me, but I don't know if I'm there yet."

Joseph's shoulders slumped almost imperceptibly, but he nodded. "Fair enough."

MISTY PRIMPED FOR HER DATE. THIS WAS THE LAST CHANCE SHE WAS GOING to give him, and if he didn't behave himself, it was over. There was only so far a junior high crush and a confession of undying affection went. Sure, being adored was heady stuff, but it wasn't enough to overcome the strong eau d'douche Joseph was regularly dousing himself with. It was worse than that body spray that the teen boy population had been obsessed with a couple years ago.

She'd never been someone who cared much about fashion. Well, except for her penchant for rockabilly librarian style dresses. And cute eyeglasses. And her frankly embarrassing collection of twee cardigans to pair with the aforementioned dresses.

Fine. She was a clotheshorse, and she wasn't afraid to admit it. Growing up, she'd never been one of the popular ones. She'd never stood out for her looks or her charm or her style. She'd always been a bit too chunky, a bit too nerdy, and a bit too dowdy. But when she'd gone away to college, she'd found that with a little bit of confidence and the application of a cute dress that accentuated her curves, she felt pretty darn good about herself more often than not. She adopted the style of the people she'd made friends with freshman year, and her appreciation for the dresses, cardigans, and hairstyles lasted much longer than the friendships with the people whose names she couldn't even remember.

She finally settled on a white dress with a red cherry pattern and a low-cut, tight bodice, a navy blue cardigan to keep her shoulders and arms warm, and the hottest pair of high heels she owned— cream pumps with navy trim and the cutest little bow on the heel.

She eyed her reflection in the mirror, pursed her lips, and nodded. No matter what happened tonight, she would come out on top.

She grabbed her gloves and purse from the console near the front door and headed out into the rain towards her car.

Thirty minutes later, she pulled into the parking lot of a small Italian restaurant in Long Beach. She grumbled as she got out of her car and prepared to make the high-heel-parking lot dash to the front door. "This either needs to work out or end so I don't have to keep having dates in a different town to avoid gossip."

The interior of the restaurant was warm and softly lit. The burgundy couches near the front door promised a comfortable wait, and the quiet guitar music soothed her annoyance at the rainy drive.

"May I help you?" the hostess asked.

"I'm meeting a friend here," she started. "I'm a bit early, though, so I'm not sure..." she trailed off.

"What's the name of the party you're meeting?"

"Joseph McEwen?" she asked, then shook herself. "I mean, Joseph McEwen. That wasn't a question."

The hostess smiled at her, then checked her list. "I have a reservation under that name, but he hasn't checked in yet. You can either wait for him here or in the bar."

"I'll head into the bar," Misty said.

"Very good. I'll let him know you're here when he arrives."

Misty walked through the too-fancy gilded archway into the bar, which was, if possible, even warmer and more burgundy than the entryway. When the bartender came over, she said, "I'll have a glass of your house red, unless it's Pinot."

"Our house red is a Cabernet Sauvignon, but we also have a good local Merlot from Chateau Ste. Michelle if you'd rather."

"Mmm... I love Cab, but I love that winery. This is a hard choice."

The bartender winked at her, leaned over the bar, and whispered conspiratorially. "Have the Merlot. It's happy hour for..." she checked her watch, "...three more minutes, and it's on special. Once you finish that glass, you can try the Cab."

"You've twisted my arm," Misty said. "Sold."

The glass of Merlot arrived a couple of minutes later with another wink and smile from the bartender, and Misty leaned back, took a sip, and relaxed for the first time since her landlord and ostensible boss had called her to announce he was making an impromptu visit to Oracle Bay. She'd meant to savor the glass of wine, but nerves and a sense of impending doom, courtesy of her handshake with Vincent Bryson earlier today, caused her to finish it faster than she'd intended. Oracle Bay was in a whole lotta trouble. If Vincent was forced to sell off his holdings to a developer, the whole feel of the town would change, everyone who rented one of his properties, whether for business or residential purposes, would be subjected to rent increases or, even worse, eviction as the buildings were torn down to make way for a more cookie-cutter, chain store, generic coastal town look. She wasn't sure if it was better or worse that she was in a position to do something about it, especially since she didn't know what—beyond a psychic flash when she shook his hand —she was supposed to do.

The bartender grabbed her empty. "A glass of the house red?"

"Yes, please," she said, handing over her credit card.

She deliberately paced herself on the second glass of wine and was on her third sip when she felt a hand at the small of her back. She tipped her head up and glanced over at Joseph. "You're late."

"The goats were particularly cantankerous tonight. Our table will be ready in about fifteen minutes."

"Want a drink?" she asked, waving the bartender over.

"I'll take whatever local porter you have available," he said.

"I have a Brimstone Smoked Porter from The Pour House."

"That sounds good."

After the beer arrived, Joseph turned towards her and said, "Thank you for meeting me here."

"I've been thinking," she said. "I wish you'd told me you had a secret you couldn't tell me. It would've been easier to take. I'm still not ready to carry them; I'm not sure we're there yet. But, instead of acting like a jerk, you could've said, 'Hey, Misty. There are some things—family things—I can't tell you right now. I might act weird, but it's not you, it's my secrety secrets that I'm keeping until I've initiated you into the dark McEwen arts."

"I guess that's fair," Joseph said. "That's not how I'd put it, but it makes sense. I'm sorry I didn't trust you—trust us—enough to tell you that I had secrets."

"The key is communicating well about what we can't share. Neither of us has been in a serious relationship in, well, years. It won't be easy for either of us. We all have secrets. Well, not me. You know just about everything there is to know."

"Everything?" a lightly accented voice asked. There was an extra half syllable on the end of 'everything,' and Misty froze. "I think you have left out a few details, no?" That accent—almost Italian with hints of Greek and something she couldn't place—was familiar. She felt Joseph's stillness mirror her own, and she knew he recognized her as well. It was the woman from her shop. The one who was so interested in Joseph.

She wanted to engage, to challenge the woman for her secrets, but that was not the point. This woman was dangerous. "Why are you here?" she asked, throwing as much chill into her voice as possible.

"What?" the woman asked. "You don't want to talk about the secrets you hold back from tu amore? The secrets you just said you don't have."

"No, I don't. Any secrets I might have are nothing but incidental. I want you to leave."

The woman turned to Joseph. "And what about you? Don't you want to know what your lady is holding back all the while berating you for committing the same sin she is guilty of?"

"Are you the woman who left me a hundred messages? I am not in the least interested in anything you have to say. You are not setting yourself up to be the most trustworthy woman in town. Please leave us alone."

"How are your goats tonight, Mr. McEwen?"

"They were fine when I left them, and they'd better be fine when I get home. If they are otherwise, you'll be hearing from the police."

She laughed, a trilling noise that set Misty's teeth on edge. "Why do you think I am a threat to your precious animals?"

"Just go," Misty said.

"In a minute—I need only one more thing." She held out her hand as if to shake, and Misty reciprocated before she could stop herself. The woman grabbed her glove with one hand, yanked it off, then grasped her hand and smiled.

Images bombarded Misty, and she gasped as they overwhelmed her. She tried to pull her hand free, but the woman held on too hard. "Stop," she begged. "Please." Tears streamed down her face and she left her rocking back and forth on her bar stool in an effort to clear the images from her mind.

"Baby, baby..." Joseph's voice broke through the scenes of murder and chaos. His arms were around her although he was very carefully avoiding her ungloved hand. "She's gone, it's over. Come back to me."

"Joseph?" Misty peered up at him through tear-soaked lashes. "What happened?"

"I don't know. She took your glove, grabbed your hand, and then you just...went blank. It was so weird to watch. Your face went slack, and your eyes were vacant. Then you started crying and rocking. I finally got her to let go, and she left before she could be kicked out. Did you..." he looked around then lowered his voice, "...see something?"

"I can't right now," she said, rubbing her temple with her ungloved hand. "Where's my other glove?"

A brief search turned up nothing. "Damnit," Misty said. "That... whatever she is...has my glove. This was my favorite pair, too."

"I'll get you some new ones," Joseph promised. "This is my fault."

"I know I'm a little bit hazy, but how is that even possible? Did you invite her here to mess with me?"

"She's interested in me—or at least, she's interested in my goats to an almost creepy degree."

"That's also on her." Misty saw movement from the corner of her eye. The bartender was hovering a bit, holding a large glass full of ice and amber liquid. "Is that a Long Island Ice Tea?"

"Yes. I thought you might want one."

"I can't," she said regretfully. "I have to drive home."

"I'll take you home—in your car if you want—and we can come back for the other vehicle in the morning."

"You drive a hard bargain."

"It's part of my charm."

Misty waved away Drew's offer of wine. "The last three days have not been good, and wine will only make it worse."

"Wine never makes anything worse," Morgana said.

"I need to tell you all two things before I can have a glass. Is everyone here?"

"Everyone but Sandy," Drew said. "She's on her way, though. I hope she brings bubbles. She's never had a French 75, and I need to initiate her into the club."

"I'll save item number two for when she gets here, but I have got to tell you all what happened last night."

"Will the rest of us need drinks for this?" Jezebel asked, settling into the couch next to Misty.

"Remember that woman who came in to get her star chart done after stopping by my shop for a palm reading?"

"Yeah, there was something off about her."

"I heard through the grapevine that after I told her I saw haruspicy and goats in her future that she started harassing Joseph."

"I heard a similar thing," Paska said. He looked at Drew out of the corner of his eye before turning his gaze back to Misty. "Anonymous grapes, of course. Has something more happened with this woman?"

"I saw her last night. She pulled off my glove and grabbed my hand."

A chorus of gasps echoed through the room. "She did what?" Morgana asked, hand to her throat. "Didn't you say she was an oracle herself? She should know better."

"What did you see?" Paska asked as Drew pushed a glass of wine into her hand.

"Death. Chaos. Blood. The woman holding a liver in a circle of dead goats."

"Ewww," Ceri said. "Were you seeing her future, or was she pushing images at you that she wanted you to see? If she's as strong a psychic as you are, or stronger, maybe she could control what you pick up?"

"She's older," Jezebel said. "A lot older. Older than Morgana."

"What do I do?" Misty asked.

"Call Farmer Boy and tell him to double his security," Drew said. "Or I can call him if you'd rather not."

"I'll do it," Misty said. "I don't know how seriously he'll take me, but I'll do it."

Someone knocked on the door. "That must be Sandy," Drew said.

"Now you'll be able to tell us the other terrible news you're holding onto."

There was a moment of pregnant silence, and then the doorbell rang.

Jezebel stood up with a huff. "I'll get it. She apparently doesn't know she can just walk in if she's expected."

"She's still got the city mentality," Drew said. "Give her some time."

There was a murmur of voices from the entry.

"Sandy!" Drew called, heading into the kitchen. "Please tell me you brought bubbles! I am going to make you the most amazing drink you've ever had in your life. You're not driving, are you?"

Misty tuned them out and looked around the room at the others. "Is anyone else getting anything weird lately?"

"Something is brewing," Ceri said. "I can feel it in the water. I don't know what it is, though. A storm is coming to Oracle Bay."

"The stars are aligning in a way I've never seen," Jezebel said. "I don't know what it means, but I'm reaching out to others. My astrology skills aren't quite up to predicting global events, at least not with any accuracy. I need to find a teacher. I'm maxed out on what I can teach myself. I have the power, just not the knowledge." She shook her head. "My struggles are neither here nor there, though. Short version is that something is happening, but I don't know what."

"That's all I have, as well," Morgana said. The testiness in her voice gave away her displeasure. "Maybe we should all grab a couple farm animals and see what's coming."

"No," Ceri said. "Absolutely not.

"Absolutely not what?" Drew asked, following Sandy into the room.

"Absolutely no animal sacrifices," Ceri said.

"That seems reasonable. Paska's ideas are never that great."

"It was Morgana this time," Jezebel said.

Drew shook his head. "I don't want to know what brought that on. Misty, what's the big news?"

She took a fortifying sip of wine, then set the glass on the end table. "Vincent Bryson, the man who owns nearly every building in Oracle Bay, is selling it all to a developer." Amid the muffled gasps, Misty pulled her tablet out of her purse, tapped on it dramatically, and said, "This is what the developer did to the last coastal town he got his greedy little paws on!"

She scrolled through pictures to demonstrate the cookie-cutter design of chain restaurants and shops. Everything was homogenous.

"It's like the Stepford Wife of towns!" Ceri whispered.

"Not a single punny shop name to be seen," Paska noted.

"This is what'll happen in Oracle Bay," Misty said. "Rents will be raised until we can't afford them, then everything will be razed and rebuilt in this image."

"Is there anything we can do to stop it?" Sandy asked. "I know I'm a newcomer here, but Oracle Bay feels more like home than anywhere I've ever lived."

Misty glanced over at Morgana and grinned a little. Their newest recruit definitely belonged.

"Why's he selling?" Ceri asked at the same time Sandy said, "Oh! I read his cards."

Every head in the room swiveled to look at Sandy.

"What'd they say?" Jezebel asked.

"He really went to a psychic?" Misty exclaimed. "I was pretty sure he thought it was all a crock of hooey."

"He might still," Sandy admitted. "He was definitely even more skeptical than me about it all."

"What did his cards say?" Jezebel asked again.

"Hold your pants on, Jezebel," Drew said. "I want to know why he's selling, and then we can talk about what Sandy got from him.

"I shook hands with him, too," Misty admitted.

"Gloveless?" Ceri looked shocked.

Misty nodded. "He told me he needed the money to clear his name of the embezzlement charges brought against him, but that he was innocent. I believe his company doesn't quite believe his guilt either, regardless of the proof offered, because they're willing to settle for having funds returned rather than pressing charges. But if he can't come up with the money, he'll probably have to go to jail. And the only way he can come up with the money is to sell his largest real estate holding—Oracle Bay."

"Do you believe him?" Ceri asked.

"I do. He didn't commit the crime he was accused of."

"And the reading?" Morgana demanded.

"His past mirrored what we know," Sandy said. "Loss, financial ruin, betrayal. There was an intern, or someone much junior to him, a younger man, who I believe betrayed him. Perhaps this man was instrumental in framing Vincent?"

There was a murmur of agreement and an impatient hand gesture from Morgana.

"He got the Wheel of Fortune in the present. That could be interpreted as a continuation of the negative change in fortune, or alternatively, prison time instead of whatever he's being accused of now. But the other cards were more positive—kind of—and gave a warning to look beyond the material to the spiritual.

"His future is dependent on a choice. He was worried about making the wrong choice but worried about the outcome either way. If he chooses correctly, he will win at life—"

"Is that what you told him?" Jezebel asked, her voice tinged with amusement.

"I'm paraphrasing," Sandy retorted. "If he can let go of the material and focus on the spiritual, he'll achieve true happiness. But to do that, he'll have to take a chance on losing everything he's held dear. It's all down to a choice on his part, and the future was wavering back and forth so much that it was difficult to give him any clarity."

"Do you always remember the readings you do so well?" Misty asked. She already knew the answer, but wanted to hear Sandy say it.

"Only since coming to Oracle Bay," Sandy replied with a wry smile.

"It's clear what needs to happen; what his choice needs to be," Morgana said.

"Don't you need a cup of tea to be clear?" Drew asked.

"Don't be an ass," Ceri said. "What needs to happen?"

"He can't sell, and we need to find a way to clear his name."

seven

Joseph looked around the gym. Crowds of costumed people milled about, most carrying cups of green punch. The sheer number of adorably tiny witches and goblins was almost overwhelming. He looked down at his outfit, wondered if anyone would believe it was a costume, and found an empty section of wall to hold up.

He scanned the crowd for Misty. He'd spent the last week in Seattle helping out at home while his mom recovered from routine surgery, and had just gotten back to town this morning. The local kids he'd hired to help out with the goats reported there'd been no trouble, but they had reported a strange woman lurking just over his property line.

Misty'd warned him that the mysterious and erratic stranger was after the goats—which was weird unless the mysterious woman knew more about the goats than almost anyone. He held himself back from pacing. She'd appear soon enough, and he'd at least get a glimpse, even if they couldn't talk tonight. They'd spoken every night for hours, much to the amusement of his parents, who'd threatened to ground him and take away his phone privileges.

He caught a glimpse of a man wearing gold lamé with weird writing all over him and knew that was where he should focus his attentions. He stared at the group on the other side of the gym for a couple minutes before figuring it out. They were dressed up as characters from The Lord of the Rings, and the lamé guy, who he didn't recognize, was the ring. One of the blondes in the group turned around, and he recognized her immediately. Misty was Legolas, complete with a bow and quiver of arrows.

Their eyes met, and even though they were across the room, he knew she was looking at him with the same longing he felt. His body almost involuntarily straightened up from the slouched lean against the wall and he'd taken two steps forward before he could stop himself. He hadn't seen her, hadn't touched her since he'd driven her home after their near disaster of a date in Long Beach over a week ago. He'd been unable to say everything he wanted that night. She'd been dazed after their encounter with the woman who was doing her best to ruin every aspect of his life, and he didn't want to burden her with more.

But before she'd gotten out of his truck, she'd leaned over and kissed him with more heat than should be legal. Within seconds, they were making out like teenagers in the cab of his truck, and only the streetlight shining directly on them kept their clothes on. Remembering how they'd left things, and some of the more heated texts they'd exchanged, made him impatient. Maybe it wasn't the agreed upon time to reveal they were dating, but she had to know this was more than a fling by now. He took another step towards her, then stopped. He might want nothing more than to pull her under the bleachers and kiss her until they were both weak in the knees, but she was intent on her night. She loved Halloween, loved dressing up, and really, really wanted to win the group costume contest this year. He could wait.

He headed back to the wall and leaned. Bill would likely show up soon, too, to check out Drew's costume while pretending to be completely indifferent to Drew. Maybe now that he and Misty were dating, they could find a way to get Drew and Bill back together. He grimaced. A few dates and a hot make-out session, and all of a sudden, he fancied himself a matchmaker? Relationships were dangerous.

His phone vibrated in his pocket. He read the text while keeping one eye on the sexy elf across the room. "This is your last warning. If you don't pay, your secrets will be revealed. I have proof that you practice the dark arts, and your pretty girlfriend won't like that. $1mil or the photos will be everywhere."

Joseph bit back a curse. He wasn't sure what kind of photos the guy had—but they couldn't be that bad. His dad had advised him to ignore the person, assuming they had nothing but some video of him talking to a goat. He wanted to know, though, what the person had on him. So, ignoring the advice of his parents, his best friend, and the one cop he'd consulted, he texted back.

"Show me the pics or leave me alone. I'm not giving you any $$$ without knowing what the threat is." He put the phone back in his pocket, looked around for Misty again, and settled in to wait.

"Has it started yet?"

Joseph jumped. He'd been so intent on staring at Misty without getting caught by the rest of the Fellowship that he'd completely missed Bill's arrival. "The little kids have gone, but that's it."

"Aww...who won?"

"The West triplets dressed up like Harry, Hermione, and Ron and gave their dog a couple extra heads. It was so freaking adorable it almost melted my cold, dead heart."

"I like that about you," Bill said.

"My inability to remain stoic in the face of near-terminal cuteness? The dog had three heads and kept trying to lick everyone. Who wouldn't feel just a little warm and fuzzy?"

"I like that you're not afraid to admit it. You might be a jerk about your deep, dark secrets, as well as crotchety well before your time, but you've never felt the need to pretend to be someone you're not to shore up the perception of your masculinity."

Joseph shrugged. "In the end, what does it matter? People will believe what they want, and it's easier to be myself."

Bill socked him in the shoulder just as his phone buzzed again. He pulled it out and looked at it. "Here's your proof." There were a half dozen photos, each weirder than the last. The first was, as he'd expected, him kneeling next to Billie Holliday with a huge calendar spread out in front of them. Weird, but not damaging. The next was of a similar bent, but instead of a calendar, it was the Wall Street Journal stock listings. He winced. That had been toeing the line, for sure, but the photo was nearly ten years old, and it showed in his baby face.

The next four were where things took a turn. There was a man, who, from the back looked a lot like Joseph, standing in front of a goat who looked nothing like any of his. The man was inside a painted pentacle and brandishing a knife dripping with blood. The next pictures showed various stages of satanic animal sacrifice culminating in the robed figure standing in a pool of blood holding what looked like a liver above his head while the dead goat lay at the edge of the frame. Joseph knew his face was screwed up into an expression of near-permanent confusion.

"What is it?" Bill asked.

Joseph passed over the phone.

"Are you asking your goat to pick stocks for you?"

"Keep going," Joseph said.

"Oh my god. What is that?"

"I wish I knew. This is the blackmail. That isn't me. Those aren't my goats. That's not even my barn."

"You might know that, but will anyone else?"

"Does it matter? I'm pretty sure that butchering a goat isn't illegal, any more than reading the newspaper with one, so why would I care?"

"Your blackmailer, who has clearly been around a long time, based on the second photo, thinks your reputation will be ruined."

"My reputation as a cranky goat farmer? I think I can handle ruining it."

"Now you'll be a satanic goat farmer."

"So? It's not like I'm running for office."

"I don't know. People might not want satanic cheese."

"There will be enough people who only want satanic cheese to make up for the people who don't. Besides, it's not like I have a million dollars to pay this guy off for his fake photos."

"Good point," Bill said. "This will make for an interesting couple months. You'd better give Misty a heads up. If she finds out on Facebook that you're satanic, she's gonna be mad."

"I'll tell her tonight. I hope she'll still want me to participate in the Bazaar."

"You do? You hate participating. You make her guilt trip you... ohhh... You were pretending so you'd get to talk to her more? Dude. You need several lessons on how to be a functional adult."

Joseph shrugged, snagged his phone back, and typed his reply. "Lol. No."

"That was short and to the point."

"I didn't want to leave him wondering what I meant. Although I suppose it could be a her."

They looked at each other and laughed, only quieting down when the announcer called the group costume contenders to the stage.

BILL AND JOSEPH WALKED UP TO THE POUR HOUSE. THERE WERE THREE GUYS passed out in a pile of muscle and bad decisions while a fourth guy desperately tried to rouse them. "Get up, you guys. The cops are coming."

Another guy stomped out of the bar, glared at Bill and Joseph, and said, "This town is full of freaks."

"Who was that?" Joseph asked.

"Sandy's ex-husband. He is a real piece of work."

"Oh, right. I've heard about him. Why's he here if the town is full of freaks?"

"Sandy's in there, right? He's showing up everywhere she is. Total stalker."

"Looks like Andy's having a lively night already."

"Halloween always brings out the jerks and various lowlifes who pass through town." Bill held the door open for Joseph and followed him in. The bar was decked out for Halloween; red, flickering lights behind silhouettes gave the impression of lost souls dancing in hellfire.

They found a spot at the bar, accepted the free beers Brandy insisted they'd earned even though they'd arrived after all the excitement, and then looked around the bar. The booth of psychics wasn't hard to find—they were all still in costume, including the man dressed in the gold lamé jumpsuit, and they were laughing. Joseph smiled at the happiness apparent on Misty's face and was still watching her when she spotted him. She froze, and a feeling of smug certitude crept over him. It was good to know that she was as affected as he was. He blinked, noticed Bill and Drew were playing the same staring game, but without the smiles, and then raised a glass to Misty. Someone at her table—it must be Sandy, he recognized almost everyone else—raised her glass and the rest of the group followed suit. They clinked glasses and drank deeply.

Joseph turned back towards the bar and his best friend. Bill had stopped staring and was looking morosely into his beer. "You can talk to him, you know," Joseph said.

"I called him a liar and a fraud," Bill said. "I did it without any evidence, and then when he walked out on me and into the arms of someone else, I called him a few other choice things as well. There is no walking back from that."

"I see the way he looks at you, Bill. He still loves you. Tell him you're sorry. Tell him you believe in psychics. You can fix it."

"I can't believe you were so anti-psychic. Your goat tells the future."

"That's a secret," Joseph said, looking around the bar. "And besides, it's not the same at all. Having a goat point her hoof at the best days for certain activities or pick stocks doesn't make her a psychic goat."

"It won't be a secret tomorrow when your ridiculous blackmailer posts pictures of you and your goat picking stocks."

"I think the satanic goat rites will get more attention than me and Billie reading the paper together."

"But you. You had a very fancy goat this whole time and still believed the local psychics were frauds?"

Joseph shrugged. "I am at least as much of a jerk as you. More, probably. I knew there was the possibility of it all being true and still denied it without proof. One slightly magical thing seems a lot easier to believe than a lot of really magical things? That's my only defense, and I know it's a terrible one."

Bill held up his glass. "To us, the dumbest guys in all of Oracle Bay."

Joseph clinked his glass against Bill's and took a long drink. Out of the corner of his eye, he saw Misty get up and head towards the bathrooms. He set down his glass and followed her, hoping no one noticed. "Hey," he whispered as he crept up behind her in the line.

She jumped, muffled a shriek, and then smiled at him. "Hey. You scared the crap out of me."

"Shouldn't you have known I was coming?"

"Ha ha. Like I've never heard that one before. You know it doesn't work that way for me."

"Meet me outside in thirty minutes? I need to tell you something important before you find out from someone else."

"Of course." The bathroom opened up, and she walked towards it. "Thirty minutes."

Joseph returned to his seat, picked up his beer, and started counting the minutes.

"What's wrong with you?" Bill asked.

"What do you mean? Nothing."

"You're tapping your foot so hard against the bar you're vibrating the whole thing, and you look like you're doing a warm-up minute on the mechanical bull. I know you're on edge lately, but this is a bit much."

"I'm worried about my goats, about whatever's going to come out tomorrow regarding my satanic goat newspaper rituals, about my stalker, and about my mother's continued health. Isn't that enough?"

"It's not enough to make you vibrate like a tuning fork. It's Misty, isn't it?"

"Why'd you ask if you already knew the answer?"

"It's fun watching you squirm. It's been ages since I've been able to tease you about a woman. I've got so much lost time to make up for. After years of only teasing you about goats and grumpiness, I feel like I've hit the motherlode."

Joseph rolled his eyes. "I was hoping you'd matured since last time I was in a relationship."

"You hoped in vain. Now I'm gonna pull out some of the same material I used last time you were dating someone. I hope it aged well."

"Knock yourself out."

"Dude, do you think she'll let you get to second base?"

"You have got to be kidding me."

Bill aimed an exaggerated wink at Joseph. "I owe you. You have given me so much shit over the years. I've been waiting for the proper time to get my revenge."

Joseph looked at his watch. "Oh, look at that. I have somewhere to be."

"Will you be back?"

"Probably in fifteen minutes or so. I don't think we'll run off together so I can get to second base in the back seat of my car."

"You drive a pickup."

"Exactly. I'll be back. Order me another beer when Brandy comes back, will you? And don't worry, no one noticed you sneaking surreptitious glances at Drew. No one at all."

Joseph pretended not to see the middle fingers Bill was aiming at him as he glanced casually over at the psychic's table, noted Misty's absence, and hurried outside.

· · ⋆ ★ ★ ★ ★ ⋆ · ·

"Hey," Misty said when he found her leaned against the side of the bar that wasn't visible from either the parking lot or the large, mostly empty patio.

"Hey, yourself," he replied, then opened his arms. "I missed you."

She walked into his embrace and wrapped her arms around his waist. She pressed her face into his chest for a moment before tipping her head back and looking up at him. "I missed you, too."

He lowered his lips to hers and paused with an almost imperceptible amount of space between them. He closed his eyes and savored the moment, the longing, the heat surging between them. Before he could give in to the anticipation, Misty rose up on tiptoe and pressed her lips against his, snaking her arms around his neck in the process. He slid his hands down her sides, grazing her breasts with his thumbs, and then settled them on her hips, tugging her closer.

He felt her stretch up and further into him, and it was all he could do not to take the requisite steps backwards to press her against the side of the building and take things further than either of them wanted out in the cold salt spray of the almost-November northwest air.

Her tongue outlined his lips, and he opened to her, allowing her to explore his mouth. It wasn't until the faint thunk of her back hitting wood reached his ears that he realized she'd been leading him back to the building he'd resisted pushing her against.

Misty twined one leg around his and pulled him closer, pressing her length against his. He pulled back. "Misty, I need to tell you…"

"Shh... You can tell me in a minute. There's been too much talking and not nearly enough kissing in the last week. In the last decade."

There was no way to argue with that, and he wasn't particularly inclined to argue anyway, so he surrendered to her insistent hands on his body and fell into her—into her heat, into her power, into her body.

A smattering of rain brought him back to his senses and forced him back. He looked over his shoulder towards the ocean and saw sheets of precipitation rushing inland. "Baby, we should go in," he said.

She followed his gaze, grimaced in the low light of the distant street lights, and straightened her clothes. He followed suit, buttoning and tucking in his shirt, then ran a hand through his hair. "I do have something to tell you." The wind picked up and pulled his words away.

"Later. Call me," she yelled, pantomiming a phone. She turned to head back into the bar, but before she got too far, he grabbed her arm, turned her around, and kissed her hard.

"Later," he promised.

She disappeared around the corner, and he walked closer to the front door, looking for a place to shelter for a moment to both give Misty time to get back to her table and to give himself time to calm down. They were playing a dangerous game, and if they didn't tell people in town they were together, that choice would be taken from them. There was only so much semi-public makeup sessions a couple could get away with without being spotted.

He adjusted his belt, took a deep breath, and went back inside.

eight

Misty settled into the back table at The Pour House with the rest of the psychic gang. Sandy's divorce hadn't been finalized, and they were here to administer companionship and cheer. Andy had asked to join them, though, and that made things a little weird.

Brandy followed them into the alcove and took everyone's beer orders as well as the request for two large plates of nachos and a hummus plate.

"What's going on?" Sandy asked once Brandy had retreated to grab their drinks.

"I'm not sure," Drew said, slowly. "Something must have happened for Andy to come to us and risk outing himself."

"Outing himself how?"

"As other," Ceri said. "He's not quite normal, and none of us have ever known who—or what—he is."

"He said he wouldn't give up his true name," said Misty.

"There's more to an identity than a true name," Jezebel said. "He might offer enough clues to lead us to the what if not the who."

"I'm more concerned about what could've prompted this," Ceri said.

"As are we," Paska said, sliding into the chair next to Misty. Morgana slipped into a chair on the other side of the table next to Drew. "I didn't really need to spend a penny; I merely needed a moment to confer with Morgana about what we would and would not share with our favorite brewmaster."

"What did you decide on behalf of us all?" Jezebel asked. There was so much snark in her voice, Sandy was surprised that Paska didn't recoil.

"We decided nothing on behalf of the rest of you. We decided only for ourselves. You all know that we're a bit older than you and have known each other for a fair amount of time. You are free to make your own decisions about what you share, whether it's about your name or your craft. If you're using something other than your true name, though, I'd recommend keeping that piece of information to yourself. You don't have to answer if you don't want to, but who here is still using their true name?"

Sandy, Misty, and Ceri raised their hands.

"I've only ever lived here," Misty said apologetically. "It seemed like a hassle to change."

"I came here when I was young, and by the time I'd developed my reputation, the name change thing seemed like a waste of time," Ceri agreed. "My surname has changed, but I'm using my given name."

"You know me," Sandy said. "I literally just got here. I haven't had a chance to even think about it."

"You don't have to decide today," Morgana said. "Now let's pause while the most excellent Brandy distributes our drinks."

The conversation turned to lighter things after Brandy left. Sandy shared the story of her not-divorce-day, and everyone spent a few minutes trash talking her ex-husband, Aaron.

"You guys are the best," she said. "I'm so glad I have friends."

Misty reached out and squeezed her hand. "We're glad you're here, too."

Andy walked into the space, immediately overwhelming it with his sheer size. "I got everyone another round of drinks." He started passing out pints as Brandy handed them to him. When all the beers were distributed and the nachos and hummus situated, he sat, picked up his own pint, and said. "I have a story, and it will be weird."

"Weird is our specialty," Drew said.

"If you please, I'd rather not be the subject of levity right now. This is serious."

"My apologies."

"Accepted, although not needed." He took a long pull of his beer. "In this time and place, I go by Andy Sterling. I am...not exactly human."

"Not exactly how?" Jezebel asked, leaning forward.

"I think I will leave that unanswered for the time being. Suffice it to say, I am much less human than all—" he looked around the table "—or at least most of you. Something happened on Halloween that leads me to believe that I, and by association, Oracle Bay, will be targeted by a group of...more non-human combatants."

"What happened?" Morgana demanded.

"Do you remember that fight? The one where I had to kick the guys out?"

Several affirmative nods encouraged him to continue.

"They turned out to be...old enemies. And my actions that night, although necessary for the security of this bar and my patrons, will have repercussions beyond that evening."

"What questions do you have for us?" Paska asked.

"What are your skills? Can you see the coming storm?"

Paska leaned forward, folded his hands on the table, and appeared to be trying to look through the man across from him.

"What are you looking at?" Andy asked. He tapped his fingers against the table until he realized what he was doing, then pulled them down quickly and hid them in his lap.

"Don't worry. I can't tell your future by looking into your soul. If you want me to look forward, you'll need to stop by my house and let me cast the bones for you. The only one who'd be able to do something right here, right now is Misty, but you'd have to let her touch you, and she has little control over what she sees without a specific destination in mind."

"Do any of you?"

"To a certain extent. The more we know, the more we can focus. Tell me more about the storm."

"Then none of you know what's coming?"

"We've been rather preoccupied," Jezebel said. "The immediate future of Oracle Bay was in danger. I can't tell the future of a town, though. Only a person. I don't have a birthdate to help me build a star chart, and I haven't mastered interpreting the movement of the heavens."

Ceri grabbed the water glass that was in front of Morgana and the bottom plate shielding the table from the nachos and set them in front of her. She spilled a little water on the plate, placed her hands on either side, and stared.

Misty hadn't watched anyone but Sandy ply their trade in far too long and watching Ceri's eyes go wide and vacant caused an involuntary shiver.

The plate started shaking in her hands. "There's too much. I can't. There's too much."

Morgana reached over and yanked the plate away, dumping the water on the table. She put an arm around Ceri, whispered something into her ear, and then pushed her beer closer.

"What did you see?" Andy asked, leaning forward and jostling the table with his eagerness.

"Give her a moment," Morgana snapped.

Drew drained his beer, looked around, and announced, "I'm

getting another round. Andy, why don't you and Jezebel help me? By the time we're back, Ceri should be good to go."

Andy grumbled but followed him out into the main part of the bar.

"Are you okay?" Misty asked.

"Andy is right," Ceri whispered. "A storm is coming. But before it hits, there will be nothing but trouble. The almost-sale of Oracle Bay was just the beginning." She leaned back, picked up her beer, and drank. She refused to say another word about what she'd seen until everyone was back. "I'm not going over it twice. I can't." Tears traced a path down her cheeks and disappeared into her collar.

When the new round was distributed, and everyone was situated, Ceri opened her eyes and looked at Andy. "I know what you are, even if I don't know who. What's coming is terrible, and there will be casualties. It's happening because of you. It's happening here because this is where you are."

Andy blanched and hunched in on himself. "I know. I mean, I suspected. I'll have to go."

"It's too late for that. The wheels are turning. We haven't an angel's chance in hell of avoiding this." She stared at him, and he fidgeted under her attention. "You have to stay. The only way this town can be saved is if you're here to save it. This time, you can't run away."

"How much did you see?"

"Too much. So much. Centuries. Millennia. It's all in the forefront of your mind and is irrevocably tied to the storm you referenced. I won't share your secrets, but they won't be secrets much longer."

"I'll keep them as long as I can."

"Don't keep them too long; a lot of pain can be avoided if you trust in others. Pride goeth before the fall, if you remember."

Andy nodded and pulled back into himself. His eyes, usually twinkling and jovial, were now grim and haunted.

"There's more, though," Ceri said, looking around the table. "Misty and Drew—I'm not sure what the next couple months will bring, but it won't be easy for either of you. When the time comes, don't hide. The advice I gave Andy goes for both of you. Don't keep secrets for the sake of keeping them."

"Sharing is caring, eh?" Drew quipped.

"Pain shared is pain halved, my friend. You don't have to be an island."

"This is taking a turn for the crappy," Drew said. "We are here to commiserate with Sandy about her not-divorce, not get horrific flashes of the future that come with dire warnings for everyone."

Misty steeled herself. "What did you see about me?"

"Nothing specific. Something is going to happen in the next few weeks that will affect you and Drew. I can't tell if it's the same event, or if two different things are going to happen. Most of the vision was tied to Andy. That will affect us all on a larger scale. Not that your stuff isn't important, it is, but..."

"It's okay," Morgana said. "There's a lot to process, and no one thinks you're downplaying anything by being worried about the storm." She turned to Andy. "I echo Ceridwen's advice. Do not wait too long to tell us what's going on and how we can help. The best allies are those that know what they're getting into."

"I don't think any of you can help at all."

"Don't discount us. While it's true that some of us are young, there are those here that have—if not as many years as you—more years than would be assumed by any regular human. And all of us are strong. If I were you, I'd take advantage of the collected power you currently have access to. Between us, we can offer not only looks into probable futures but advice on the best ways to deal with what's coming. Sandy is the best tarot reader I've ever encountered. She's been reading for less than two months, and being in the same room while she reads is like standing too close to a lightning storm on a hill."

Andy stood up, shoved his fingers through his hair, and said, "I'll think about what you've said. I don't want to put any of you in danger—"

"Too late," Ceri said, a trace of her regular humor returning.

A smile ghosted over his lips, and he continued, "I'll probably need to talk to someone again to nail down the timeline."

"Christmas. The storm will break on Christmas Day."

"As long as it's after the Yule Ball," Misty said. "And the Bazaar." She looked at Andy, pointed one ungloved finger at him, and winked. "Don't mess up my parties."

"I wouldn't dream of it," he said, a bit of the smooth bartender persona returning.

"Shake on it?" She offered her hand.

"Not today. You all already know too much."

"There's no such thing as too much knowledge," Sandy said, finally finding her voice.

"You say that now...tell me if you still feel that way on New Year's Day." He turned and started to walk out of the small alcove. Before he got too far away, he turned back. "Drinks are on me, tonight. Sorry your divorce isn't final yet, Sandy. When it is, come back, and I'll see if I can make you a French 75."

Misty stood in the kitchen, arranging cookies on trays and counting out the wine glass charms. She looked at the deck of cards charm, and the corners of her lips tugged downwards. Sandy hadn't been part of their group long, but her temporary absence—especially due to a gunshot wound, probably caused by her almost ex-husband— made a huge dent in their gatherings. She put that one away and pulled out the wine she'd selected for the evening. The others would be here soon, and they had a full agenda. They'd had nothing but full agendas for the last two months. They'd had so many emergency meetings, that she was considering proposing that they put once a week meetings on the calendar instead of the monthly meetings that were currently there.

There was a quick knock at the door, and then it opened. The first of the group was arriving. Misty took a deep breath, pasted a smile on her face—not too bright, because Sandy was still recovering, and called out, "Everything's set up in the living room! Red wine or white?"

"Red please," Morgana said.

"Same for me," Drew's voice echoed through the house.

"I'll have sparkling water," Ceri said. The response was shocking enough that Misty popped her head out of the kitchen and looked at the trio of oracles settling in in the living room.

"Are you okay?"

"Just a headache." Ceri smiled with what Misty assumed was supposed to be reassurance, but her lips wavered a bit before she pasted it into place and she looked even paler than usual. Misty poured wine for Drew and Morgana and cracked a can of La Croix for Ceri.

In the next ten minutes, her house filled with people, and she was kept busy enough not to think about all the impending problems by filling glasses and setting out trays of fruit and sweets. Once everyone had a drink in their hands, she sat down, looked around the room, and said, "We have a number of things going on right now. The last week has been busy. How about we take things in order of least to most important?"

No one objected, but the way Paska looked at her made her certain he knew more about her secrets than she was letting on. She shook off the feeling that she had something to confess—now wasn't the time nor the place to give up the thrill of her secret love life—and got down to business. "I haven't seen nor heard from our Oracle Bay goat stalker since last time I updated you. From what I know, Joseph hasn't either. Anyone else?"

"No," Paska said. "But there is still something weird going on at the farm. I do not trust this silence, and I do not trust that farmer."

Misty opened her mouth to protest but closed it again when she realized she had no idea what to say.

Paska gave her a penetrating look. "Do you know his secrets?"

"No," she heard herself answering much more honestly than she'd intended. "Only that he has them."

"You should find out. He will not be at the center of the coming storm, but he will play a role in bringing it here."

"What role?" Misty asked as a chorus of other questions rang out.

"I don't know," Paska admitted. "There is too much uncertainty, too many variables. I'll tell you when I have something that makes sense."

"Maybe it's time to move on to the second item?" Morgana's smooth voice interrupted. "Should we discuss Vincent and Sandy next, or the coming storm? I don't want to gossip about their relationship. Lord knows we've done enough of that already, but he is staying with her at the hospital, right?"

"He is, and everything is going swimmingly," Jezebel said. "I'd rather talk about the town. If Vincent isn't successful in his ploy to get the charges dropped, does it even matter what will become of it? A storm in a town that isn't home is a natural disaster but not a tragedy."

Drew looked over at her, "You've been spending too much time with Morgana if that's what you believe. It might be time for a weekend with me. We can find a way to refill those much-needed empathy stores."

Jezebel flipped him off and continued. "What I meant was—" she glared at Drew then turned to the rest of the room, "the coming storm is coming for something. Would it still be here if Oracle Bay was normal? If we were gone, and Andy...would this town still be a target? Or as much of a target?"

Morgana leaned forward, leaned her chin on her folded hands, and said, "I see where you're going with this. If Oracle Bay is no longer anything but a quirkily named town, will the storm damage and not destroy? Will it go somewhere else entirely? It is a good question, but I think there is no way to divert a storm in motion. Not to mention all the residents of this town who are...touched. There are plenty of people here who have a gift, just not to the extent that we do. Joseph's haruspicer is more than enough evidence of that, as is Joseph himself, not to mention Russell, everyone's favorite bartender, Andy, the mysterious and dark brewmaster, Natalie, the mistress of charcuterie and best bacon purveyor in the land, as well as countless others."

"What do you mean, Joseph?" Misty demanded at the same time Jezebel asked, "Natalie? Seriously?"

Jezebel sank back into her chair and tipped her head forward, hiding her cheeks with her hair. Misty was glad for the distraction; Jezebel's obvious interest in Natalie's supernaturalness took the attention away from hers.

She shook off her speculation with a reminder that her friends' love lives were none of her business until they chose to make it her business, and tuned back into the conversation. Morgana was refusing to elaborate on anyone else's potential gifts, including Joseph's, and Jezebel was eying Misty with the same speculation she'd just been directing at the astrologer. Jezebel offered a half-smile and a quarter nod to Misty, who returned it with a surreptitious wink.

"I think it's fairly certain we're not going to pack up and leave the town undefended on the off-chance that it'll make life easier for those left behind."

"Undefended?" Jezebel asked. "Other than my sassy mouth and Morgana's and Paska's willingness to kill anyone in their way, what do we have in terms of defenses. We are psychics, not battle mages."

"We can teach you," Morgana said after sharing a look with Paska. "There is a way to weaponize your powers—all of your powers."

"Even mine and Sandy's?" Jezebel asked, doubt evident in her voice. "Not sure what an astrologer and a tarot card reader can offer in a war."

"Even yours," Paska confirmed. "There are some who will find it easier—Ceri's and Drew's scrying powers, specifically—but it is possible to use your psychic powers as defense, and, in some cases, offense."

"So, we will learn to defend this town against whatever comes, we will believe that Vincent will prevail in his attempt to clear his name from the embezzlement accusations, Sandy will recover quickly from her gunshot wound, and we'll keep an eye out for the goat lady who wants to tell the future with one of Joseph's goats?" Misty asked, trying to wrap up.

"We should plan a real celebration for Sandy," Ceri said. "She's had a rough couple months, and our last celebration didn't work out.

"She'll be divorced when she comes back," Paska said. "Vincent will be exonerated of the false accusations, and Sandy's evil ex-husband will end up in jail for a very long time."

"Vincent bought the house across from mine," Drew announced. "He'll bring her there the day after they return from Portland. We can let them have the first night together with her as a single lady, and then ambush them in the house the next afternoon. I still have a key."

Morgana clapped her hands. "It is decided, then. Anything else?"

"The bazaar," Misty said, almost reluctantly. "It's only two weeks away."

"Other than the bazaar chairperson getting shot, do we have any other wrinkles?" Jezebel asked. "I can step in for anything Sandy would be doing as she recovers."

"That should take care of it," Misty agreed. "It's quite the well-oiled machine by now, and all the bake-off competitors, judges, and other artisans are confirmed. Sandy hasn't really had much time, so I've been making arrangements."

"I'm off, then," Morgana said. "Thank you for the wine."

They trickled out of her house until finally, she was alone in silence again. She dug her phone out of her pocket and checked. Three texts.

One from her aunt on her mother's side, "Watch yourself, Mystic. There's something coming, and I don't know what. Keep 'hold of that heart." A chill ran down her spine, and she shivered. Her aunt was who'd taught her the rudiments of how to use her sight, but although she was retired and living in San Diego, she still caught flashes and usually forwarded them to Misty. She'd call her in the morning.

The second and third were both from Joseph. "I can't stop thinking about last week, pressed against the side of The Pour House, your lips on mine. I am weak for you, Misty."

The next one, dated three minutes after the first, "Dinner tomorrow? I'll pick you up, and we can go to Long Beach. I promise to be good."

Misty smiled and started typing. "Tomorrow is perfect. I'll pick you up. Don't make any promises I don't want you to keep."

· · · ★ ★ ★ ★ ★ ★ · ·

MISTY TUGGED ON A PAIR OF JEANS AND CHECKED OUT THE VIEW FROM THE back. She grinned. She might not be skinny, but her ass rocked a good pair of tight jeans. After the jeans, she put on a shell pink camisole with a low, lacy collar, then layered on a soft, forest green sweater that almost perfectly matched her eyes. One pair of high heeled booties later, and she was almost ready to go.

She stepped into the bathroom, ran a brush through her hair, then added mascara and lip gloss before putting on her glasses. "Misty," she told her reflection, cocking her finger guns, "you are damn cute."

A knot formed in her stomach on the way to Joseph's. Last time she'd picked him up, the date hadn't exactly ended well. The knot burst and a million butterflies started milling about, causing a faint sheen of sweat to break out on her brow. And now, now she had to tell him something uncomfortable. Something that was going to seem a little unbelievable. He might be on board with her abilities— at least partially—but this was going to be some high-level weird.

Rain spattered her windshield and she turned on her wipers.

It'd been unusually dry this fall, and objectively the rain was good, but she hated driving in it. An unfortunate reality of living in the Pacific Northwest was that she often found herself driving in the rain. "Ugh," she said, smacking the steering wheel. Joseph had said he had something to tell her, too. It'd been a week since Halloween, since their make-out session at The Pour House. Another week when they'd had to make do with nothing but phone calls and texts.

She'd been seeing clients and finalizing bazaar plans, and he'd been busy on the farm with something he was reluctant to discuss over the phone—just the refrain of "We'll talk about it when we're together." What if he was going to end things for her own good again? What if she should let him? Things were going to get dicey in Oracle Bay in the next couple of months, and regardless of what Morgana said about Joseph being one of the 'touched' people in town, Misty was pretty sure he wouldn't want any part of the mystical madness.

She was about thirty seconds from talking herself into turning around and delivering the warning via breakup text when she saw the turnoff to Joseph's farm. She hit the blinker, slowed down, and began the sharp left turn. Three-quarters of the way into the turn, her headlights illuminated something that didn't quite look right. She slowed the car even further and squinted, trying to make out whatever had briefly reflected in the headlights' glare. She was nearly at a standstill when she saw it again. There was something draped over the fence that lined the road.

Misty rolled to a stop, put it in neutral, and engaged the emergency brake. She left the door open and engine running—just in case. With the flashlight of her smartphone, she walked through the damp, waist-high ditch grass towards the object, which was taking on more and more solidity the closer she got to it. When she got within ten feet, she paused. The shape looked familiar. She shone the flashlight all around, then pressed a hand against her mouth to stifle a scream. There was a distinctively three-dimensional cylindrical shape hanging down, all-but-hidden in the drapes of dark fabric that swathed the figure.

Her heart raced, and the butterflies that had been unnerving her on her drive to Joseph's became bats and took up residence in her chest. Her hand shook, and her thoughts raced. Should she call the cops? Call Joseph? Check on the body to see if it was a...body? She took a deep breath, reminded herself that she was a badass, and took a step forward. Her steps were slow and deliberate. She knew she needed to check on whoever it was, but she wanted to be mindful of a possible crime scene, too.

She was within three feet when she realized that part of the wrongness she'd been sensing from the shape was that it wasn't human. It was a goat, and underneath it was a liver sitting in the middle of a large puddle of blood.

Misty returned to the car so fast she practically flew and was dialing 911 the second she was in the car with the doors locked.

As soon as she'd relayed what she'd seen and where, the dispatcher promised to send someone else and asked her to stay put as long as she felt safe to do so.

Misty hung up and called Joseph.

"Misty, hey. What's up? Running late?"

She took a deep breath but found she couldn't answer. Her tongue was plastered to the roof of her mouth, and she was three seconds away from hyperventilating.

"Misty, baby. What's wrong? Take a breath and talk to me."

She took a deep breath, a gulping sob of a breath, and said, "Come out to the road. I'm here."

"Are you okay?"

"I'm okay. Just come."

"Be there in five." He hung up, and she stared at her phone, wishing there was someone to keep her company. She called Drew.

"Hey, Misty. Wanna hit up the bar at the Sleeping Inn, drink cocktails 'til we're giggling fools, and flirt with Russell? We haven't done that in ages."

"I can't. Something's happened." She choked on a sob and had to scrunch her eyes closed and count to ten to be able to focus on Drew.

"Tell me if you can, or I can try to find out. Do you need me?"

"Just keep me company for a couple minutes on the phone?" she asked.

"Of course. Do you need me in person?"

"No. Joseph will be here soon."

"Joseph? Joseph McEwen? Cranky Joe?"

"Don't call him that," Misty whispered.

"If you are having a secret love affair with the goat farmer, and you didn't tell me, you and I are going to have words. Mystic Greene, I thought we were friends."

"We are, or I wouldn't have called you first. Well, second."

"Second after Joseph," Drew guessed.

"It's his land and his...goat."

"Do you want to talk about it?"

"I found a goat. Like in my vision. I think it's one of his—who else's could it be, especially here?"

"And you're alone right now? Misty, someone did this. That someone could still be there. You need to hang up and call the cops."

"I did. They're coming now. I just can't be alone. I'm more freaked out than I've ever been, and I have seen some weird stuff. Please don't hang up until Joseph gets here."

"Okay, whatever you need Misty. Wanna hear a dirty story?"

"Please."

Misty was grinning—not quite ready to laugh—as Drew finished up the story just as Joseph drove up. "He's here."

"Okay. Call me later if you need me. Call me even if you don't, although that can wait until tomorrow."

"Love you."

"I know." He hung up, and Misty got out of her car, shoved her phone in her back pocket, and watched Joseph get out of the car. She rushed over to him and threw her arms around his waist, burying her face in his chest.

"Hey baby, what's the problem?" He wrapped his arms around her and held her while she shook. The lightheartedness Drew'd shared with her sloughed off, and she was left with terror and shock.

"It's over there," she waved towards the fence. Joseph turned towards the fence and squinted.

"Is that a body?"

"It is," she said. "But not human."

"Did you call the cops?" he asked as he started towards it.

"Yes. They're on the way. It's not human.

"If it's not human, what is it Misty?" Joseph asked. He paused and looked back at her over his shoulder, sounding more like someone who was dreading an answer than someone who was genuinely curious.

"It's a goat," she said. "But there's more."

"More goats?"

She winced. "No. More to it. It was…sacrificed or something. The liver's been cut out, and it's in a pool of blood.

"Stay here. I'll go look and be right back."

She didn't argue.

He didn't stay down for long and was as careful as she'd been not to disturb the scene. He was noticeably pale when he got back to the car.

"I have something to tell you," he said.

"I need to tell you something, too. Before the cops come."

"You first," he said.

She sighed, looked around, and said, "I saw something the night that woman took my glove."

"I wondered."

"I know you don't believe in what I—what *we*—do in this town, but it's real."

"It's more than parlor tricks, that's for sure. I have no room not to believe, and I don't know why I couldn't before."

Misty cocked her head and looked at him in curiosity. "What do you mean?"

He waved his hand. "Story for later. Continue. What'd you see?"

"Death and chaos. The woman standing in a circle of blood holding a goat liver."

"That is abstract yet disturbing," Joseph said. "And strangely fitting with..." he waved his hand towards the fence behind them... "all that."

"The feeling behind it was worse than it sounds. It was dark and terrifying. It's hard to describe."

"You don't have to unless you think there's more that I need to know."

"I should've told you sooner. Everything was so jumbled when it happened. Usually, I'm in at least some amount of control over what I see, but that was a tsunami of information, and it took a few hours to get it sorted. Then, once I did know, I was afraid you'd scoff at me." She leaned her head against his shoulder so she wouldn't have to meet his eyes.

"It's fine. It wouldn't have prevented this. I don't know what could've."

"What did you want to tell me?" Misty asked.

Joseph sighed. "I've been trying to tell you for a while, but first you said you didn't need to know yet, and then we made out instead of talking, and I wanted to tell you in person."

"It's fine," she repeated his words back at him. "Tell me now."

"My family is different."

Misty started to say something, but Joseph held up his hand. "Let me finish. This is hard." He went silent; Misty took his hand and squeezed it gently. "My family is different and has been for as long as we can remember. We've raised goats for generations. My great-grandmother emigrated from Italy with her prize goat and met my great-grandfather, fresh off the boat from Scotland, in New York. They came west, first settling in South Dakota, but after just a few years, they continued the journey to Oregon and started this farm. But that goat—the one Nonna Maria brought over—was Billie."

"Her name was Billie? Do you name all your favorite goats Billie?"

"No. It's the same goat."

"That's impossible," Misty sputtered. "That'd make Billie at least...seventy? I don't know the lifespan of the average goat, but I think I'd know if it was seventy years."

"I don't know how old she is. No one really does. Well over a hundred at this point, and likely older even than that."

"Your family secret is that you have an immortal goat?"

"That's not all she does." The faint sound of sirens broke the relative silence surrounding them. "I'll make this quick. Billie always gives birth to twins who aren't blessed with abnormally long lives but are blessed with abnormally creamy milk, and she can tell the future."

An almost hysterical laugh burst out of Misty before she could stop it. "You have an oracular goat?"

"She helps us predict the weather, lets us know when to prepare for kidding, and helps me play the stock market."

Misty found that she had exactly nothing to say to that. She nodded and swallowed, trying to moisten her mouth and throat enough to speak. "Anything else?" she rasped.

"Someone's trying to blackmail me with a series of pictures they somehow took of me and some that are staged. One of the staged photos is meant to look like me sacrificing a goat and holding the liver up over my head."

"That is seriously messed up," Misty breathed as the cops pulled up. "Did you report it?"

He sighed. "No. The pictures weren't released as threatened, and it's pretty ridiculous all around."

"You should, though. This person could be in collusion with the woman, who really needs a name so I can stop calling her 'the woman.'"

He squeezed her hand, then dropped it and turned to face the police officers who were walking up to them. "Hello Roger, David. Thanks for coming out."

"No problem. I understand you have a dead animal?" Roger

asked, putting just enough incredulity into the question to raise Misty's hackles.

"Yes," she answered. "If it were just road kill or something, I wouldn't have called, but this looks weird."

"Well, let's see it," David said.

TWO HOURS LATER, MISTY FOLLOWED JOSEPH TO HIS PLACE. HER SEXY DATE boots were caked in the same mud that now spattered that back of her jeans and her hair was soaked and plastered to her head. The sprinkles that had started on her way to Joseph's had turned into a full-blown downpour an hour into the endless questions.

The cops had been sent copies of the goat sacrificing photos earlier that day, and although they allowed that there was no way to identify the person in the photo definitively as Joseph and that the goat in the pictures looked nothing like the goat—Goatzilla—that was draped over the fence, they maintained the timing was suspicious.

Misty was exhausted and more than a little cranky. Although they'd gotten through their big exchange of weird news, it had definitely not been the evening she'd planned. She was torn between her desire to salvage their date and her desire to go home, draw herself a bath, pour a glass of wine, and read one of the new romance novels she'd picked up at Title Wave earlier that week.

Joseph pulled into his garage, and Misty followed, parking on the concrete slab behind him. She was just about to tell him that she needed a raincheck and would talk to him tomorrow when he jogged up to her car. She got out, but before she could say anything, he handed her a set of keys. "The silver one's for the front door. Let yourself in, help yourself to a beer from the fridge, or if you'd rather, there are a couple bottles of red on the counter along with a corkscrew and glasses. Now that the cops have finally let us leave the scene, I need to check the flock and make sure no one else is missing.

Goatzilla—" his voice broke for a moment, and he screwed his eyes closed and took a deep breath before continuing, "shared a small barn with Vincent Van Goat and my wethers. I need to check on all of them to make sure no one else is missing."

"Shouldn't the cops have come up to do that?" Misty asked. "This seems odd. David and Rogers are good guys. They arrested Sandy's ex-husband the other day, and then they arrested the man who shot her. They're not jerks."

"I'm not that popular," Joseph admitted. "I've been a jerk for a long time, not to mention standoffish and reclusive. That doesn't lend itself to being a sympathetic character."

"It doesn't matter," Misty repeated stubbornly. "They are supposed to be on our side."

Joseph reached out and ran his thumb along her jawline. "That they are, but it looks like for now, I'm on my own."

"You're not," Misty said. "I'll come with you."

Joseph smiled, took a couple steps forward, and dropped a kiss on her lips. "I appreciate that offer more than I can tell you, but I'd rather do this alone. The goats know me, know my scent, and I need them to be comfortable tonight. Later, I'll introduce you to everyone so they can get to know you, too, but tonight isn't the right time."

Misty pursed her lips and looked up at him. "That makes sense. Please don't take too long. I mean, take as long as you need, but I'm jumpy as all get out."

He kissed her again. "Twenty minutes." He turned and walked into the darkness, and she turned back towards the house.

After divesting herself of her muddy boots, pouring herself a generous glass of wine, and curling up on the sinfully comfortable overstuffed sofa, Misty sighed. She looked around the living room, taking in the furnishings—everything for practicality or comfort, and almost nothing that could be said to be purely decorative. There wasn't a knickknack in sight, nor was there any art on the walls. There was, however, a large red vase—nearly three feet tall—that glowed with reflected light and held a grouping of wavy sticks. It was so incongruous with the rest of the furnishings that Misty couldn't help but stare.

"Like the vase?"

Misty jumped and nearly dropped her wine. She flushed when Joseph laughed.

"Sorry. Didn't mean to startle you." He sat down next to her and set his beer bottle on the end table. "I'm sorry about tonight. Dating is hard."

She laughed out loud. "It has not been easy, that's for sure. It might almost be worth it to go public early just so we could run into town and grab a bite to eat. I am starving."

"I could grab us some takeout or I could cook a frozen pizza. There's not much else to offer here. I don't really feel like driving to Long Beach, but I will if you'd like."

"Oh, god, no," she groaned. "I'm wiped out and dirty and soggy. All I want is a little hot food and a little wine and maybe a snuggle or two."

"I'll go turn on the oven. I can make all of these things happen." He stood up, snagged her nearly empty wine glass, and headed to the kitchen.

Misty leaned against the arm of the couch and pulled the afghan over her seemingly perma-chilled body. The house was invitingly warm, and her hair was beginning to feel less like icicles. Her eyelids were getting heavier, and she knew she should fight it, but it'd been a long day at the end of a series of long days, and she was exhausted. Her last conscious memory was of Joseph chuckling softly to himself and repositioning her so he could wrap the afghan more fully around her.

She tried to say something—to protest she was awake—but he put his finger over her lips and kissed her forehead. "Shhh, darling. Sleep. I'll be here when you wake up."

· · · · · ★ ★ ★ ★ · · · ·

Misty glanced around the bar, looking for Joseph. He'd been making a point of showing up with Bill in the same places she was, lately. She didn't know why she was so hesitant to go public with their relationship—especially after the other night when she'd technically spent the night, albeit fully clothed on his couch. At this point, she knew it was more than a fling, but she still wasn't ready to tell anyone.

"It's the thrill," Paska said to her.

"What?" She knew he was powerful, but hadn't thought he could read minds.

"That's why Andras won't walk away. He thinks it's too late to save the town by leaving and that he's sacrificing himself to stay, but he's bored and is looking forward to getting a little action for the first time in longer than he can remember."

Misty smiled at Paska, unable to hide her discomfort.

"Why? What did you think I meant?"

She shook her head and scooched away from him to let Sandy squeeze into the back corner of the alcove booth they'd commandeered at The Pour House. Brandy was working again tonight, and she brought over the three large platters of nachos that Misty had ordered for the group as well as a few pitchers of the new seasonal Purgatory Porter. "On the house," Brandy said. "In fact, Andy says that for the foreseeable future, none of your money is good here."

"Thank you," Morgana said. "It's not necessary."

"You'll have to take that up with the boss," Brandy said. "I just work here." She winked and left.

"This worries me," Jezebel said. "I wish we had a better idea of what was going to happen." She looked at Ceri.

"Not yet," she said. "There are too many secrets tied to Andy, and I promised to keep them as long as I could."

"You're too honorable by half," Drew grumbled. "If it's going to affect us all, we should get a heads up as to what 'it' will be."

"If he waits too long to tell you, I'll share. But for now, he needs a little more time to process, and I can give it to him. The rest of you are welcome to try your own divinations and learn the truth your way."

"Ceridwen is right," Paska said. "We need to wait for him to reveal the truth to us, rather than force the issue. If we wait, the outcome is better. Trust is established on both sides. He will trust us because we didn't pry into his background until he was ready and because Ceri didn't reveal the secrets she learned. We will trust him because he will share with us what we need to know before it is too late for us to act. Everyone wins."

"Do they, though?" Andy asked, striding into the alcove. "We won't know who's going to win until it's over." He set a drink down in front of Sandy then turned to go. Before he took a step, the entire bar started shaking. It was a slow jerking, like the floor couldn't make up its mind which way it wanted to go. Misty grabbed the nearest plate of nachos and saw the others reach out to save the food, too. She was beginning to feel vaguely sea sick—a feeling she hadn't had since in ill-timed and extremely hungover whale watching trip in her early twenties. After what seemed like ages, but was, according to her watch, only a minute or so, everything stopped moving. She took a fortifying sip of beer, popped a cheese-drenched chip in her mouth, and tried to relax.

"Was that an earthquake?" Vincent asked once the shaking subsided.

"I think it was," Paska replied. "I haven't felt one of those in a while, at least not one that strong."

"That wasn't too bad," Ceri said. "Maybe a four, if the epicenter is close."

"I'd better go turn on the radio to make sure it wasn't something bigger." Andy glanced towards the wall of windows looking out over the Pacific Ocean.

"Good idea."

Andy strode into the middle of the bar. "Looks like everything's okay, folks," he announced. "I'm just gonna turn on the radio to make sure we don't need to remember the tsunami evacuation route."

There was a round of nervous laughter, and a few people stood up.

"If you all hang on, I'll cover the next round. Let's not rush out of here until we know if there's a reason to start rushing."

The room lit up, brighter than day, accompanied by a deafening crack of thunder. Misty was still looking towards the ocean and saw the bolt hit the water before the afterburn of the light inverted all the colors of her vision and the thunder started a ringing in her ears. The power went out, leaving the bar in pitch darkness. A few people screamed, and from the sounds of scurrying feet, more than a couple were making their exits armed only with the dim light of their cell phone screens. More people turned on their phones, casting a dim glow over the bar but barely making a dent in the darkness.

"There's no tsunami danger," someone announced. "The earthquake was a shallow one and registered as a three point eight."

"Where was the epicenter?" Misty asked.

"I think we already know the answer, don't we?" Morgana asked.

"Oracle Bay," was the response.

"It's starting," Ceri said.

Misty sat in her car a half hour later. The power was back on, and people were leaving in an orderly fashion. She picked up her cell and called Joseph. He didn't answer the first three times she called, nor did he reply to any of her texts. She shrugged. He'd be there tomorrow. He was probably calming the goats after the earthquake, something she had no experience in and no real desire to intrude on tonight.

She turned the key and flipped on her headlights. An involuntary scream filled the interior of the car. Standing right in front of her was her—the woman—the goat fiend. The woman lifted her arm, waved, and walked off into the darkness.

She had no choice. She gripped the steering wheel and headed to the farm.

nine

Joseph was trying to take a night off from worrying about his farm. He'd had additional lights and cameras installed, paying for them with the hope he'd make enough through the winter to pay off the financing. In addition, he'd hired a couple locals to do security checks on the barns and outbuildings. Even so, it was hard to relax enough to enjoy himself, but he was going to do his best.

He looked around The Roadhouse and grinned. He didn't care what anyone said—this was a great bar. Well, it had great karaoke, he corrected himself. Bill showed up and plonked two Rainiers on the table. "Ready to croon?" Bill asked, grinning.

"I do not croon," Joseph said, feigning indignation. "I rock. I am a god. A karaoke god."

Bill laughed. "Whatever gets you through the days."

They wrote down their songs and handed them in, along with a couple bucks for the KJ, and waited for their turn. It was loud enough during the karaoke that they couldn't speak, so instead, they sang along when they knew the words and otherwise sat in companionable silence.

Bill had just been called up to sing "My Way," to the heckling accusation of "Crooner!" by Joseph when the building began to shake. Joseph helped herd everyone outside and away from the questionable structural integrity of The Columbia Bar Roadhouse. The lights flickered a few times, blinked off, and then a moment later blinked back on.

The silence that had lain over the crowd like a heavy blanket in the wake of the noises that accompanied the earthquake was broken by a sudden cacophony of conversation. People had their phones out to check for news and tsunami warnings, and Joseph looked at Bill. "Let's go. We need to get back to the farm."

Bill didn't argue, just walked back inside to trade his debit card for a couple twenties, then met Joseph at his truck, ready to head out.

"It was just an earthquake," Bill said.

"They're not common, and the goats will be freaked out," Joseph replied.

Bill didn't say anything else, and thirty-five minutes later they were parked in front of the main barn.

"Check Vincent and the wethers," Joseph replied. "I'll get the does and kids." Bill saluted and took off towards the second barn.

The door to the main barn was slightly ajar, and Joseph tried to convince himself the earthquake had shaken things loose. He slid it the rest of the way open and walked in to the sound of panting and soft bleating. "Shh, shh, girls. It's okay." He flipped on the overhead lights and did a quick headcount.

He checked their feed and water, then gave them each an extra pat and head scratch before walking out of the barn and straight into Misty.

* * * * * ★ ★ ★ ★ * * *

Joseph stared down at her for a moment before grabbing her arms and pulling her in for a kiss. "What are you doing here? Are you okay?"

"I was worried about you. I tried to get a hold of you, but you didn't answer my calls or my texts."

Joseph pulled his phone out of his pocket and checked the display. No missed calls. No new texts. He showed it to Misty. She grabbed her phone and looked at it, almost as if she feared what she was going to see. "Look! Three calls and three texts," she said, relief evident in her voice. "I thought I was losing my mind for a moment."

"That is so weird," Joseph said, fiddling with his phone. "I've got nothing. No signal or anything."

"Maybe the earthquake did something to it?" Misty offered hesitantly.

"That's as good a theory as any. But why drive all the way out here just because I was incommunicado for an hour?"

"It does sound a little stalkeresque when you put it that way," Misty admitted. "But I had a bad feeling, and then, in the parking lot of The Pour House, I saw..." she trailed off as a figure started towards them at the same time a cold, steady rain began to fall.

Joseph saw her shoulders tighten and her eyes widen as her gaze caught on something behind him. He reached out a steadying hand and grasped her shoulder before turning to follow her line of sight. At first, the rain obscured the figure from him, and he tensed. Then the person walked into the splash of light left by the nearest yard light, and Joseph's shoulders slumped. "It's Bill," he told Misty quietly. He watched the tension drain out of her shoulders. Relief lightened her face for a moment before it shuttered again. Joseph brushed a thumb along her jawline. "What's wrong?"

She shook her head and set her jawline. "Nothing. I..."

"What's going on here?" Bill asked. "Did someone plan a wet t-shirt contest and forget to invite me?"

Misty rolled her eyes, and Joseph stifled a grin. He turned

around, shifting to be beside Misty instead of in front of her, and said, "Everything okay in there?"

"They were cranky, but everyone was accounted for, and they calmed down once I pointed out that they still had food and water. Well, mostly calmed down. Vincent seemed a little jumpier than usual."

"Maybe I'll just pop in and make sure he's okay," Joseph said. "He's the most sensitive buck I've had in a long time, and hasn't been himself since Goatzilla..." Joseph's voice trailed off, and he stared at the barn, not meeting either Bill's or Misty's eyes.

Misty slipped an arm around his waist and pulled him close. "Go on and check. I'll wait here for you. Tonight is probably not the night for goat introductions."

He dropped a kiss on top of her head. "Thank you, baby. I'll be back in ten minutes. Bill will—"

"I'll come with you," Bill announced.

"Good idea," Misty agreed.

"It's pouring. Why don't you go inside and get warm and dry? You know where everything is." Joseph dug his keys out of his pocket and handed them over. "There's a bottle of Pinot on the counter."

Misty hesitated, but then took the keys. She winked at him— barely visible in the dim light and rain—and asked, "Are the pajamas from last time still in the same spot?"

Tension rushed through Joseph's body, and he was barely conscious of Bill standing next to him. Checking on his goats was feeling less and less urgent. He took a step forward, and Bill caught his elbow. "Are we checking on the goats or what?"

Joseph glanced back at Bill then at Misty. He poured all the longing he felt for her into his eyes and hoped she could see it. "Ten minutes."

"I'll be inside, warm and dry, drinking a glass of wine," she promised.

He watched her turn and walk away, keeping his eyes on her until she reached the front door of his house and stood illuminated on the front steps. Only when she disappeared did he allow Bill to drag him back towards the barn.

"I thought I was gonna lose you there," Bill teased.

"I almost wish you had," Joseph grumbled. "There is a desirable woman in my house—in my bedroom—right now, possibly taking off her clothes."

"You'd never forgive yourself if there was something wrong and you didn't check on the guys yourself."

Joseph furrowed his brow and pressed his lips together. "I know you're right, but somehow this still feels very, very wrong."

Bill laughed. "Come on, Romeo." He pulled open the barn door, and they walked inside.

"Why didn't you stay with her?" Joseph asked. "I can do this alone—in fact, it probably would've been faster."

"She doesn't trust me, and I don't think she likes me very much. She's not yet forgiven me for what happened with Drew, and I didn't want to make things harder on her by forcing her to spend time alone with me."

"That was very thoughtful," Joseph said.

"There's no need to sound so surprised. I'm a nice guy," Bill protested.

Joseph laughed. "Sometimes, maybe. I'll allow it." He walked into the barn, and Vincent van Goat immediately started rattling the door to his pen. Joseph walked up to him murmuring soothingly. "It's okay, goat. You're a good goat. Everything's okay now." He opened the pen and walked inside. There was something on the ground, and he bent over to grab it, earning a head to the butt for his troubles. He reached behind him and stroked the top of Vincent's head. "I'll take this now. You're okay."

Vincent bleated once, then settled, went to the back corner, and laid down. Joseph stepped out, locked the pen and double checked the rest of the doors, then held up the item he'd retrieved from Vincent's pen.

"A glove?" Bill asked.

"Misty's glove."

"Oh, damn."

Joseph led Bill into the house so Bill could wash up and dry off before leaving. He left him with a bath towel at the guest bathroom and headed to his room to do the same. Misty was on the couch, glass of wine in hand, looking very cozy and exceedingly kissable in the flannel shirt and boxers she'd borrowed from him last time she'd spent the night.

Desire suffused him, and he almost stopped and made a beeline straight for her without the detour to his bedroom to change into clean, dry clothes.

"I'll be right back," he said, surreptitiously checking to make sure her glove was tucked into his pocket and not dangling free and waving at her while he walked by. Once he'd stripped and started to dry off, he realized how cold he was from the rain combined with the coastal November air, so he jumped in the shower to rinse the last of the day's stress and grime from his body before putting on his favorite pair of jeans and a soft, button-up shirt. He stopped by the kitchen to grab a glass of wine for himself before rejoining Misty in the living room.

Bill had beaten him there and was perched at the edge of the recliner, ankles crossed, longneck in one hand, with the other forearm laying across his knees, looking for all the world like a man who didn't know how to use a comfy chair.

The air was thick with tense silence and Misty and Bill both looked very determinedly at everything in the room but each other. Joseph looked back and forth between his best friend and the woman he was quickly coming to...he cut himself off with a swig of wine before he could go any further down a path he wasn't ready for. He ignored the nerve-quickened heartbeat and sat down next to Misty, pulling her glove out of his pocket as he did so.

Her hand trembled as she reached for it, and Joseph swiped her glass of wine and set it down on the end table before they could put the Scotchgard to the test.

"Where did you find this?" Her voice was softer than usual but didn't waver. Her eyes were wide, and the vertical lines between her eyes coupled with tremors still evident in her hands belied the calmness of her words.

Joseph wanted to lie. He wanted to claim he'd found it on the floor of the restaurant she'd left it in, and was just now getting around to giving it back. He wanted to be able to reassure her, to protect her. He also knew that while she might need his support, she didn't need his protection or his lies.

"It was in Vincent's pen," Joseph said.

Misty wrinkled her nose and angled her head. "What? What was Vincent doing out here? I didn't know you guys even knew each other."

It was Joseph's turn to be confused. "Vincent van Goat? My... goat? I guess that last bit was a bit redundant."

"Vincent Bryson is the guy who owns most of the business district," Bill said. "Misty's shop, mine, Natalie's, the bookstore..."

"Drew's," Misty said. She had the glove clenched in one one-knuckled hand and reached over Joseph to retrieve her wine. "All the properties I manage."

"Drew's," Bill agreed, meeting her eyes for the first time since Joseph'd entered the room.

"You guys, you're two of my favorite people. I am not looking forward to years of needing a machete to cut through the tension you two generate when you're in the same room. You don't have to work it out tonight, but you're going to have to work it out somehow."

"Years?" Misty said.

The corner of Joseph's mouth quirked up. "You heard me. I'm not taking it back."

Pink stained her cheeks, and the look she gave him fanned the flames she'd lit earlier. Before he could crawl over to her and pin her to the sofa for a taste of her wine-stained lips, Bill cleared his throat.

"Apologies. I'll do better in the future. I truly don't mean to make anyone uncomfortable, particularly not either of you."

Joseph leaned back into the couch, shifted slightly in an attempt to get more comfortable, then gave it up as a bad job. He took a drink of wine, then said, "We should call the police."

"And tell them what? That your goat had my glove?"

"After what happened with Goatzilla, this could be another attempt to kidnap and harm one of my flock."

Bill snorted and immediately took a sip of beer to try to cover his lapse.

"Are you laughing about Goatzilla's murder?" Joseph demanded, voice too loud for the room. The heat he felt now had nothing to do with the way Misty's sweater hugged every curve.

"No, of course not. A million times no," Bill said. "It's just...you said kidnapping. And baby goats are kids. And..." he trailed off, finished his beer in one long swallow, and stood up, forgetting to uncross his ankles and nearly taking a tumble. "I'm grabbing another. You guys need anything?" He bolted out of the living room.

Joseph caught Misty's eyes. Her shoulders were shaking, and she was biting her lower lip. When she noticed him noticing her suppressed laughter, she whispered, "It was kinda funny."

He let go of the rest of his tension and grinned, then guffawed. Misty joined his laughter, although there was a note of rising panic in hers. She leaned into him, and he wrapped an arm around her, squeezing her tight. "It'll be okay," he said. "Whatever this is, we'll figure it out, and we'll fix it."

Bill walked back into the room with the bottle of wine. He filled the two nearly-empty glasses, then sat back down in the recliner, this time fitting his whole body in the chair and leaning back instead of forward. "Are we going to talk more about the glove?" he asked.

"What more is there?" Misty replied. "That woman took it from me, and she returned it via goat mail, which is not much slower than snail mail, really."

"She's clearly after you both," Bill said. "Although Joseph seems to be her primary target right now."

Misty gave Bill a sidelong look, then took another sip of wine. "I have thoughts, but I don't want to be mocked."

"No one will mock you here," Joseph said.

Misty pursed her lips, tilted her head, and pointed at Bill. "He's an unbeliever."

"He's not. Not really," Joseph assured her.

"That almost makes it worse. If he does believe and he still..." she shut her mouth with a snap.

"People change," Bill said. "Billie—"

Misty set down her wine glass and stood up. "I understand why you'd believe Joseph, why that would make you change your mind about the locals. What I don't understand is why the man you purported to love, the one with whom you were planning on spending your life, wasn't worth as much to you."

She turned back to the couch, ignoring Bill's rising flush and unhinged jaw. "Joseph, I'm glad you're okay and that nothing happened to the goats tonight. I'll grab my stuff and go, but if you don't mind, I'd like to wear the shirt out. My clothes are likely still soaked."

"Of course, wear whatever you want. I wish..."

She interrupted him with a kiss. "I'll grab my things from your bedroom and be back in a second."

A few minutes later, jeans and shoes added to the flannel shirt she'd been wearing, Misty reappeared.

"I'll walk you out to your car," Joseph said.

"That's not necessary. Just walk me to the front door so I can kiss you without an audience."

Joseph wanted to protest, to find the words that would convince her to stay, but again, her lips interrupted his attempts to change her mind.

"Let me know when you're home safe," he said.

"Of course. Call me tomorrow? Can we have a real date? Dinner, drinks, just the two of us?"

"There is nothing I want more." He kissed her again. "Tomorrow. Seven. Meet me here?"

As soon as she'd driven off, Joseph headed back to the living room. "Dude!"

"What?"

"I had a woman in my living room. A beautiful woman wearing nothing but my clothes. Here. For me."

"And?"

"You didn't leave. Do you know how long it's been since there's been anyone, much less something I cared about? Why didn't you go?"

"It's guys' night," Bill said.

"I thought you had my back," Joseph said.

"I thought it was best you stayed focused. Someone is out to get you, and you shouldn't be distracted."

"I can't believe people think that you're the nice one," Joseph shook his head.

"Well, if you want me to leave that badly." Bill stood up, took his half-full beer to the kitchen while Joseph stared after him in surprise.

Joseph followed him out. "She's right, you know. You suspended your disbelief for me when you wouldn't for Drew."

"What's interesting is that you did the exact same thing to her, and you get the pass that I don't."

"Hurting her friends is worse than hurting her," Joseph said. "That's why she'll forgive me when she won't forgive you."

"Whatever," Bill said. "I'll see you later." He walked out into the storm.

· · · · ★ ★ ★ ★ · · · ·

It was a little past midnight when Joseph finished the last of the wine and decided to do one last check of the barns and head to bed. Misty hadn't texted him to say she was home safe and hadn't replied to any of his four texts and three voicemails. He checked his bars—nothing. Maybe their messages just weren't getting through, like earlier. Something weird was going on.

"Understatement of the year," he said, pulling on a raincoat and grabbing the flashlight by the front door. His phone vibrated in his back pocket, and he cursed under his breath as he dug through the layers of jacket and too-long shirttails to grab it.

"Hey! I miss u. Wanna meet me @ the brewpub 4 a drink & a walk on the beach? Let me know ttyl xoxo"

The message was so odd that he double-checked it was from Misty. It was her number, but he'd never known her to eschew proper spelling and punctuation, even for the sake of text message brevity. The downpour outside and the fact that they still weren't Oracle Bay public further backed his theory that this was not, in fact, Mystic Greene. He didn't know how someone could send a text that looked like it was from someone else, but he knew enough of the world to know that there were always going to be more things he didn't know than things he did.

"Sure," he texted back, then pocketed the phone, turned on the flashlight, and headed for the barns.

Vincent van Goat and the wethers were all asleep, and everything looked undisturbed. He turned to leave, stumbled a bit, and shook his head to clear the wine. His phone buzzed again, and he fished it out of his pocket while locking the barn and heading to the second one. There was light shining under the door which was slightly ajar. He shifted his flashlight to his right hand, shuffling the phone to his left, and opened the door as quietly as he could. There was a figure at the far end crouched over...he squinted but couldn't quite see. He took another step and realized she was standing over the bodies of Billie's two kids, with Billie trussed up beside them. He raised the flashlight and sprinted forward.

She turned the minute he stopped trying to be quiet, grimaced, and said, "You're supposed to be in town." Then a bright flash erupted from the hand she waved casually towards him, white hot pain erupted through his body, and he dropped to the ground, letting go of the flashlight and the phone. The last thing he saw before unconsciousness overtook him was the woman—that same, damnable woman—look at Billie and say, "I am the goddess of lightning and weather, the mother of haruspicy. I am She Who Remembers, and you thought you could hide from me? I am Menrva, and I will have my answers and my revenge."

ten

Misty drove into Joseph's long driveway at precisely ten minutes to seven. It was dark, but at least not a stormy night. The house blazed with light on the otherwise dark farmstead. The yard lights near the barns as well as the barns themselves were dark—which was unusual. She'd always assumed they automatically came on when it got dark. She scraped her front driver's side wheel against the shrubbery lining trying to get as close to the front walk as possible and squeezed through the narrow opening she'd left herself.

Something was wrong, and Misty wasn't about to start ignoring her finely honed instincts out of fear of looking silly in front of her new boyfriend.

She rang the doorbell and knocked. The shaking in her hand turned the planned *rap rap* into a snare drum's staccato. She steeled herself, swallowed the fear that was threatening to spew forth, and tried the doorknob. The door swung open with a screech she didn't remember from any of the other times she'd been here. Light splashed over the vacant entryway creating demonic shadows bobbing in the corners. A shiver started at the base of her spine and chased goosebumps up to her neck, chattering her teeth.

"Joseph?" she called. "The door was open. Are you here?"

Silence answered her. She took two grudging steps forward, breaching the doorway to the living room, and peered in. When she'd left the night before, the place had been immaculate. Now, the pristine cream couch cushions were ripped open and scattered around the floor. The tightness in her chest got worse, and her breath came in shallow bursts. She pulled her phone out of her purse, unlocked it, and dialed 9-1-.

She walked back through the kitchen and dining room, both of which were more cluttered than usual but didn't bear the signs of the destruction in the front room, and headed to the back hall. Four closed doors greeted her, and ice spread out from the growing fear and chilled her veins. She opened the first door on the left—the guest room. It was undisturbed, not that there was much to disturb. A queen-sized bed anchored by two end tables and an empty armoire were the entirety of the furnishings.

Misty backed out of the room and pulled the door closed behind her, wincing as the latch snicked into place with an obscenely loud echo. The first door on the right was the shared half-bath. Nothing out of place here except the lid of the toilet tank was broken in half on the floor.

The next door on the right was the room Joseph used as his office. She gritted her teeth and walked in. The tall bookshelves that lined two walls were devoid of books—their inhabitants were strewn across the room in haphazard piles. Bent and torn pages, ripped dust jackets, and broken spines littered the floor—a sight almost painful enough to interrupt the strengthening pulses of panic reverberating through her body.

The desk drawers were pulled almost all the way out and hung precariously. Papers were in untidy clumps near the desk. Joseph's iMac was tipped over, a sight almost as heart-wrenching as the damaged books. She couldn't tell if anything was missing. They'd only been dating a couple of weeks, and she'd only had a glimpse before. The glimpse she'd had, though, had been of a tidy room. The desk had nothing on it but the computer, a notebook, and a pen. Every book had been in its place, and there'd been nothing on the floor.

Misty swallowed hard. There was enough here to warrant calling the cops. Joseph's place had clearly been ransacked, and there wasn't a Joseph around. The door had been unlocked, he'd had plans with her, and the lights by the barn were off. It was enough. She looked at Joseph's bedroom door and took a deep breath to try to combat the near-hyperventilation she was currently doing.

She was going to look.

One step. Two. The hallway first stretched to be impossibly wide —it'd take an hour to get to the other side—then folded in on itself, and she was in front of the door. Her hands were clammy in her gloves, and she almost took them off until she remembered about fingerprints. Everything was damp. There was a slow trickle of sweat tracing her spine through the curve of her lower back, and she wished—not for the first time—that bras were made from terry cloth.

A deep breath and another and she was ready. She opened the door, grateful that her gloves protected the doorknob and any potential evidence from her sweaty palms, and walked into Joseph's bedroom. Unlike the other rooms, it was undisturbed. Eerily so. The bed was made, the dresser drawers were shut, the closet was closed, and the large black and white photograph of Haystack Rock was perfectly centered over the bed, not even a degree off of square.

Misty backed out of the room and was pulling the door closed when something caught her eye. Something red. Her heart pounded so quickly and loudly in her chest, breaking the silence, and causing her to scream in shock. She unlocked her phone again and hit the last number she was waiting to dial.

"Nine-one-one, what's your emergency?" a smooth, calm voice answered.

"I'm at a friend's place, Joseph McEwen, and something is wrong. He was supposed to be here, and he's not, and his house has been ransacked."

"How long has he been missing?"

"I don't know. I spoke to him yesterday evening to confirm that we were meeting tonight, but haven't talked to him since."

"I have officers on the way. They'll be there soon. In the meantime, please hold on and don't touch anything. Can you tell me your name?"

Misty tried to answer the dispatcher's questions, probably mostly designed to keep her calm and functional, until she heard the wail of sirens in the distance. She walked to the front door and met the officers. "Hi, Roger. Hi, David."

"Misty Greene. You were not the person we were expecting to see," David said.

"Yes, she is," Roger contradicted. "Dispatch told us who was here."

"Also, last time there was a Joseph related crime, I called it in," Misty said helpfully.

"You're also well-known to dislike him strongly," David said. "Which means, we're going to have some questions. The first one— did you touch anything?"

Misty gave them a run-down of where she'd been and what she'd touched, then reminded them that she always wore gloves, so hopefully, she hadn't contaminated too much. David and Roger looked around, made interested sounding grunts, and then returned to where Misty was waiting.

"Doesn't look like too much to me," David said. "Joseph probably took off in a hurry and forgot to straighten up."

"Wha—?" Misty couldn't even articulate how completely ridiculous that sounded. "The couch cushions are ripped to shreds. Every single book is on the floor. The toilet was broken."

"Reasonable explanations for everything," Roger said. "Pets could've ripped up the couch and knocked down the toilet lid. As for the books, maybe he was looking for one or two specific ones to take on his vacation and knocked everything down to find them."

"That is the least reasonable explanation I've ever heard," Misty said.

"Or maybe you did it, and called us to cover your tracks?" David said. His eyes met hers, and the blank menace was enough to cause her to take a step back.

"We should check the barns," she managed to say. The wrongness was getting worse, and she one hundred percent did not want to go to the barns with these men—men she'd known for almost a decade—but she needed to make sure the goats were okay.

The first barn, the small one, everything looked just like a goat barn should look, at least what Misty imagined a goat barn to look like. The four goats bleated at the intrusion. She checked the water and noticed there was no food. She had no idea when they'd last been fed, didn't know what to feed them, and certainly couldn't determine how much. She was going to have to call Bill.

The second barn, the one with the babies, was not in order. One pen was empty, the straw inside disturbed, and there was blood on the floor.

"They're just hungry and cranky," David said. "Best leave you to it if you're here to take care of things while Joseph's away."

"There's a goat missing, and her baby." She did a quick scan of the room. "I think it's Billie Holliday, so that means two babies missing."

"That Joseph's a goat farmer! Probably took them to the goat doctor."

"Or on a goat vacation," Roger added. "I've read about goat yoga. Maybe they're at a yoga retreat."

"That is..." words failed her. After a minute, she found herself again. "Something has happened. Joseph wouldn't leave his goats unfed, unwatered, and unmilked. He wouldn't leave his house unlocked and in disarray. You've known him for an age. You know this isn't normal. So, do something. Investigate. Find him."

"He'll be back," Roger said, reaching out to pat her shoulder. She flinched away.

"Call if anything comes up!" David said, then followed his partner out to their patrol car.

Hot tears snaked down her cheeks, and suppressed sobs shook her chest. She would not give in. Not now. Now she had to take care of the goats and then find Joseph. She girded her loins and dialed Bill's number.

Misty stood at Vincent's front door. Sandy hadn't moved in—yet—but it was Vincent's first official night in the house, so they were probably both there. Unless they weren't. Maybe they were off celebrating.

"Get ahold of yourself, Mystic Green," she muttered, then pressed the bell before she could change her mind.

Vincent opened the door, and for a moment, neither of them said anything. He recovered quickly. "Come in. Please. Are you okay?"

"Is Sandy here?"

"Of course. One moment." He walked to the stairs, never taking his eyes off her, and called, "Sandy. It's for you."

Less than a minute later, Sandy appeared holding an empty glass that she passed off to Vincent when she saw Misty standing in the entryway. Her eyes ached from crying, and she knew she looked a mess.

Sandy rushed forward and pulled her into her arms. "What's wrong? What's happened? Are you okay?" She turned her head to look behind her. "Can you get Misty a French 75? Another for me, too, please." She led Misty into the living room, and they sat down on the sofa. "Misty. Please. What's wrong?"

"It's Joseph. He's gone."

"Joseph?" Sandy looked at Misty. "Joseph the goat farmer?"

"He's missing. He's gone, and so is Billie Holiday." She knew how preposterous it sounded the moment the words left her lips, but there was no other way to describe it.

"Billie Holiday? The singer?" Sandy wrinkled her nose and furrowed her bow.

"Billie Holiday! His prizewinning goat! The one that produces the best milk, the richest cream, and always gives birth to twins." Her voice was getting too loud too quickly, and she desperately searched for her internal off switch. She said again, her voice barely more than a whisper, "Joseph is gone."

Sandy leaned back into the couch and gazed at Misty. "That is upsetting. I'm assuming you contacted the police. What about his parents? Or Bill? Surely they can take it from here."

Misty ducked her head and pulled her phone out of her pocket to escape Sandy's gaze. She had to come clean, she wanted to come clean, but for some reason, the words were sticking. "There's something more. But missing people are concerning no matter what."

"How long has he been missing?" She reached a hand towards Misty and patted her knee.

Misty looked down at her phone again, then met Sandy's eyes. "I was supposed to meet him at his place tonight at seven. When I got to his place, he was gone, his place was tossed, and Billie Holiday was missing. I called the cops, but they're just saying it could be a messy house and a farmer out of town."

"Did you tell them you were dating?" Sandy asked softly.

Misty flushed. "No."

"Why not?"

"It's a secret?" She hated the way her voice canted up, making it a question.

"Why, though? What's going on with that?"

Misty felt the tears overflow into her eyes, spilling down her cheeks before she could even try to stop them. "I saw this. I knew something was going to happen, and I didn't say anything."

Sandy scooted over to sit next to her and put an arm around her shoulder. "It's not your fault."

"What if he's gone and I never get the chance…"

"We'll find him," Sandy said. "I promise."

"How? All I have is a vision I got from that creepy stalker lady and a ransacked house that the cops think looks like a typical bachelor pad."

"Is it? I mean, had you seen it otherwise?"

"Yeah. He's not a neat freak, but there wasn't much for clutter or mess last night."

"You were there last night?" Sandy was trying to sound casual and completely whiffing the attempt.

Vincent walked into the room. "I took the liberty of speaking to the man who showed up on the front stoop but who couldn't be bothered to ring the doorbell. Drew will rally the rest of the troops, and we'll break in our new house with a psychic meeting. I'll run out and get some supplies. We're pretty low on groceries."

Sandy smiled up at him and the naked adoration in her eyes—in both their eyes—made Misty's stomach do flip-flops. "Perfect."

"Argh, it's your first night in the new house. I shouldn't be here— no one should be here. I will take my sad story and leave."

"Sit down," Sandy said. "Vincent's already told Drew, so there's no point in leaving now. We're having a team meeting, like it or not."

Misty sank back into the sofa. Sandy was right. Now that Drew knew she was distressed he'd be there to call a meeting to figure out why and determine whose ass needed kicking.

The doorbell rang, and Sandy got up to answer it. Drew came and sat down on the couch next to Misty and enveloped her in a great bear hug. "What's wrong, sweetheart? Who do I need to take out? And why didn't you call me?"

His response was so predictable that she let out a shaky laugh. "I did call you. And Ceri. And I stopped by both your houses. No one was there. That's the only reason I came here; it was right across the street, and the lights were on. The others are coming?"

"Of course."

"I'll wait then. I don't want to explain more than once."

"As you wish."

Misty slumped back into the sofa. She pressed her fingers to her temples trying to press out the knots causing the dull ache spreading throughout her head. Things had been weird, but she'd never expected to be here—terrified for a man she'd professed to hate only a few weeks ago, a man that she was more than a little certain she was growing to love.

The door opened with no fanfare, and Vincent walked through, followed by Ceri and Jezebel.

Ceri sat next to Misty and grasped her gloved hands with her own. "We'll find him," she promised.

"How can you be sure?"

"Who do you think you're talking to?" Ceri asked, her eyes slightly unfocused. Misty followed her gaze; she was staring at the hallway mirror. Her hair rose in a halo around her head, and her pupils expanded until her iris was nearly invisible. "We are oracles, and we have enough power to save this world or damn it with the truths that we can see."

Misty's jaw dropped a bit, and goosebumps ran over her body, prickling her uncomfortably. "What have you seen?"

"The echo of your seeing when the woman tore your glove away, the events that transpired last night, and a vague but probable end. If you learn to utilize your powers to their fullest extent, you can help save Joseph, save the goats, and eventually, save this town."

"Holy crap," Vincent whispered. He'd followed Jezebel into the room carrying three bottles of wine and was staring at Ceri with the awe and amazement she'd inspired.

Twenty minutes later, everyone had arrived and settled in. Misty was still keeping a tight harness on her emotions but had taken a break to clean up her mascara.

Vincent pulled a chair into the living room and positioned it unobtrusively in the corner. Sandy gave him a peck on the cheek and settled into the sofa beside Misty.

"Do you want to tell us what happened, or do you want me to do it?" Sandy asked.

"No, I'll do it. It's my story." She took a deep breath and a fortifying sip of wine, sketched in her burgeoning relationship with Joseph, and brought everything back around to the mysterious woman, her own vision, the goat murder, and last night. She skirted around Joseph's family secrets, muttering something about the goat being special, and then floundered to an end. "I left Bill caring for the rest of the goats—he knows what he's doing, and they know him. And here I am. We need to find him."

"We need a plan," Drew said.

"Ceri said I'm not utilizing my full potential, but I'm not sure I have the ability to find Joseph and the goats in time."

"In time for what?" Morgana asked, speaking for the first time.

"In time for..." Misty trailed off. "I don't know. Just in time."

"Hold onto that feeling," Morgana said, nodding. "As I told you all and Andras before, we can do so much more than most of us believe. We are more than receptacles, more than mere oracles. Knowledge is power, and we have so much of both.

eleven

Misty pulled into the driveway at Joseph's farm and parked in front of the house for the third time in three days. She and Drew hopped out of the car and walked over to the barn where Bill was standing with Roger and David.

"Howdy, ma'am, sir," Roger said, tipping his police cap at them.

Howdy? Ma'am? Misty stopped walking before she got within arm's reach. When had the Washington state born and bred Roger Webster become an extra on the set of "Stereotypical White Cops of Texas?

Drew grabbed her hand and squeezed three times before letting go. He was just as freaked out as she was. The weirdness factor had just increased by a factor of infinity. David King was standing motionless next to his partner. Something was off about him, too. After a minute of staring, Misty realized what it was. He hadn't blinked. Misty didn't know how often people blinked, but she was positive that it was more frequently than once every couple minutes. "David?"

He blinked, and that simple motion animated him. Color flooded his cheeks, his limbs jerked a bit, and his eyes focused on her.

"Is it me, or is this the eeriest thing that you've ever seen?" Drew whispered.

She reached out and took his hand again. "David? Roger? Can you tell us why we're here?"

"Of course," Roger said. "Since the three of you were closest to the missing person, we thought it would be useful to have you here to answer questions as we do a secondary search."

"I thought you said there was no reason for alarm," Bill pointed out.

"New information has come to light," David said in a near-perfect monotone.

"What new information?" Misty asked. She wasn't sure what to believe but didn't mind grasping at straws. Maybe if she caught one, she could take a long drink of hope before it dissolved.

"New information," David repeated.

Bill skirted the police officers, leaving a wide berth, and came to stand next to Misty and Drew. She almost grabbed his hand, too—a united front of scaredy cats was better than a loosely grouped flock of chickens—but thought better of it. She still didn't like him. He might be her boyfriend's BFF, but he'd hurt her BFF, and Misty had never been one who was quick to forgive and forget. She didn't know how to have an emotion that didn't run down to her soul, whether that emotion was disdain, dislike, or devotion.

"Hey," Bill said, not looking at either of them.

"Hey," Misty responded, once it became apparent that Drew wouldn't. All three of them kept their eyes on the cops.

"We will do another search," Roger said. "David will do the barns and surrounding out building with Bill and Drew, and I'll do the house with Misty. It will be good teamwork."

"Oh, hell no," Misty said. "That is, by far, the worst idea you've ever had, Roger Webster. There is no way I'm going anywhere with you."

"If we have to split up, why doesn't Drew go with you and Misty," Bill said.

Misty looked at the men she was with. Bill was a big guy. He was an inch or two over six feet and had the broad, muscular shoulders of a linebacker and the softer middle of a professional baker. His dark hair and eyes rounded out his look. There was nothing in his physique that suggested messing with him would be a good idea. Drew was shorter by a good half a foot, had a permanent five o'clock shadow, and the most beautiful blue-grey eyes she'd ever seen. His build reminded her more of a wrestler than a football player. Sleek, muscular, and quick, but not a visual powerhouse.

She contrasted their appearances with that of the cops. Both on the young side—early thirties—and both average in about every way. Roger was a bit slimmer than David, but neither looked like they did more than the bare minimum to keep in shape. More importantly, neither was a match of Bill. Roger and Drew were friends— had been since Roger had moved to town—and as freaky as he was acting, at least he wasn't a creepy automaton like David.

"That would work for me. Drew?" she asked, tilting her head over to look at him. He avoided her eyes and looked up and over her head to the man on her other side. She couldn't see Bill's expression without being totally obvious, so she watched Drew instead. The wide-eyed hopefulness slowly pinched in on itself until there was nothing but resignation.

"That's probably for the best," Drew said.

"I think Roger's plan is best," David said.

"I think you can go—"

"To the barn, where I will help you with your search," Bill said. "We should go now. It's nearly dusk, and I'll need to milk and feed the goats soon. Let's get this over with."

Misty smiled tightly at Bill, realized what she was doing, and looked away. She was almost positive that the suggested group change was to protect her rather than for Bill to avoid Drew, and she was both relieved and annoyed by his presumption.

"Does anyone have a key to the house?" Roger asked.

"I do," Bill said. "Do you Misty?"

"No, I left mine behind the night of the earthquake," she said. "I was in a hurry to leave."

Bill handed his key to Misty, bypassing Roger's outstretched hand. This time she didn't stop the smile that aimed itself at her former almost-arch-enemy and unexpected ally. He responded with a lopsided smile of his own, and then the grim weirdness of the situation reasserted itself and erased the brief moment of camaraderie.

"Let's go," Roger said, reaching out to grab Misty's arm.

She jerked back, no longer caring how rude it might make her look. "Please don't touch me, Roger. I'm a little jumpy after the events of the last couple days. Weeks. Whatever."

"Why?" He sounded genuinely curious and Misty wrinkled her nose and looked sideways at him.

"Goat murders. Earthquakes. My friend disappearing. My other friend was shot, in a property I manage. Andy..." she trailed off before she could say anything she shouldn't.

"What about...Andy," Roger asked. A note of avaricious interest colored his words. "He is old."

"He just had a little trouble at the bar with Sandy's ex-husband," Drew said. "The guy you arrested in Caffiend Dreams. That guy couldn't go anywhere without causing trouble."

"Oh," Roger said, his voice returning to the flat tone he'd been using before. Not as monotone as automaton-David, but not animated enough for human—and generally dramatically flamboyant—Roger.

Misty squeezed Drew's hand and led the way up the sidewalk to the front door, painfully aware of the armed and creepy cop behind her.

Forty minutes later, skin still crawling, Misty and Drew rejoined Bill outside. Bill widened his eyes at them in what Misty was certain was supposed to be some kind significance, but she had no idea what he was trying to say.

"Find anything?" Roger asked.

"No. Find anything?" David answered in an almost-identical monotone.

"No."

"Now what?" David asked.

Roger said, "It's time."

"Time for what?" Bill asked. Impatience edged his voice, and Misty flinched at the sharpness. "Sorry," he said, walking over to where she and Drew waited a little ways back from the cops. "I'm frustrated, anxious, and more than a little freaked out."

"Solidarity," Misty said, then took a brief moment to appreciate their first civil conversation in more than a couple years.

"It's time to look in the field, now," Roger said.

Misty twisted her body to catch the western horizon out of the corner of her eye. The sun was hovering less than an inch above the ocean. "It'll be dark soon," she said. "We won't be able to find anything."

"We should go to the field," David said. "We will find a clue."

"No. That's about enough," Drew said. "What the hell is wrong with you guys?"

"What do you mean?" they asked in unison.

Drew, Misty, and Bill took a step back, and Misty edged her car keys out of her pocket.

Roger shook himself, smiled too wide, and said, "My apologies. We've had more crime than usual the last couple weeks, and I, for one, haven't been sleeping well. We're generally underemployed—focusing mostly on speeding tourists and drunk and disorderliness, which are usually also tourists. Lately, we've responded to a domestic dispute in your business, an attempted murder, a satanic-looking goat sacrifice, and now a missing person case. It's a bit over-whelming.

"We'd really appreciate it if the three of you would walk through the field with us," Roger said. "It's not that big of an area, but it'll go faster with five rather than three, and when we don't find anything, we can go home."

Misty looked at David, mute since Bill'd called out their weird behavior. "David? Are you okay?"

"Of course, I'm okay. Just tired as my partner Roger said."

"Let's do it," she said. "I want to get it over with so I can go home and find my bathtub."

"Is your bathtub missing, too? Would you like to file a report for it? Ha ha ha. That was a joke," Roger said.

Misty forced a smile onto her face and exchanged wide-eyed looks with Bill and Drew.

Roger and David led the way to the field. The others, through unspoken communication, hung back ten feet or so, and followed. They clamored gingerly over the barbed wire fence, spread out the distance of two arm's lengths away from each other, and started walking. They made it to the other end without finding anything, scooted down one group's length so as not to walk over any ground already covered, and started back. The sun was slipping into the ocean by now, turning the sea and the sky a brilliant orange. Dusk was settling on them, covering the stubbled field with a purple cloak and softening the harsh, stubbled edges, while hiding the obstacles they'd encountered on the way in.

Misty took off, a little faster than she'd walked on the first length, and after a few steps, pulled out her cell phone and turned on the flashlight. She hadn't gone more than a few dozen feet farther when something caught her eye. She pointed her flashlight towards the uneven break in the landscape and followed the beam of light.

"I found something," she said hoarsely. Her breath was coming in shallow pants, and her pulse accelerated in her throat.

"What is it?" Bill asked, voice cracking with strain. "It's not..."

"No. It's just his stuff. Clothes, wallet, key, cell phone. And a Polaroid."

Bill reached her side and squatted down next to her. The beam of his flashlight joined with hers, and they stared at the picture in silence until Drew and the cops showed up.

"Is that...Joseph?" Roger asked, sounding completely natural for the first time in...weeks.

"Yeah," Misty confirmed.

The Polaroid showed a man clad only in boxer briefs. His hands were cuffed behind him, and the cuffs were wrapped around a wrought-iron fence post. There was a paper bag over his head with a smiley face drawn on it.

"Can we go?" Misty asked. "I didn't touch anything, and I want to get home. The dullness in her voice gave her a monotone almost as uncharacteristic as David's.

"Yes," Roger said.

Misty didn't look back but took off across the field towards the house and her waiting car. She was in the car, ignition on and heat blasting by the time Drew climbed in beside her.

"Ready?" she asked.

"More than," he replied. "Let's get out of here."

"Bill..." she started. "He—"

"He's staying here to take care of the goats. He'll be okay. But just to be on the safe side, you should call him when you get home."

"Why don't you?"

"Maybe next time," he said. A wistful smile flickered across his face, and Misty was overcome with the urge to hug him and tell him everything would be okay. It was neither the time, nor the place, though, and she couldn't make any such promise, so she put the car in gear and took off down the absurdly long driveway.

"If you're up, come to the farm." Misty squinted at the text message, rubbed her eyes, and read it again. It still didn't make sense, in part because it was from a number she didn't have in her contact list.

"Who is this?" she replied, then jumped in the shower. Last night when she'd gotten home, she'd taken a bath with a glass of wine, then gone straight to bed—at the very late hour of eight o'clock. She'd slept for a full twelve hours, but her rest had been plagued by nightmares of zombie goats, the mysterious woman wielding a knife, and a sky filled with winged creatures intent on destroying Oracle Bay.

The shower didn't help her grogginess, and neither did the two cups of French press coffee she made herself. A tired like this called for the big guns. She dressed down—worn blue jeans, a t-shirt proclaiming her affiliation with House Stark, and an old pair of hiking boots, pulled her unruly hair into a ponytail, perched her glasses on her nose, and headed out to brave the beast in his den.

Twenty minutes and what felt like twenty inches of rain later, Misty pushed open the door of Caffiend Dreams. She'd been the property manager for the last few years and the owner now for the last few days, but this was the first time she'd set foot in it for anything other than business since Drew and Bill had split.

Bill looked over the short line in front of the register and the beginnings of a grin crooked up the corners of his mouth. He took orders, engaged in small talk, and made coffees while she waited. She knew he wasn't deliberately slowing things down on purpose, but she was caffeine-deprived, exhausted, hungry, and a bit on the cranky side.

When she was finally at the front of the line, Bill asked, "Flat white?"

Misty was a little surprised and a lot touched that he remembered her regular order. "Not today. Can I get a Quad Shot Americano with a bit of room? Also, a ham and cheese croissant, please."

Bill rocked back on his heels. "That's a whole lotta caffeine, Misty."

"It's been a rough few days, and I'm not sleeping well." She hadn't meant to be so open, so vulnerable.

"I understand. It's yours. I'll get your croissant warming up and make you the coffee. But I need a doctor's note that your heart is in good enough condition to handle that much caffeine."

She grinned and held out her debit card. She hadn't remembered to put her gloves on that morning, and when he briefly brushed her hand when he took her card, the images started. Drew flickered in and out of everything, always at the center of who Bill was and what he chose. Interspersed with that were images of Joseph coated with the waxy sheen of fear and the mysterious woman who blinked between an obvious humanity and a creature made of electricity and light.

Cold sweat and goosebumps broke out over Misty's body, and she pulled her hand back, dropping her card in the process.

"Are you okay?" Bill asked, grabbing the card and swiping it. He handed it back, and she was careful not to come into contact with his skin again.

"Fine. Just..." She waved her hand around in an attempt to explain everything, and he nodded.

"Everything is difficult right now. I feel the same. Did you get my text?"

"Your text?"

"Yeah. I told you to come out to the farm."

"Oh. That text. It didn't come from the number I have for you, and you didn't respond to my reply."

Bill frowned, dug his phone out of his pocket, and checked the display. "I don't have a reply from you."

Misty pulled her phone out and showed him the texts. "This keeps happening."

"Maybe there's a dead zone at the farm," Bill said. "Although that wouldn't explain why it looks like it came from an unknown number."

Her breath caught in her throat for too long and she choked back a sob. She knew what he meant and knew how illogical her response was, but all she could think of when he'd said 'dead zone' is standing next to the man she probably loved while looking at a dead goat and imagining him in its place.

"Shi-oot. I'm sorry," Bill said.

The line behind her was ten deep now, and she could hear the beginning murmurs of discontent. She took his iPad, finger-signed her name, nodded in what she hoped was a reassuring fashion, and found the most out of the way seat she could find.

"Get a grip, Mystic," she muttered to herself, catching the notice of the nearest tourist downing a latte and staying out of the heavy rain that had been nearly incessant since the earthquake. She switched to her inside voice. *Everything will be okay. You are strong. You are worthy of affection. You do not need to rely on the approval of others.* Oops. Internal pep talk had become the therapy mantra she'd used in her late teens and early twenties to deal with her burgeoning powers and subsequent ostracization from certain elements of her family. *Too many issues, not enough subscriptions.*

She shook herself and turned her attention out the window. The western sky was gray and heavy with another oncoming storm—the fourth in as many days to batter the coast. The waves rolled in, dark and capped with white foam, pounding the shoreline and discouraging the few late-season tourists from approaching the shore.

Her phone buzzed. She tipped it up, expecting another encouraging text from one of the union members, and instead was greeted with an appointment reminder. In one hour, she was to meet with the event manager of the auditorium, as well as this year's chairs of entertainment and guest services to finalize the logistics for the Fall Bazaar.

Bill placed her croissant and coffee in front of her. "Once you get caffeinated and settled, you should head out to the farm."

"I don't know. I've spent too much time there the last couple days. It eats at me, you know?"

"I know, but Joseph's parents are there, and they'd like to see you."

Misty took a deep breath and drew back. She'd always adored

Ann and John, and she felt even closer to them now due to the vicarious connection through Joseph. "I'll go, but I have a Bazaar meeting first."

"I'll see you there. Any pastry requests?"

"Whatever you have leftover is fine with me. Later."

twelve

Misty balanced the grocery bag on one hip and tentatively knocked on the door with her free hand. The rip of paper distracted her from the door, and she looked down in time to see a huge tear snake along the outside edge of her bag. She grabbed it as it slid down her leg and awkwardly juggled the brown paper sack trying to rebalance the contents. The door opened as she lost control of it, and the contents spilled into the open doorway at John McEwen's feet.

"Misty!" he exclaimed, pulling her into his arms for an enthusiastic bear hug.

"Mr. McEwen! It's good to see you, although these aren't the circumstances I would've hoped for."

"That they're not," he confirmed, bending over to retrieve her spilled groceries. He placed the three bottles of wine back into her nearly useless bag, grabbed it carefully and held the open side against his body, then ushered her in. "Please call me John," he said. "We're all adults here. If you call Ann Mrs. McEwen, I can't promise I'll be able to protect you." He shook his head and widened his eyes.

"She's vicious as all get out when she thinks people are calling her old."

Misty was almost positive he was kidding. Almost. Mrs. McEwen —Ann, she reminded herself—had been the high school librarian and was known for her research assistance and uncanny ability to pick the perfect book for any individual student than her fierceness.

Butterflies took wing in her abdomen, and she plastered a smile on her face. She'd hoped to see them again when being introduced as their son's girlfriend, not because they were in town to take care of the farm left behind when Joseph went missing.

She stopped in the doorway of the kitchen abruptly enough that John ran into her. "Keep going, lass. You can't put off 'til later what you've come here to do now."

He was right. She breathed in deeply, filling her lungs, closed her eyes to remind herself that she was strong and capable, then let the air out with a whoosh, opened her eyes, and walked forward to meet Ann McEwen.

Ann was ensconced in the big recliner, blankets carefully tucked around her and pillows propping up her head. She looked paler and smaller than Misty remembered. It'd been ten years, but she hadn't expected this much change.

Some of what she'd been thinking must have shown on her face because Ann smiled and beckoned her closer. "It's not as bad as it looks," she said, and even her voice had lost breadth and power. "The surgery I had a couple of weeks ago hit me a bit harder than expected. I'm healing up quickly now, though, and should be ready to take a four-wheeler out to aid in the search tomorrow."

John walked into the room and handed a glass of wine to Misty and one to his wife. "You will not be out on any vehicle tomorrow, woman." He held up his glass. "To Joseph, wherever he is. And to Misty, the woman he loves. When he comes back to us, I am going to give him so much grief for missing this moment."

Ann and Misty held up their glasses, then took small sips.

"Tell me, now, dear," Ann said. "Where do you think my boy is? And what do you think happened?"

"All we know is what he told us when he and Bill came up, and then the bits and pieces he was able to add to the story since then."

"You know about Goatzilla's death?" Misty asked. "And the weird woman?"

"Yes," John confirmed. "Does anyone know who she is?"

"No. Only that she's old," Misty said, frustration creeping into her voice.

"How old?" John asked. "Do you mean old like us? Like our parents' generation? Or do you mean something else—old like Billie?"

Misty shook herself. It was still so weird thinking about the goat as something *other*, but there was no reason to doubt the story told by both Joseph and his father. "I don't know how old Billie is, but this woman is ancient."

Ann drummed her fingers against the bowl of her wine glass then looked at her husband. "The legends."

"Don't talk to me of legends, woman."

"Don't call me woman. You know I hate that. You only do it when you're trying to distract me or someone else. The legends may not be truth, but they started somewhere."

"It's a game of telephone. Any truth they once possessed is long since gone."

"Then why do you keep passing them on? If it's nothing but a children's story with no meaning, why does it get passed from parent to child? Your mother told you, as her mother told her. You passed it down to your child."

"Does the line run patri- or matrilineally?" Misty asked.

"Into every generation a seer is born," John intoned.

Misty barked out a laugh, then covered her mouth and tried to push it back in.

"It's okay to laugh," Ann said. "I always do when he makes odd Buffy references. But to answer your question, the gift passes to the first born, regardless of sex. Joseph was our eldest, and John the eldest of the prior generation. His mother, Sylvia, was the firstborn of her parents. Tracing the lineage gets difficult a few more generations back, but anecdotally—and the records kept by the family—the line goes back more than five hundred years. Billie—who has not always been called by that name, of course—is always present at the birth of the eldest."

"Always?" Misty asked, aghast. "But hospitals?"

"I had a home birth for Joseph, although the others were lucky enough to be born in a hospital. It took more than a little convincing on John's behalf, but whatever her abilities encompass, her presence eases the birthing process. The nurse midwife who consented to deliver my child was a little skeptical of having a goat present, but in the end, the promises of a little extra money and that Billie would stay back and out of the way were enough to persuade her. It was the easiest birth I had. John's mom says the same. When it's your turn—"

"Whoa. Let's not get ahead of ourselves here. I had a simple question, and it had nothing to do with my reproductive capabilities or desires."

Ann reared back in her chair for a moment and fixed her gaze unflinchingly on Misty, then laughed. "My apologies. I was moving too fast. The same magic that makes Billie always have twins equally ensures that the line won't die out. If you can't or aren't interested in having kids, the gift will jump into the eldest of the next eldest—in this case, my niece Siobhan."

Misty gusted out a sigh of relief. "I didn't mean..."

"I know. But now isn't the time. What we do need to discuss is the legend John is so eager to forget."

"I need more wine," he muttered.

"And then we'll talk," Ann said.

"Whatever you say, woman."

"He's not nearly as big an ass as he pretends to be," Ann said. "Most of it's for show."

"I can hear you," he roared back from the kitchen.

"That was my intent," she replied before turning back towards Misty. "We don't always bicker. He's stressed about Joseph and worried about me, and a good bicker makes him feel better, so I try to help as much as possible with that. Tell me now, dear. How are you? Are you holding up okay? Have you talked to your Aunt Sybil recently?"

"I'm okay. No, that's not true. I'm decidedly not okay. The last few weeks have been stressful, and the only bright spots were the few days when Joseph's and my stars aligned and we could spend time together without fighting or being interrupted. Things will get worse here before they get better, and I can't even care right now, because Joseph—" her voice broke and she choked back the sob that threatened to erupt.

"I know, sweetheart," Ann said. "I'm scared for him, too. But you have the advantage here. You can reach out into the future and find more information. I can only hope."

"My gift doesn't work that way," Misty said. "I only see the future of the one I'm touching. I can't direct my foresight any more than that."

"How well can you direct your visions of the person you're touching?" Ann asked. "Can you look into a specific part of my future, if I ask you to? Can you see who attends my funeral?"

"What? No! Why? Ann!"

"Calm yourself. I only picked that specific event because it seems most likely that if Joseph still lives and is found, he would attend my funeral. As he would attend Bill's wedding or Siobhan's high school graduation. So, if you touch me, as opposed to Bill or Siobhan, and concentrate on the guests at my funeral, you'd be able to see if he's there. And if he's there, we know we find him alive. It'd work, would it not?"

Misty considered the frail-looking woman in front of her. "It might," she allowed. "But if you outlive me, I might get inconclusive results."

"I'll not outlive you," she said, taking another sip of wine.

Blood drained from Misty's face. "What do you mean?" she whispered.

"Nothing more than I am older than you, and you come from a line of people who are generally blessed with extraordinarily long lives. I've known your Aunt Sybil since I was a little girl and she was the wizened church organist. She never made much of an effort to hide her true age, but there comes a point when you need to force people to accept you for your elderly self or skedaddle out of town and pretend to fade into nothing, instead of going on a cruise to celebrate her one hundred and twentieth birthday—and subsequently getting banned from the entire cruise line for shenanigans not befitting a woman of her age."

"I don't think I know this story," Misty said. Then waved her hand. "It's not important now, though. What is important is finding Joseph. Can you tell me the legend that may or may not be relevant?"

"I'd like to wait for Bill to arrive if you don't mind. In the meantime, could you try your gift on me?"

Misty steeled herself and put down her wine. She might want another sip or five before concentrating on the future funeral of the woman she'd begun to hope to call her mother-in-law, but wine clouded things, and she didn't want to take any chances that she'd miss something.

Joseph deserved better than that.

She pulled off her glove—the same one she'd had stolen then returned, she wore it to regain the confidence lost when that other woman had come into her town, messed with her people, and stolen her property—and reached out a hand.

Ann clasped her hand and squeezed, "I trust you. I always have."

Misty's lips turned up in a tremulous smile, then she closed her eyes and braced herself. She pulled as many funereal images to mind as she could, making sure to keep this woman in the center of it all. Ashes and urns, caskets and roses, the Irish wake and the Italian mass. Everyone in black, red roses being the only splotches of color at the graveside. And through it all deep, nearly unbearable sadness.

Pictures raced through her mind as she tried to look forward in time to this specific event. John's face blinked in and out more often than anyone else's, and it was reminiscent of how centered on Drew Bill's thoughts and future were. She raced faster and faster until the images slid by in a blur unless she focused on them, then skidded to a stop on a green hill overlooking the Pacific Ocean. Grey skies hung heavy and low with the threat of rain, and a thin film of salt spray coated her lips. She looked around, recognized Oracle Bay Cemetery, and settled in to observe.

There was no way to tell when she was or how much time had passed. All she could do was observe and not focus on how much time Ann had left. More than fifty people filled the rickety white folding chairs that were ubiquitous at every graveside service, and a dozen or so more stood at the back of the seated crowd. A priest— one she didn't recognize—stood alone next to the gaping hole. Misty kept her eyes away from the headstone, half of which was completely filled out while the other half was still blank—and instead scanned the crowd for familiar faces.

She saw Sandy and Vincent, Jezebel next to a person she didn't recognize, and Ceri next to someone she did. Morgana and Paska were nowhere to be seen, and neither were Drew, Bill, or Joseph. There were people she recognized from town, more than a few strangers, and no children. Someone squeezed her hand, and she leaned into the strength offered and accepted. There was no sound, not even the breeze whipping in from the ocean ruffling hair and dresses, and that made the tableau eerier.

People's heads turned, and Misty followed their gaze. The coffin, carried by six pallbearers, was entering. She squeezed the hand she was holding and tried to turn to look at the person who was there to offer comfort, but every time she turned her head, he was just out of eyesight. She gave up and turned back towards the solemn procession. The first two pallbearers were Joseph's siblings Thomas and

Isabella. Bill and Drew carried the side closest to her, and tears filled her eyes at the implication that Drew and Bill—long considered an honorary child of the McEwen's—were close again, close enough for Drew to have a place with the other children. She stood up on her tiptoes, trying to see the two on the other side, but couldn't see around them. She let go of her invisible friend's hand and ran out to the front to stand next to the priest.

She had a moment of worry that she'd be seen, the way whoever'd held her hand and seen her grief had noticed her, but no one gasped and pointed and stared. The two people she'd been unable to see were stacked—she could only see one of them. It was Patrick, Isabella's husband. Misty tried to move around to get the sixth person's face in her eyesight, but much like her mysterious hand holder, this figure stayed just out of recognizable eyesight.

She heaved a frustrated sigh.

"Annoying, isn't it?" someone said beside her. "Trying to see a future that isn't quite decided."

Misty jumped back and teetered on the edge of the coffin hole, arms windmilling in an attempt to keep from falling in.

"I wonder what happens if you die in one of your visions? Would you die only here and come to yourself gasping with the memory of taking your last breath? Or would whoever's palm you're reading get to feel the life leave you. Would the method of death leave marks on your body? Would blood appear? Bruises? Burns? Or would you expire quietly?"

"I don't know who you are," Misty gasped as her balance finally settled.

"Don't you?" A hand shot out and caught her in the chest. Misty waved her arms, but couldn't save herself this time. She fell backwards and landed flat on her back, knocking the wind out of her so painfully she gasped wondering if she'd ever get a full breath of air again. Everything hurt—pain was radiating throughout her whole body is pulsing waves, and the dim light of the sun was dotted with black swirls and spirals.

A presence crouched beside her, and a cold hand briefly caressed her face. "Won't it be interesting to see if the bruises blooming on your body now will follow you back? Don't go too far into the future, little sister. You haven't the reach nor the skill, especially compared to me."

"It's you," Misty managed to spit out. "Who are you? Why do you sound so different?"

"I am the goddess of lightning and weather, the mother of haruspicy. I am She Who Remembers, and you thought you could hide from me? I am Menrva, and I will have my answers and my revenge."

"You used that line already," a dry voice said from the other side of her body.

"Joseph?"

"I don't know what you're doing here, or what I'm doing here, but you need to go. Now."

"I need to know where..."

"Misty, go!" A new voice yelled. "We can talk about this later."

She looked up at the woman who'd interrupted. It looked like... her Aunt Sibyl. Surprise broke her hold as this future dissolved and she flew backwards through time, the elastic of the slingshot stretched too far to keep going.

She felt her consciousness ricochet back into her body and pain erupted through her head.

"Misty?" Ann asked. "John, get in here! There's something wrong with Misty!"

Everything went black.

MISTY OPENED HER EYES TO TWO CONCERNED FACES STARING DOWN AT HER. "Do you need an ambulance?" John asked.

"No," she replied, then took a mental inventory of her body. "No. How long was I out?"

"Less than five minutes," Ann said, tapping her phone screen and turning it for Misty to see. The face read 4:27. "If we'd gotten to five, we were going to call an ambulance."

"I'm okay." She struggled to a sitting position, wincing as her body made known the results of the traumas she'd experienced. "Oh, no..." Her head dropped into her hands.

"What's wrong?" John asked, an edge of panic in his voice.

"She's fine, John. She just needs a glass of water and a whiskey. I'm a medical professional, and I've got this."

"You're a retired school librarian," he retorted, but he stood up and headed to the kitchen anyway.

"I read a lot. It's almost the same."

"What did you see? Did you find my funeral?"

"I did, but it didn't tell me what we want to know. The future's too uncertain now—there was a figure there, one I couldn't see—because Joseph's fate hasn't been decided yet. I'm sorry I didn't get more..."

"That's enough," she interrupted. "If it hasn't been decided yet, then we know he's not dead. There's room. There's hope."

"I don't know—"

"Let me have this."

Misty bowed her head in acquiescence.

"Now, give me the dirt. Who else was there?"

A grin cracked across Misty's face. "I'm not sure I should..."

Ann pouted. "At least tell me if Doris was there."

Misty searched her memory. "I wasn't paying attention to most of the attendees, so I'm not one hundred percent positive, but I don't think so."

Ann pumped her fist. "Yes! I outlived that horrible old biddy."

"You mean Ms. Morgan, right? The English teacher? I didn't know she was horrible."

"Ugh. The worst. She used to switch people's lunches around in the teacher's lounge fridge and request ridiculous book lists as supplemental reading that were often either unavailable or nonexistent. Just to mess with me."

Misty stifled her smile.

"I see you smirking over there. It wouldn't be so funny if your sandwich was eaten every day and you were subjected to student complaints about not being able to check out "Lady Chatterley's Brother," the little-known sequel that no one's talking about."

"My senior year, it was "The Old Man and the Seal." Most of us knew it was a fake, but there were a couple..."

Ann sighed gustily. "Yes, I remember. She was a menace to society, and if she'd outlived me, she would've been there to gloat."

John reappeared with the whiskey and the water and helped Ann back into her chair, fussing about her plumping up pillows until the doorbell saved her from his mother-henning.

"That'll be Bill," Ann announced. "Before the men come back, tell me, is there anything else? Anyone else?"

Misty weighed all the possible answers in her mind before shrugging. "Nothing that seems especially relevant to the question at hand."

Ann narrowed her eyes. "I see what you're doing there, but if you promise it's nothing about my boy..."

"Pinky swear," Misty replied, then took a sip of her whiskey.

"Little early in the day to be hitting the hard stuff, isn't it?" Bill asked.

"She fainted," John announced before Misty could make up an excuse.

"Using her mystical powers," Ann added.

Misty avoided Bill's gaze and took another sip of whiskey.

"I don't want to know," Bill declared. He stalked into the kitchen and came back with a bottle of coke.

"You accepted our story," John said. "What's so different about this? When it comes down to it, Misty's a lot more believable than a psychic goat who reveals the future to the eldest in each generation."

"A psychic *immortal* goat," Ann clarified.

Bill was edging further and further towards the hall and escape. "It's because of Drew. He's holding himself back from believing because if he believes me, he has to believe Drew, and if he believes him, he'll have to apologize."

The mild panic in Bill's gaze was replaced by sheer, unadulterated anger. "How dare you," he started.

Ann held up a hand. "William Shakespeare Walters, you sit yourself down right now," Ann said. "If you can't behave, you won't get any pie."

To Misty's eternal shock, he did as he was told. "Your middle name is Shakespeare?" she asked. It was the only thing she could think of to say.

"My parents had grand aspirations for me," he said. Bitterness tinged his voice, and she winced. She knew his relationship with his family was nearly non-existent and kicked herself for asking a question that would remind him of them.

"Bill, I'm sorry," she started.

He shook himself. "It's fine. Everything's fine. You're all right. I'm being a jerk to Misty because I need an excuse not to tell Drew I was wrong."

"Why don't you want to, though?" Misty asked. "You could fix everything."

Bill shook his head and took a swig of Coke.

"If he apologizes and says he's wrong but Drew still walks away, that's worse than not trying to change things at all. At least this level of misery is known." Ann didn't look at Misty as she explained; her attention was entirely on the man she regarded as a third son. "You can't live your life alone because you're too stubborn to admit you were wrong. That doesn't make you strong, it makes you foolish."

"Thanks, Mom," he replied in a tone caustic enough to peel paint from the walls.

"I wouldn't be a very good mom if I didn't lay out the tough love."

Misty set down the whiskey—hard liquor, unless mixed in a Long Island Ice Tea, wasn't usually her thing. She didn't want to interrupt, but she needed to get this show on the road. "Is it time for the legend now?"

"I think it's time for pie!" John announced. "It will be substandard because I made it, but the crust was all Ann, so it should at least be edible."

"Absolutely not. No pie until you tell your story. The kids will have places to go and things to do, and I'm not going to delay Misty any longer than necessary. Tell the darn story, John, or I'll tell it for you. You know how much you hate it when I tell your stories and add my special touches."

He growled but acquiesced.

"Legend has it that my great- great- many times great-grandmother was widowed with five children under the age of six, and in her despair, she left her small village of Castiglioncello, went into the Livorno Hills, and sacrificed the twin kids that had just been born to her only aged doe. She prayed to the gods—all of them, whether she knew their names or not—to send her a way to preserve her family.

"When she returned to her farmstead, she found a new doe waiting, one that was ready to kid. The doe gave birth to twins, a replacement for the ones she'd sacrificed, and from there, her fortunes started looking up. The new doe gave the sweetest milk, and my ancestor, whose name is lost to the annals of time, was one of the first in Tuscany to make goat cheese.

"The sale of the cheese and the fact that the new doe seemed ageless and unusually fecund greatly improved the fortunes of my forebears. The doe was pushy, and often sticking her literal nose in where it didn't belong. When the first-born of my many times great-grandmother reached twenty, he spent the night in the barn, waiting for her to kid, and spent the night dreaming instead. Those dreams —which come around the age of twenty for every firstborn, teach the dreamer how to communicate with Billie and unlocks her divination powers for the next generation. It's helped immensely for farming purposes and other agricultural planning."

"And the stock market," Bill added.

"It doesn't work that well for the stock market," Ann said. "Everyone tries, and everyone does moderately well, but there seems to be a kind of stopgap that prevents the McEwen's from getting too big for their britches."

"Didn't keep me from feeling confident enough to court the prettiest girl I'd ever met when Billie picked her picture out of the yearbook."

"Hush, you," Ann said, blushing prettily.

"That's a very interesting story," Misty said. "But what does it have to do with finding Joseph?"

John and Ann exchanged looks. "There's a bit more to the story that John let on."

"It's silly," he said. "The whole story is a bit silly, but this is the nail in the coffin."

Misty winced at the imagery and ran her hand through her hair, scattering remnants of grave dirt on the couch.

"Fine," he said when no one spoke up to let him off the hook. "The legend specifies that the prayer was answered by a goddess, and she imbued the goat with her essence to make her immortal."

"Which goddess?" Misty asked, setting down the water she'd been drinking and leaning forward. "Was it Menrva?"

"No, but funny you should ask. What brought that name up?"

"Which goddess?" Misty pressed.

"Uni, an Etruscan goddess on whom Juno was modeled. The supreme goddess of the Etruscans—and the mother of Menrva."

"Get out of town!"

"Who's Menrva, besides what we just learned, I mean," Bill asked.

"She's the woman—the mysterious creepiosa who's been wandering around, getting psychic readings, calling Joseph a million times, and stealing my gloves. I also think she's the woman who took the goats and Joseph."

A mild cacophony followed the pronouncement, and Misty was unable to understand any of the questions the other three were throwing at her. She let them go on, though, and pulled out her phone. She typed Menrva into a search engine and was disappointed by the lack of results. Even on the few pages that did come up, there wasn't a ton of information. Her parents were Uni and Tinia, and together they made up the triad of major gods in the Etruscan religion. She was considered a forerunner of Minerva and was the goddess of war, art, wisdom, and medicine, as well as having lightning powers. She recounted her meager findings for the others, and no one had any insight.

That was about it, no fun stories, no information about consorts. She was out of her depth. The Oracle Bay origin story might contain gods, and Drew claimed to have been seduced by a demigod, a story she whole-heartedly pretended to believe, but had never really given the credence it was due—she thought it more likely Drew was seduced by an exceptionally pretty one-night-stand—but she'd never thought they'd be back to cause problems.

She typed out a quick text, finished her water, and stood up. "I need to do a little research and investigation," she said.

"Of course," Ann said. "We're anxious for whatever information you can give us. Let me know if there's anything I can do."

Misty gave John a one-armed squeeze and dropped a kiss on Ann's cheek. "See you later."

· · ★ ★ ★ ★ ★ ★ ★ · · ·

"Why are we here?" Jezebel asked. "Don't get me wrong, I like the Sleeping Inn, but I'd rather be at The Pour House keeping an eye on Andy."

"I'll try not to be offended that you aren't interested in keeping eyes on me," Russell said, placing three coasters in front of the women sitting at the bar. It was late afternoon on a weekday, and there weren't a lot of patrons.

"Russell, you know everyone's always got eyes for you," Jezebel said, batting her lashes and pursing her lips at him.

He laughed. "You can take that back down a couple of notches. I'm just teasing you. What can I get you, ladies?"

"Long—"

"I wasn't even going to ask you, Misty," Russell said. "You have a thirst about you. Jezebel? Ceri?"

"Just a mineral water, please," Ceri said.

"I'll have a margarita on the rocks, no salt," Jezebel said, then turned to Ceri. "Still having the headaches?"

"A bit. I saw too much, went back too far. I keep having flash-backs, like a bad acid trip that haunts you forever."

"You've been on acid trips?" Jezebel asked. "You seem so...wholesome."

"Oh, no. Not actually. I've mostly read about them. I'm only guessing that this is what a bad acid trip flashback is like. That's not why we're here, though. We can talk about my wholesomeness any time. What's going on, Misty?"

She drew a deep breath and smiled gratefully at Russell as he set her drink down in front of her. She took a swallow, then turned towards her friends. "Joseph's mom asked me to See her funeral, to see if Joseph was there. Her reasoning is that if he was, he's obviously still alive. It made sense, so I tried it."

"Oh, honey. Are you okay?" Jezebel asked.

"Mostly. It was weird focusing so specifically on an event and person, but I got there. No one could see me, but someone was holding my hand?"

"Probably whoever future you brings to the funeral," Ceri said. "You would've used your own body as an anchor point if it was there. It's easier that way, and instinctive if you don't know what you're doing. It takes time and practice to stop doing that, and a little bit of training. I can help you next time you decide to dive deep like that."

"What else?" Jezebel prodded, taking a slow drink of her margarita.

"That woman showed up, the one who's been around causing all sorts of trouble. She pushed me into Ann's open grave, told me her name was Menrva, and then Joseph and Sybil both told me to run away."

Jezebel leaned back, taking her drink with her. "That is some serious weirdness."

"Your Aunt Sybil?" Ceri asked. "What was she doing there? Is she an oracle, too?"

"Yeah. She left town when I came back from college, sold her house and business to me, wished me luck, and gallivanted off into the sunset."

"Did Menrva talk to you, too? Tell you what she wanted?" Jezebel asked. "Or just Joseph and your Aunt?"

"She said she was the goddess of lightning and the mother of haruspicy and she's out for revenge. I know I'm missing something, but it was all a bit fast and more than a bit weird."

"She's a storm bringer, then," Jezebel said.

"Haruspicy fits, too," Ceri said. "If she's reading the future in the entrails of the goats, that might be helping her hone in on whoever she needs to seek revenge on."

"That's the real question," Misty said. "I don't know if she's really a goddess and what kind of revenge she's seeking. She's focused on Joseph and his goats, but the family doesn't seem the type to aggravate a goddess..."

Russell held up the bar phone. "Morgana is on the phone and requests the three of you finish your drinks and meet her at The Pour House. She told me to tell you that 'something interesting has happened.'" Russell did an almost perfect imitation of Morgana's formal diction and nearly over-bearing primness that had to be inauthentic, and Misty didn't bother to smother her laughter.

"I can hear you," Morgana yelled through the phone Russell was still holding.

"Tell her we'll be there soon," Misty said, downing her Long Island. "It feels like it's gonna be a long, long night."

thirteen

Ceri led the trio into The Pour House, but before they could get very far, the new bartender who'd started right before Halloween, popped up in front of them. "Andy wants you in the private room. Can I bring you a drink?"

Jezebel gave him a once over and then a second glance. She opened her mouth, "I'll take a—"

"I'm celibate," he said.

"—Pilsner. And don't flatter yourself."

Misty carefully didn't look at either of her friends; she wasn't sure she could keep a straight face. "Same for me."

"Soda water, if you have it," Ceri said.

"I'll be right behind you with the drinks unless you need me to show you to the private room."

"I think we can manage," Misty said. The rest of the psychics, along with Andy, were already seated.

"Where's Russell?" Morgana demanded.

"Russell?" Misty repeated, unsure if she'd heard right.

"He should be here. His input could be valuable."

"Did you ask him to come?"

"No, of course not. I told him his presence was required."

"Even if he could take off work at the drop of a hat, telling him what to do is the exact best way to ensure he won't do it," Jezebel said. "He's not a part of this group and hasn't resigned himself to following your orders."

"Yet," Morgana muttered. "Yet."

Impatience washed over Misty, and the pain of it caused her to hunch in on herself. "I need to be looking for Joseph."

"Of course. And you're free to do so as soon as we finish here. There are a few items we need to take care of, first."

Zeke walked into the room and handed out drinks.

"You said you had news, Andras. News you couldn't share unless we were all here, so here we are."

"Something's happened. I have more information on the coming storm."

"Are you going to tell us who—and what—you are?" Sandy asked. She was running her finger around the rim of her soda glass and darting glances at the door.

"You know who I am, and what I am is irrelevant. I am Andras, Oracle Bay's not quite mortal brewmaster."

"Stop." Ceri held up her hand. "It's not irrelevant. It's very relevant, in fact. I said I'd keep your secrets until it became imprudent to do so. That time is quickly approaching. Choose your words carefully, Andras. We aren't your only allies, but we're the only ones who are here right now. There are other things, more immediate things, happening that require the attention of at least some of us, but if you can't speak straight, you'll lose us all. I've no patience for prevarication and procrastination. Especially not when it puts other lives at risk."

She leaned back and grabbed Misty's hand, giving it a gentle squeeze.

Andy tipped back in his chair balancing on the back legs with his feet hooked over the rungs. Misty stared, head tilted to one side, trying to suss out how he was so perfectly steady even though his body wasn't still on the chair. He was fidgeting and shifting and once he opened his mouth to talk, gesticulating.

"Beings are starting to trickle into town. I have no control over them, and they're not all here because of the coming storm, but they're being drawn here. Oracle Bay has long been a nexus of power, but one that is easy to ignore if you want. Most of you were drawn here. Only Misty has never left."

She wanted to protest, to say she'd left for college, but he was right.

Andy continued, "I'm not sure who will come and what they will do. There will be a battle, and sides will be chosen, lines drawn in the sand."

"What's the battle over?" Drew asked.

"Pardon?"

"Why is there going to be a fight? We know that you set the storm in motion when you kicked those guys out at Halloween, but a huge supernatural battle drawing powerful participants and spectators seems a little over the top to get revenge for being eighty-sixed from a small brewpub in a small town on the edge of the world."

"Supremacy," Andy replied. "It's as simple as that."

"I don't understand," Sandy said. Her attention was now fully on Andy, and she no longer had one metaphorical foot out the door.

"Whoever wins the battle is on top."

"You're saying nothing at all and doing so in such a condescending manner that you deserve a smack upside the head from your mam, if you even had one," Paska said. "It's a load of—"

"Poppycock," Morgana interjected primly. "He's right, though, Andy. If you want our help, tell us all the truth; now is not the time to tell it slant."

"Dickinson."

Morgana inclined her head to him. "More or less."

"Very well. The battle will be over the world. There are three factions. The first are what you would call the hosts of heaven. Angels, cherubim, seraphim, and the line. The second represents what most consider the hosts of hell. Demons, fallen angels, imps, et cetera. The third are the gray wings. Those believe that earth should be left as it is—to the humans and non-divine supernaturals that inhabit it and that any of the other two factions who wish to renounce their respective sides can also live in peace."

"To which group do you belong?" Misty asked. She was trying very hard not to let this revelation cause a physical reaction. She was willing to have an abstract belief in gods, but this sounded a little more apocalyptic than she was comfortable with.

He leaned forward, and the chair landed with a solid thump. "There've been times in the past that I've been allied with the dark and the light."

"And now?" Jezebel asked. "Your current alliance seems more important than your past."

"I guess I'm a gray wing."

"And what can you offer us in return for our assistance in the coming storm?"

"I will fight on your side!" The surprise in Andy's voice hinted that he'd never previously considered there'd be anything else.

"Actually," Drew said, "We will be fighting on your side. You brought the fight here. Your actions revealed your location and amplified the signal, drawing tourists in addition to combatants. We have agreed to help, but what can you do to help us?"

Andy swung his head back and forth, taking in the room full of psychics staring at him expectantly. "What do you want?" he asked slowly, tipping his chair backwards and balancing on the back legs again.

"Misty?" Drew nodded at her.

"I need help finding and banishing the goddess Menrva."

For the second time, Andy's chair crashed down, and this time accompanied by the unmistakable sound of splintering wood.

"Why?"

"She's in town, and she has something of mine. I want it back, and I want her gone."

"Does she know I'm here?" Andy's normally dusky complexion paled, and now it was his eyes darting to the door.

"I think so. I saw her here the night of the earthquake."

Andy scrubbed his hand through his hair. "This has gone further than I expected. I can help you find her, but I'm not sure I can help you get rid of her. That may lie beyond my skills."

"That's a start," Misty said.

Before she could go any further, they were interrupted by a knock on the door. Andy frowned. "Enter."

Bill walked in, glanced around the table, carefully avoiding Drew, then focused on Misty. "We need to go to the police station. They're finally starting an official investigation, and you and I are to be questioned first. Do you want a ride?"

"Yes, thank you."

She gathered her things and looked around.

"We'll work with Andy to get some answers," Ceri promised. "Take care of yourself."

"The bazaar—"

"Bah! I can manage that as well," Morgana said. "And isn't Sandy technically in charge this year? Share your calendar and notes with us, and we will make sure everything is fine."

Misty almost tripped as the surprise of Morgana volunteering to have anything to do with the bazaar overtook her. "Thank you."

"Don't thank me. It's time for me to take a turn. I'm sure we won't mess it up too much."

With those less than promising words, Misty allowed herself to be escorted out the door for her date with the cops.

Misty stopped by her house after leaving the police station and changed. The day had already been too long, but according to the six text messages she received during what had passed for an interrogation, her presence was required back at the Pour House. "We have nachos," Ceri's last message promised—a guarantee that spurred her along a little faster.

The entire crew minus Andy but plus Vincent was in the back room with the promised nachos when Misty arrived. The rain had started falling a little more seriously on the walk to The Pour House from her place, and water was dripping uncomfortably down the back of her neck and trailing along her spine. She shook her head slightly to dislodge the stubborn rain drops.

There were five more plates than people at the table, and when she grabbed the chair Drew was shaking suggestively at her, she looked around to do a headcount. "Who else is coming? Do we even know other people?"

"Bill will be back soon," Ceri said. "And Russell, as opposed as he was to coming with us earlier, will be here as soon as his shift ends."

"And the other two?"

"Those are for us," Ann said.

John helped Ann get seated next to Misty, then sat next to her and filled a couple small plates with nachos. "Your young friend Ceridwen invited us out for dinner since neither you nor Bill were going to make it back. Fortunately, we have enough pie for everyone. That lovely bartender Brandy took them off our hands and said she'd bring them in after dinner. We came because the lot of you are the closest thing Joseph has to friends anymore. I know the situation. He's kept everyone but Bill too far away for fear of revealing his secret, and that's his loss. When he comes back, we're not going to let him return to his old habits. He will have friends, and he will like it." John thumped his fist down on the table, rattling the chips and causing a mild tsunami in some of the fuller glasses. "Sorry. I may have gotten a bit carried away."

"You're fine, dear," Ann said, patting his hand. "We figured—at least Ceridwen figured—that the information we have about Joseph and Billie and the legends would help with what you can do. Your jobs are no secret to me. I don't know what each of you does specifically, but I lived in Oracle Bay for a long time. Sybil—which is definitely not her real name, the pretentious hag—let me in on a few secrets, back when it was just her, Morgana, and Paska in town, so I knew what to watch out for. I've always been a believer, and I used to pretend that I had the power to see the future, too, but alas! I was destined to marry into oracular greatness rather than develop it myself."

Andy came back in with two more chairs and place settings, followed by Zeke and Brandy with trays of drinks and Bill and Aunt Sybil, looking not a day over one hundred and fifty years old. Misty's jaw dropped.

"Close your mouth, Mystic. You'll catch flies."

"This is too many people in this room," Andy muttered.

"Stop your belly-achin'. No fire would dare go against this much power." Sybil sat down, grabbed a stein almost as big as she was, and drained her drink. She let out a loud and resonant belch, took a second beer—this one in a slightly more manageable sized glass— and glared at Zeke until the protest he was about to offer died on his lips. "I ordered two when I came in. They're both mine. Travel is thirsty work, especially when you're this old."

"How old are you?" Ceri asked in fascination. "I thought Oracle Bay acted as a preservative."

"If you stay, practice your craft, drink the waters, and breathe the salt air, it holds your aging in stasis, as long as you have the gift. There are other places in the world that offer the same kind of fountain of youth gift, but none so powerful as Oracle Bay—at least none that I've visited."

Misty noted that Sybil didn't answer Ceri's question. "Aunt Sybil, how old are you really?"

Sybil smirked at Misty. "Old enough to know you don't ask a lady her age."

"I've known you since you were a little girl, and the one thing you've never been is a lady," Paska said.

"You stop it right now, Paska Cooper," Sybil giggled.

Misty still hadn't managed to close her mouth, so she grabbed the nearest beer and took a good, long swallow.

Andy grabbed a pint for himself, and slouched in the seat closest to the door, regarding everyone under half-closed lids. The door opened one last time, and Russell walked in. He looked around the room, nodding slightly as he inventoried each face, but was held up when he got to Bill. "Bill? You, too, man? Or are you just here in the capacity Vincent's here?"

If looks could kill, the daggers Bill shot at Russell would've hit a deadly target. "I'm here in the capacity of Joseph's friend. No other reason."

"Sure. Whatever you say." He moved on to Sybil, and when their gazes met, Russell slow-collapsed onto the nearest chair. "Aunt Sybil? You disappeared three years ago...have you been here?"

Sybil shot a glance at Misty who was valiantly trying not to choke on her beer. Drew was patting her back harder than necessary, and every side conversation in the room stopped. "I've not been here. I would've stopped in to say hi if we'd been in the same neighborhood. You make the best AMF in this hemisphere, and when you get as old as me, you develop a powerful thirst."

"What's an AMF?" Misty asked.

"It's short for Adios, mother—" Sybil said.

"It's like a Long Island Ice tea but with curaçao instead of cola. It's not for the faint of heart," Russell said.

Misty took a deep breath and tried to quell the anxiety that hadn't plagued her in years. She compartmentalized everything so she could focus on her missing boyfriend and the rogue goddess who'd taken him. It settled enough for her to pay attention to Morgana.

"Will anyone but Bill, Misty, John and Ann need to speak on the disappearance of Joseph McEwen and his goats?"

"I will go at the end," Sybil said. "I saw a few things Misty wouldn't have been able to catch when we met at the cemetery."

There was no way Misty was going to get through the rest of the day without the constant shocks causing a full-blown panic attack. She dug in her purse, found the little-used prescription bottle, and popped a Xanax while John and Ann took turns relaying the family legend, complete with Uni and the magical immortal goat. Bill told his story next, and by the time it was her turn, Misty was even-keeled enough to relay her part without hyperventilating. She told her version of looking into Ann's future, not leaving anything out in this telling, and then finished up with the events at the police station and weirdness that was the local fuzz.

"It's your turn, Sybil. What more do you have to offer that the rest of us haven't seen?"

"You don't have to get your knickers in a twist. The only reason I saw more than you was due to my connection to Misty and to the town in general. Our family was one of the first white families here. We were here long before the rest of the colonizers came—although we were no better than those who came after us. We opened the door enough that others were able to get through. The wrongs committed by my family could fill a book, but won't help us find Misty's young man any faster, though." She sighed heavily and seemed to age another five years with the exhale. "I was in the cemetery, paying my respects to the family I'd neglected since leaving town ten years ago when I felt the pull of family magic near the McEwen section. I hobbled over in time for a funeral to appear before my eyes. I took a vacant seat and watched the tableau unfold. The woman who calls herself Menrva isn't just blowing smoke. She's the most powerful being I've encountered in a good long while." Sybil's hard stare weighted down Paska, Morgana, and Andy in turn. "Some of you know the significance of that."

A blanket of silence weighted down the room.

Misty shattered it. "Has anyone besides me tried looking?"

"I can't catch hold of him," Ceri said. "He's there and hasn't passed beyond death's veil, but there's nothing to grab hold of."

"My experience is similar," Drew said. "It's like he's made of smoke."

"I've tried every layout and question iteration I can think of, but I can't get any answers. The cards just aren't speaking to me. Maybe if I read your cards instead of trying to read his in absentia..."

Morgana shrugged. "I can try something similar if you and Bill want to come over for tea, but my powers work better directly rather than indirectly."

"I'm in the same boat," Jezebel admitted. "I looked up his chart earlier, and with the help of Ann could get more detail, but I never do as well when the person whose chart I'm reading isn't the one who requested the reading."

Misty growled.

"Don't get frustrated, dear. We'll figure something out," Sybil said. "There's one person yet who hasn't answered."

Paska shrugged. "I haven't tried, but I will if you want me to. Runes are but a poor substitute in divination, and it's unlikely I'll get any better result than the rest of you."

"I have bones," Misty blurted. "Or I can get some, at least. Goat bones have to be almost as good as human bones."

"Bones, you say?" Paska perked up.

"The police didn't take Goatzilla's remains as evidence, so Joseph buried him on the farm. Goatzilla was likely sacrificed by the same person who has Joseph now. Maybe those bones could lead you to her."

Paska stroked his chin. "That could work. I'll need to find a power boost, though, because animal bones don't work as well for me as...other types, and I don't want to be looking for some powerful goddess and get caught in her web without the strength to extricate myself. I was a fly once, and I don't intend to ever play that role again."

"I can boost you," Andy said. "It'll further pinpoint my location, but it's only a matter of time before that happens anyway, now that I've been spotted."

"I'll be ready as soon as we have the bones." Paska looked at

Misty, and she suddenly realized she'd volunteered herself for a little Pet Cemetery robbery.

"I'll help you," Drew and Bill said at the same time.

She looked back and forth between them. "Thanks. Should we meet at the farm at eight? The sun will be up, so we at least won't have to do any in-the-dark grave robbery."

"I'll be there with shovels," Bill said.

"Are there any particular bones you'd prefer?" Misty asked, cringing a bit.

"As many as you can get. Preferably cleaned."

She blanched.

"I'll take care of that part," John said. "Your job is to show us where to dig."

fourteen

Misty led Bill, John, and Drew to the rock cairn where Goatzilla was buried. She helped move the rocks and then stepped back with John to watch Bill and Drew dig, a feat they managed without saying a word to each other or even making eye contact. Somehow, they managed to completely ignore the existence of the other man while never getting in the way of the other's shovel.

Once they'd cleared a layer of loose dirt, the digging slowed. Misty gagged as the smell of putrefying flesh hit her, and she had to take a few steps back.

"That is foul," Drew muttered.

"Grave robbery is not as glamorous as it sounds," Bill replied.

"It's because we don't have flashlights, lighters, and a box of salt. Sam and Dean would be very disappointed in us."

"We should've come at midnight. It's much too bright to do a proper grave robbing."

Drew and Bill exchanged grins, and then the smiles fell off their faces at the same time, and their attention returned to unearthing the rotting corpse of Goatzilla.

"This seems really wrong," Misty said to John.

"It does, but if Goatzilla had been able to sign a living will, I'm sure he'd have stipulated that his body could be used in death to help save the lives of the people he loved, as well as his mother and brothers."

"I'll try to hold on to that. Thank you."

"We'll find him, and he will be okay," John said. Then, quietly in a tone that seemed to be directed to himself and not her, he repeated, "He will be okay."

Misty reached out and slid her hand into John's. They watched Drew and Bill finish digging up Goatzilla then began the arduous and stinky task of hauling the remains to an out-building that had once housed the cheese making facilities but was no longer in use. It still had a long table in the middle and an old wood-burning stove that was burning merrily. John put on an apron and gloves and after directing Bill and Drew to lift a huge pot of water to the top of the stove, dismissed everyone.

"None of you need to stay for this part. I'll get the bones clean and let you know when they're ready for the next step."

Paska appeared in the open doorway, also in an apron and gloves. "I can help. This won't be my first time, and this way I can keep an eye on the bones. It's important that they don't get too soft, or I won't get the information I need from them."

John handed Paska a second knife, and they bowed their heads over the table. Misty made a hasty retreat, followed closely by Bill and Drew. "Do you guys want to come in to clean up and have a glass of water?" Misty asked, gesturing at the house.

"That'd be nice," Bill said.

Drew shook his head. "I have a client meeting in about an hour. I'll come back when it's over, though, so I can be here when Paska is ready to do his thing. I've never seen him use bones before, and I'm curious. The others will come, too. Text me when it's time."

"Okay. See you later."

Bill watched Drew drive away with an inscrutable expression.

"Do you want to talk about it?" Misty asked.

"No." He walked into the house without a backwards glance and Misty kicked herself for even trying.

ABOUT AN HOUR BEFORE SUNSET, THE PSYCHICS, JOHN, ANN, BILL, ANDY, and Sybil—who'd shown up without anyone inviting her—stood in a rough half-circle around Paska in an unused pasture behind the barns. A goatskin was spread on the ground in front of him, and the bones were in a basket by his side. He cleared the ground at the hind end of the goatskin, made a ring of rocks, and built a small fire, feeding it larger and larger sticks until it burned hot and strong.

"These bones are a bit bigger than those I usually work with," Paska said. "I am going to start by asking a question then drawing three bones, much like Sandy would with her cards. Then I will burn the scapula for more answers. If you have any questions, please ask them now. I'll need complete silence for the ritual."

"What do you need me to do?" Andy asked.

"Stand beside me and channel your power into me. Do you know how to do that?"

"I do. Do you know how to receive?"

"This isn't my first time. Concentrate on keeping us from being noticed, if you can do that as well as channel."

"I'll do my best."

"That's all I ask. Anyone else have any questions?"

No one else said anything, so Paska set down the bleached skull at the head of the skin, then closed his eyes and reached into the basket. He tossed the bones down, then squatted in front of them and stared. Just when Misty began to believe he'd stay there all afternoon, he rose from his crouch, a troubled look on his face. He scattered the remaining bones then knelt beside them.

Andy stood behind him, and Misty noticed that sweat was beginning to break out along his brow line. She wanted to offer him a handkerchief but didn't want to break his concentration.

Paska stood up and walked around the bones in a slow circle, not taking his eyes off the patterns made. After completing three circles, he reached down and picked up a scapula that was covered in markings that'd been carved out and filled in with red marker. Paska set the scapula in the fire and watched the flames lick the bone. The sun was dropping below the horizon before Paska reached in and pulled the bone out.

Misty gasped, hand over her mouth, until she saw that he was wearing a glove. He set the bone down on what looked like an oven rack, pulled off the glove, and finally acknowledged his audience.

"You can stop, Andy," he said. His voice was rough and scratchy like he'd developed a two pack a day habit during the last hour. "Thank you. Your power is...interesting."

Andy collapsed onto the ground, breathing heavily. Ceri handed him and Paska bottles of water. They drained them simultaneously. When the bottles were empty, Morgana passed over a flask. They each took a long pull of whiskey, then Paska handed the flask back to Morgana.

"Joseph is hidden from divination. This is something we all suspected based on our individual efforts. The goats, too, are hidden. That was not something I expected. It didn't occur to me that the witch—or whatever she is—would think to shield the animals as well as the human. That leads me to believe that she knows more of their true nature than she should."

"So, we got nowhere?" Misty asked, shoulders slumping in defeat. She hadn't realized how much weight she was putting on Paska's abilities.

"I wouldn't say that. She didn't hide herself. I don't know if it was due to arrogance, the belief we wouldn't try to find her through divination even though she'd used at least two of our own oracles to see into the future herself, or if she couldn't anticipate the connection she had to this goat by virtue of his own parentage, but I saw her.

"I couldn't see Joseph or the goats, but that means nothing, especially considering how well-cloaked they are. But I saw her. She isn't far. I didn't recognize the precise location, but it smelled of mist and salt air, and the landscape was similar to this one. There were rolling hills in the background, and I could see the lighthouse."

"Was it the Oracle Bay lighthouse? Or Cape Disappointment?" Jezebel asked.

"Oracle Bay. She was looking at the lighthouse, but I couldn't see the ocean. There was a small building behind her, one that looked abandoned to the ravages of time."

"We just need to figure out a place inland enough to be out of sight of the water, but with a view of the lighthouse, and with an abandoned shack?" Jezebel asked. "No problem."

"It shouldn't be too bad," Drew said. "Once I'm home, I'll get on the computer and figure out likely starting places. There will only be so many places the proper distance away to meet those criteria. Once we add in the topography, we'll be able to see what matches, and we can hand over our guesses to the cops, so they can go in prepared.

Bill and Misty shared an involuntary glance. "We might want to have a little more than a general idea before going to the cops," Bill said. "They aren't quite right."

"Bill's right. There's something distinctly odd about them," Misty said. "Didn't you notice when they had us search the land?"

Drew pursed his lips, then nodded. "They were weird, but I chalked it up to being the first big case they'd had in a while."

"They didn't seem weird when I was shot," Sandy said. "Were they different then, too? I don't know them as well."

"You're right," Drew conceded. "They were a little stressed, but otherwise perfectly normal then. This is different."

"Very different," Bill said. "I don't know what Misty's interview was like, but mine was full-on unbelievably ridiculous."

"I'd like to spend a little time with these cops," Paska said. "I don't know either man well, but I do know them well enough to assess their behavior.

"I'll come with you if you don't mind," Andy added. "I do know them well—nature of the bar business."

Paska nodded and slapped him on the back.

"Are we done for the night?" Ann asked.

"I've gotten as much as I can."

"You're all invited back to the house for dinner," Ann said. "I didn't have time to make more pies today, but I've had a stew bubbling away most of the day and made cornbread and blackberry cobbler."

"That sounds amazing," Bill said. "It's good you live so far away, though. I don't want the competition when you inevitably decide to open your own bakery."

"You have all my recipes," Ann said. "I taught you how to bake."

"And I still don't have the gift you do, and now all these people are going to know it, too. Speaking of baking, I should probably head home and get started on tomorrow's."

Ann smiled at him fondly. "Round up your friends and come inside. If you go home now, I'll regale them with stories of your youth. And not the nice ones."

"I think you should leave," Drew said. "I want the dirt."

An expression of astonished pleasure passed over Bill's face so quickly Misty wasn't quite sure she hadn't imagined it.

"You don't need any more dirt than you already have. I'm staying."

Misty was drinking her morning coffee and wiping the sleep out of her eyes when her phone buzzed. Like every time that'd happened over the past few days, her stomach jerked in a nauseating combination of hope and fear. She grabbed her phone and paused before looking at the display.

It was Drew. "Meet me at Paska's in an hour. I have locations."

Misty looked around the kitchen then down at herself. She was unfed, unshowered, and undressed. She headed upstairs, coffee still in hand, and turned on the water for the shower, making it as hot as she could stand. She pulled her hair back into a tight bun—no way did she have time for the hair care routine necessary to make her curly locks look presentable, much less good. She picked up the coffee again, eyed the shower, then regretfully set it back down to hop in and wash off the dirt and grime accumulated over the last twenty-four hours.

She dried off, finished her coffee, and made toast and jam before heading back up to her room to get dressed. Nothing was clean; she couldn't remember the last time she'd done laundry. She was supposed to be at Paska's in fifteen minutes, and while she knew that being late would be fine, no one would be angry, just a little surprised, she hated the idea of lateness. She dug through her drawers and found an old pair of yoga pants and an oversized t-shirt that read "Your Future is in Oracle Bay," and put them on, assiduously avoiding the mirror. She called Caffiend Dreams.

"Caffiend Dreams, how can I help you?" Bill asked.

"Hi. It's Misty. I'm having a terrible morning and am going to be late for a meeting. Can I place a to go order?"

"Of course. What can I get you?"

"Flat white and whatever you have in a savory scone."

"I have gruyere and caramelized onion."

"Perfect. I'll be there in five."

Misty hopped in her car—normally she wouldn't drive in town, but she was already running late. She pushed the button to open the garage door. Nothing happened. She spent the next minute exercising every swear word she'd ever heard, and when she ran out, she started inventing her own curses. "Llama-faced pile of maggot poop!"

She got out of the car, went back through the house, and out the front door, texting Drew as she walked towards the coffee shop.

"Everything is going wrong this morning. Can you pick me up at Caffiend Dreams?"

Misty made it to the coffee shop in record time and saw Drew parked outside. She waved, walked into the shop, and picked up her order. He waved her card away. "One flat white on the house. Go. Find him."

Misty and John passed out mugs of hot cocoa to the various and assorted people seated at the long dining table in Joseph's house.

Paska and Andy had taken the likely locations Drew had discovered to the police station—everyone wanted to make sure that every aspect of the search was on the up and up, and hiding information from the cops was generally assumed to be bad form. Paska had texted Misty that the men were on their way to the farm and everything had gone exactly as expected. Almost.

Someone knocked on the door, and Misty went to let Paska and Andy in. Instead, she opened the door to Sybil and Russell. "We need to talk," the old woman said as soon as the door was open. "Is there a place we can have privacy here?"

"Now really isn't the best time," Misty said, moving aside so they could come in.

"It's the perfect time." Sybil strode down the call, ignored everyone at the dining room table, and headed towards the back of the house. "Which of these rooms will have a place for me to sit down?"

Misty opened the door to the office. It was still in some disarray —she hadn't been sure where everything belonged—but it had enough places to sit.

"I'm not your mother's aunt," Sybil announced without preamble as soon as she, Russell, and Misty were seated with the door closed. She looked at Russell. "Not your daddy's aunt, either. My relationship to the both of you is a bit more complicated than that. Don't expect me to tell you my age, but I am old. Older than almost everyone in that room, save Morgana. I'm not older than the Dark One you call Andy or Andras or whatever he's going by, nor am I older than Paska. But I'm older than Ceri and Drew, both of whom are quite a bit older than they pretend to be. The only ones here who are as they seem are Joseph and Ann, you two, the new girl and her man, and Bill."

"You didn't mention Jezebel," Russell pointed out.

"I don't quite know where she falls," Sybil replied, a hint of chagrin coloring her voice. "I'm here because of Joseph. I am tied to all my descendants who have even a hint of the sight. But it is because of the Dark One that I'll stay."

"Aunt—or whatever—Sybil. I'm sure you mean well, but the man I was beginning to fall in love with has gone missing, and I am a little short on patience at this stage in the game." She glanced at Russell. "Sorry, Russell. I'm super excited to find out we're related. We can have a family reunion when all this is over, okay?" She stood up.

"Sit down," Sybil's voice cracked. "I don't care how much of your heart is tangled up in what's going on. This isn't about you. Young people are so self-centered." The last was muttered under her breath, just loud enough for everyone to hear.

Misty sat.

"I am the first modern oracle to have lived in Oracle Bay. I was born on the beach and rinsed in the bay. I don't remember my given name—I've been known as Sybil for a very long time. It was an honorific, rather than a name, and my name was eventually lost to the annals of time.”

Misty found herself unwillingly fascinated. She propped her chin in her hands and noticed Russell had adopted a similar pose.

“I married young, as was the custom of the time, and was blessed with six children who lived past the age of one. I watched them closely, and every single one of them developed the sight around the time they hit puberty. Their children did the same, and their children’s children. By the fourth generation, though, only about fifty percent of my descendants had the sight, and three generations after that, ten percent. You are the only two in this generation to have received the sight.”

“Finally ready to admit the truth, Russell?”

He shrugged. “It’s barely worth mentioning.”

Sybil looked at him. “That’s not true, but we can address that later. What matters now is that a storm is coming to Oracle Bay, and this town will need as much help as it can get to weather it. There will be a battle for the heart and soul of the town. People will die. The only way for the town to be saved is for everyone who has Oracle Bay magic tied to their soul to come together as a breakwater. The battle will be fought by others—that is not our role—but we can give the side we favor an edge and protect the townsfolk who have no other way to stay safe. I am here to help. Because we share a bloodline, when we link together, we can be more powerful than we would be alone. And because you both, to varying degrees, have ties to the town and the other oracles, you can pull them into the net.”

“How?” Russell asked.

Sybil looked at Misty. “It starts with her, and it starts tonight. Misty, give me your gloves.”

Misty slowly pulled them off and reluctantly handed them over, careful to avoid skin contact.

“I will teach you how to mute the effects. Our gifts manifest somewhat differently, but I can help with this.”

“Why didn’t you ever bother before?” Misty asked. “It would’ve been very handy in high school and college to be able to touch people with my bare hands."

Sybil laughed. "I never even thought about how my lack of intervention earlier would affect your love life. I knew who you were destined for, but didn't know how long it'd take you to find each other. I hope you found ways around the restriction."

Misty crossed her arms and refused to answer.

"Hold out your hands and close your eyes. Now imagine you're wearing gloves, but not ones of leather or a similar material. Rather, gloves of light and energy. That light will protect you from knowing things you don't want to know. Pull it into your skin."

Misty followed along with the exercise put before her. Heat suffused her arms as she pulled in the mental image of the light gloves. Hands grasped hers, and her eyes popped open in shock. She started to pull away and brace herself from the images she knew would start coming, but nothing happened. She stared at Russell in surprise. He mouthed 'Sorry,' at her and she shrugged.

"Now imagine the gloves thinning, spreading out, until the barrier between you and Russell is almost non-existent. Don't spread it out of existence, just enough that images start to get through."

Misty closed her eyes and concentrated, pulling the imaginary light thinner and thinner until images and feelings not her own appeared in her mind. There was longing, but she couldn't tell what Russell longed, for, and she didn't want to violate his privacy any further to find out. Instead, she concentrated on the bar he tended at the Sleeping Inn and sifted through those images until she satisfied herself that she was in control of the situation and the protection she'd imagined for herself wasn't hampering her abilities. She let go of Russell, pushed the gloves back into place, and opened her eyes. "Now that I know how, it seems so simple. I am so used to the physical gloves, though, that I don't know if it ever would've occurred to me to try. How come you didn't tell me before you left town?"

Sybil rubbed her hand along her jawline. "Hubris maybe. Or carelessness. I am old, and even though my body is still strong, I begin to forget. I have forgotten what it's like to be young and unsure. I had to make my own way, and managed, but I had the support of a village who treated me as a gift and wasn't the child of parents who hated that my blood bred true in them. I should've done better than hold the town true until you were ready to take over."

"Take over as what?"

"As The Oracle, the font of power. You keep Oracle Bay alive. My birth waked the powers that lay dormant, and my bloodline has held it stable for almost three hundred years. Whenever there's been a gap, I've come back to keep the town strong and steady until the next of my line can assume their place."

"And if we leave? All three of us?"

"The magic would fade. Oracle Bay would become nothing more than a generic beachside town."

"There's nothing wrong with that," Russell protested.

"It's a safe haven," Sybil said. "This town gives people like the two of you, and the rest of your psychic friends a place to develop their powers and be themselves. It gave the McEwens a place to settle in where no one would question their weird goat habits, and it gave Andy a place to hide. Without one of you here, any of your friends who might be running from something will be exposed."

Misty took all the information in and stared at her great-great-et cetera great-grandmother. Before she could even begin to process the information, someone knocked on the door. Ceri popped her head in. "Drew and Paska are here, and we're ready to start."

"It was as you predicted," Paska said. "Andy and I brought them the leads and polished our story until it shone with sincerity and earnestness—a chance eavesdropping on a suspicious looking woman led us to believe it would be around here. They asked us for the map, tried to convince us to turn over the extra copy we had and encouraged us to destroy the original on the computer, or they'd get a warrant to destroy the computer themselves. I wanted to argue with them—no judge would issue a search warrant to destroy evidence freely offered —but they seemed unstable enough I chose not to push the issue.”

“The judge they go to might be just as off as they are,” Andy rumbled. “It’s not worth the risk.”

“Agreed.”

“So, you do believe there’s something not quite right?” Bill asked.

“If I believed in possession, I might suggest they were possessed,” Paska shrugged. “But since possession is impossible...”

“I believe in possession,” Andy said. “There are many creatures who can take over a body for short periods of time. But this isn’t possession. At least not in the traditional sense.”

“Can I just point out how interesting it is that someone just implied, in all seriousness, that there are traditional and non-traditional possessions?” Jezebel said. “We are truly living our best lives.”

“If it’s not a possession, what is it?” Morgana asked.

“If the woman is the goddess Menrva as she claims, I think she has cast pieces of her spirit into each of these men. She can see what they see and hear what they hear and direct their speech, at least for short periods of time.”

“Can she do that to anyone?” Morgana asked.

“I don’t know. I am not familiar with this goddess—she came into her own at a time I wasn’t paying attention to world events. I would, however, conjecture that she can only thrust her consciousness into those with whom she’s had a real, physical connection with and who don’t have well-developed natural defenses. That is to say, I would venture that most of the people in this room are safe, saving only Joseph’s parents and his friend Bill. Russell is likely okay, but his powers are less developed than everyone else’s. Has anyone in this room touched the goddess?”

“I have, more than once,” Misty admitted.

“I have as well,” Jezebel said. “She came to me for a reading, too.”

“I have,” Bill said. “And I gave her everything she asked for.”

"Okay. Two people who will stay safe and one who may not. Bill, for your own protection, I think you should stay with one of the oracles of this town. I don't know if their presence will stave off a possession—it didn't deter Menrva from possessing the police officers in the presence of Misty, Paska, or Drew. But it won't hurt. In fact, all the powerless should be in the presence of a person of power until this situation is sorted out."

John made an indistinct noise, perhaps at the indignity of being called powerless, but otherwise did not object.

Paska stood up and passed maps around the table. "There are two locations that seem most likely. I've marked each with an "x." I suggest we split into three groups. One for each of the possible locations and one to stay here. The group that stays here needs an equal number of weirdos and regular folk, and no more than one individual lacking psychic gifts per search group. I'll be in one group, and Drew will head the other. We have the most knowledge of the terrain and landscape and have been staring at this map the longest. Misty, I'd like you to come with me. You have the most connection to Joseph. By that token, Bill should go in Drew's group. He's connected to Joseph, and he'll be safe."

"I will come with you, old man," Morgana said.

"I'll go with Drew and Bill, then," Jezebel said. "I'll report back any shenanigans."

"There won't be any shenanigans," Drew growled.

"Anyone else?" Morgana asked. "Ceri, you can't come. Sandy?"

"I'll come unless it'd make more sense for me to fetch Vincent. He wouldn't be a target, would he?"

"Maybe it's best that you get him and bring him out to the farm. Better yet, just call him and ask him to come out. Sybil, I don't think a back country hike is on your agenda for today. You and Ceri can stay with John and Ann. Russell?"

"I'll go with Drew's group," he said.

"Let's synchronize our watches," Sandy said, clapping her hands.

There was a round of subdued laughter, and everyone showed off their bare wrists.

"Let's check in in two hours," Paska said. "Sandy, since you're staying behind, do you mind being the communication hub?"

"Not in the least. Take care!"

The seven searchers walked out of the dining room towards the front of the house. Misty looked around at the people who were all going out of their way to find a man that most of them didn't care for that much. Drew must have sensed something in the quiet sigh she released because he ended his quiet bickering with Bill and reached back to grab her hand. She squeezed and tried to smile, but before she could talk her facial muscles into turning her lips up at the corner, Drew dropped her hand with a gasp. "I am so sorry!"

"What?"

Everyone else in the narrow hallway had stopped and were staring.

"Your gloves! You're not wearing them. I didn't notice."

"Oh. Right. That. Sybil taught me how to shield myself from unwanted fortune telling, and I forgot to get my gloves back from her."

"I didn't know that was a thing," Drew said.

"Yeah. Me neither until tonight. I think there was a whole lot of my education that was neglected in favor of Sybil getting the hell out of Dodge when I was twenty-two. I'd bet good money, too, that Cousin Russell knows more about my history than I do."

Paska opened the front door and ushered everyone out. "I can drive my group out if Misty's is still trapped in her garage."

Misty flipped him off and climbed into the back seat.

PASKA PULLED TO A STOP AT THE END OF A GRASSY ROAD. A LOW FENCE barred their way, but it wasn't buzzing with the tell-tale sound of electricity. Misty was suddenly even more grateful for the yoga pants she'd been forced to don as she hopped over the fence. Paska had armed them all with flashlights and laminated copies of the map before he walked out to take the lead.

"Aren't we pretty close to Natalie's farm?" Morgana asked. "I've been there to assess her potential power, but never from this direction. It doesn't smell as much like pig as I would've thought, and that's confusing my senses further."

"She's up over the next rise," Paska confirmed. "The other group will be skirting her borders. I probably should've called and given her a heads up."

"I'll do it now," Misty said. She pulled out her phone and got a persistent 'no signal' notice. "I guess I won't. We'll just have to rely on her good nature to not capture the rest of our party and turn them into charcuterie."

"I wonder if people taste like bacon if prepared and smoked correctly," Paska said.

"I'm surprised you don't know the answer to that question," Misty rejoined.

"I have eaten many things in my day, but I have never had human belly."

"Notice he's only eliminated the belly of a human from things he's consumed," Morgana added. She was dressed in a manner similar to Misty, but her tall, graceful body made it look like an outfit rather than an accident. Her black leggings and long, black shirt dress perfectly accentuated her spare frame, and Misty took a minute to envy the other woman's height and ability to shop anywhere to find clothes that fit. She shook off her shopping envy and started paying closer attention to where she was stepping. The last thing she needed was a sprained ankle this far away from the car.

"There's a building," Morgana said.

"Where?" Misty asked, shading her eyes from the very slight glare of the late afternoon sun.

Misty pointed off to the northwest, and if she squinted, Misty supposed she could almost make out a speck that may or may not be a building. "You have eagle eyes," she grumbled.

"Not eagle," Paska laughed. "But she can see farther than almost anyone I know."

Morgana swatted at him, and Paska easily evaded her. "Speak for yourself, Cooper."

Paska said, "I see it now. I was looking in the wrong direction." He and Morgana veered off across the field towards the building that Misty still couldn't see. Ten minutes later, the growing smudge on the horizon resolved into a building shape and Misty picked up the pace. Anxiety curdled her stomach, souring the hope that still existed. Paska reached out and put a hand on her shoulder. "Patience and caution. We don't know what awaits us in there."

Misty drew in a nervous, reflexive breath.

"Don't worry. I am armed, both traditionally as well as magically, and so is Morgana," Paska said. "The others are armed traditionally as well. Their magic armaments aren't as strong as ours, but their bullets are greater in number."

Cold fear edged its way into Misty's belly, chilling her body as they approached the dilapidated barn. Paska held his finger over his lips, then stood back while Morgana lifted the latch and pushed back the great door. It screeched on the roll bar, and Misty winced as the sound broke the perfect silence.

When no attack was forthcoming, the trio stepped forward cautiously. A piteous bleat greeted them, and after shining her flashlight into every corner of the very small shed, Misty darted forward to where the three goats were tied to the wall. "It's Billie and her kids," Misty said.

"Are you certain?" Morgana asked. She didn't walk any further into the shed.

"Not one hundred percent," Misty admitted. "But this goat looks just like Billie, and these two are obviously young twins. It seems a logical leap."

Paska crouched down next to her. "I agree. I've never seen

Billie in the flesh, as it were, but this does look very much like the goat featured on Joseph's website. I spent some time on it earlier today with the hopes I'd better recognize the lady if we came across her."

Billie butted her head gently against Paska's arm and bleated again. Misty looked around. "There's no water or food here. If they're being fed and watered, it's infrequent."

"The kids don't need much more than their mama," Paska pointed out. "But she'll give all of herself to keep them alive with no worry for herself. Any animal would, but I have a sneaking suspicion this one is more than she seems."

"I'd like to gasp in awe of your astute observation," Misty said, "but we've both heard the stories of the immortal goat sent from the Mother of the Etruscan gods. It's not really a stretch to assume she's more than she seems."

"That's a fair point, and you're right. I was getting a little carried away with my immense profundity." Paska dug in his pocket and pulled out an apple and a bottle of water. "Are you thirsty, little mama?"

Billie grabbed the apple from his hand and disappeared it before Paska found a suitable implement in which to pour the water. She took a long drink, rubbed her head against Paska's flank like a satis-fied house cat, and bleated again.

"What's that? You want to leave? Well, let's go then. Can you walk a couple of miles?"

Billie stood up and lipped Paska's coat. He laughed and removed some carrots. "You are a smart one, aren't you?"

After Billie disposed of the carrots and another apple, she nudged her kids. They both stood up, but their balance wasn't as good as their mom's. Billie grabbed the hem of Misty's shirt and pulled her over to one of them. She looked up at Misty and bleated loudly. Misty took the hint and picked up the kid, staggering under the weight. "Whoa. She is a lot heavier than she looks. This walk is going to suck."

"You can trade off with Morgana," Paska said as he picked up the other kid.

Morgana muttered something that Misty didn't catch—only the word 'off' was discernible.

"Hopefully that won't be necessary," Misty said. "It'll depend on how quickly you want to get back."

It took twice as long to get back to the car as it'd taken to get to the shed. Misty managed to carry her kid all the way back, with several rest breaks and baleful glances from Morgana.

"We're at the two-hour mark," Morgana said, glancing at her phone.

"Do you have a signal so we can call in?" Misty asked, setting down the baby goat and stretching her screaming back.

"No. We'll have to get into town."

"How are we going to get the goats back to the farm?" Paska asked.

Misty stared at him. "How do you think, person who drove out here."

Paska cursed creatively and in several different languages. "But my leather seats," he wailed.

Misty crouched down and looked Billie in the eye. "Can you and your babies behave themselves while we drive back to the farm? No bodily functions and no chewing the upholstery." Billie bleated and gently butted Paska.

"They'll be good," Misty said. "She promises."

MISTY STOOD IN THE BARN THAT HOUSED THE DOES AND KIDS AND STARED AT the scene in front of her. Billie was tearing away at the food in front of her and gently nudging away the two kids who'd pepped up as soon as they'd gotten into Paska's car. John stood beside her with an arm draped around her shoulder.

"Thank you for finding them. I'm so grateful."

"I didn't find Joseph, though," she said. "I'm sorry."

He nudged her with his shoulder the way Billie head-butted her earlier. "Not yet. But he disappeared with the goats. I've no great worry that you'll find him, too. Your friends are rather extraordinary, as are you. I only wish I'd been more explicit about what I knew about this town. You assume a kid with a magic goat might entertain the fact that the psychics in town are real, and only later find out he thinks he's a lot more special than he really is. Where did I go wrong?"

"I don't know," Misty said. "We're pretty insular about our actual abilities, so it often seems like we're playing a part when we're serious. We go out of our way to be the clichéd beach town psychics everyone wants us to be. Would you be so willing to accept me if I said I could see the future if you didn't have your own familial weirdness? How much of your ability to put aside what the world says is real is based on the fact that you have a secret oracular goat?"

"You're right. It's easier when there's room for suspension of disbelief. It's great to be awed at the psychic's spot-on reading, but it makes a person uncomfortable if they're forced to confront something they've always believed is impossible. That's how I felt the first time I saw Bigfoot. He was right there, so majestic and furry and big, and I knew he didn't exist, so my brain ran a dozen different scenarios—"

"Wait a minute," Misty said. "You saw Bigfoot? When? Where? How did I not know..." She trailed off when she saw John's smirk. "Are you messing with me right now?"

He held up his hand, index finger and thumb a fraction of an inch apart. "A little. Did it work?"

"You had me going there for a minute."

"I think Billie and her kids are good for the moment. Let's go back to the house and see if the other group had any better luck."

Misty linked her arm through his; their shared grief and angst at Joseph's kidnapping offered few chances to stop, catch their breaths, and whistle in the dark to relieve the overbearing tension. The driveway was full of cars, and the house blazed with light. It looked warm and inviting—like family. Something she'd been blessed with through her friends, but that Joseph hadn't gotten to enjoy since his parents retired to Seattle. Her heart constricted at the sudden realization that he may never get to experience the warmth and joy of a house full of friends and food.

"What made you stumble, Misty darling?"

"Just worried about Joseph. What if—" for the first time since he'd gone missing, she couldn't keep her grief private and her aura of distracted optimism front and center.

"We've got no room for what ifs. We'll deal with whatever happens, but for now, I prefer hope to fatalism. There's still time. If the other search group didn't find him tonight, once she has a chance to recover a bit more, we can ask Billie what she knows."

"Does she...does she talk?" Misty asked, aware of how ridiculous the question sounded, but not positive the answer would be no."

"Not as such, but she does have a way of communicating. We'll see what we can learn. In the meantime, let's keep our hope alive and head indoors. If I know Ann, and I think after this many years I can safely say I do, she'll have a glass of wine with your name on it and a feast for everyone...complete with another one of my pies. She was feeling a lot perkier today than she has been, and will work out that extra energy in the kitchen."

"That sounds heavenly."

John and Misty made their way into the dining room filled with people. Misty did a headcount and came up short. "Where are Jezebel, Drew, Russell, and Bill?" she asked.

"They haven't come back, and they haven't reported in," Paska said. "Neither I nor Morgana have been able to reach any of their cell phones."

Misty pulled her phone out of her pocket. Four missed calls and a text. She checked the text message first. It was the school superintendent wanting to quadruple check the schedule for this weekend's bazaar. She closed her eyes and took a breath. Everything would work out. It had to. Morgana and Sandy were handling it. She let out the breath she'd drawn in and held too long, and forwarded the message to Morgana and Sandy.

Then she pulled up the incoming calls. The first call was from the superintendent; there was no message. The next two calls were from local participants in the bazaar—Viviane Lake, a tattoo artist new to town who was going to use henna to draw temporary tattoos on anyone willing and Natalie Dale, Oracle Bay's charcuterie queen. She didn't listen to either of those messages—they'd keep for tomorrow. The fourth call was from Drew, and he'd left a broken, staticky voice mail.

"Found...shed. Empty. Someone...here. Natalie...oh no!"

Misty hung up and played Natalie's voicemail. It was regarding table signage at the bazaar and had been left about five minutes before Drew's."

She looked up. Everyone in the room was staring at her. She shrugged. "It's mostly bazaar questions—"

"Bazaar or bizarre?" Paska asked.

She tilted her head. "What?"

"Festival or weird questions," he clarified.

"Fall bazaar. The last voicemail was from Drew. It sounded like they found a shed, but it was empty. Then someone came in, and he yelled 'Natalie.'"

"Natalie? Natalie Dale?" Morgana asked.

"That's what I assumed, but I might be biased because the call right before that was from Natalie, asking a question about the bazaar."

"We need to go out there," Paska said.

"Agreed," Misty replied. "But it's late. It's dark. And if there is a threat, it's not one we want to walk into blind. Let's have the dinner Ann prepared, get some sleep, and go find everyone in the morning." She beamed at everyone, and they started to sit at the table. She backed out of the room and headed towards the office and a working phone.

"What are you doing?" Sandy asked.

"Calling the cops. Gotta report the group missing. I don't want there to be any questions later. They'll laugh at me, tell me to call when they've been gone longer than a few hours, and hang up. But I'll make sure there's a record of it. I don't know what's going on with Roger and David, but I will not be complicit in letting them get away with this."

Sandy pulled Misty into a quick hug. "You're a good person, Misty Greene."

Misty hugged her back. "So are you, Sandy Franklin. So are you."

sixteen

Misty met her crew of Paska and Morgana the next morning shortly after sunrise. To her surprise, Andy was waiting for them, too. "We know where the group started, and we know they found a shed almost two hours into their search, based on the timestamp of the voicemail that Drew left Misty. We'll start where they started and follow their trail. I will be texting Sandy every fifteen minutes with our coordinates and any pertinent information, so if we also go missing, they'll have our last known location within fifteen minutes."

"Sounds like a plan," Misty said. They piled into Paska's car and headed out. They found Bill's vehicle parked at the end of a road similar to the one where they'd parked the day before.

They followed the map's suggested route, but it was slow going on foot. The ground was rutted and rocky, full of stealthy rocks waiting to turn unsuspecting ankles, unexpected low spots that had turned into foot-sucking mires with the recent rain, and hills so steep they pushed the boundaries of her physical fitness. Every fifteen minutes, Paska's phone beeped, and he'd text a location update to Sandy.

A little over two hours into their hike, Paska spotted something on the horizon. "Found the shed."

The path transformed from rocky and rough to so smooth it almost felt paved. In minutes, they were in front of the shed. Morgana looked around. "We're definitely on Natalie's land now, aren't we?"

Paska looked up and sniffed the wind. "We are. I smell bacon."

"You're not supposed to call pigs bacon," Morgana chided.

Misty tried—unsuccessfully—to stifle a snort of laughter. Paska winked at her. The smokehouse must either be close or downwind; the air had an aroma of maple-glazed bacon. Misty looked around. A mist was beginning to roll in and devour any recognizable features of the landscape. "There's the lighthouse," she pointed.

"And I smell the mist and salt air from my telling. There wasn't bacon then, but I don't know how often there are things in the smoker."

"So, do we call the cops or do we go in, metaphorical guns a'blazing?" Morgana asked, smoothing the lines of her jeans.

"I'll go in first," Andy said. "I have the best metaphorical guns of all of you, although I'd prefer not to use them."

Morgana smirked at him, then inclined her head and stepped back out of his way. Andy led the way around the shed to the door. It was six inches ajar, and warm light spilled out onto the concrete. Andy stepped lightly forward, grabbed the door, and flung it open. He rushed in, followed closely by the others. There was a figure in front of a long, metal table. They were clad in a white apron and were wearing heavy-duty boots that framed a drain on the floor. The head sported giant, red wireless headphones that matched the red spatters on the table, floor, and person.

In one corner were two bodies, stripped of their skin and hanging from what looked like metal hangers attached to a dry-cleaning facility conveyor belt.

"Hey!" Andy yelled. His voice reverberated off the walls of the slaughterhouse and rattled the boards.

The figure whirled around, bloody knife held aloft. Her hair was covered by a scarf, and her dark skin was splattered with drying blood.

"Natalie?" Misty asked.

She dropped her knife, cursed loudly and creatively, and glared at the intruders.

"What are you doing in here? How'd you even find it? I don't advertise where I butcher for very good reasons."

"What are you doing?" Misty asked, jutting her chin towards the hanging bodies.

"Butchering pigs, as is my job. However, since this is my property and you're the intruders, and since you didn't return my phone call last night, I think I have the right to answers. Tell me now why you're here and how you found this place or I'll call the cops."

"There's no need for that," Paska said. "We're looking for a few people."

"A few? Did someone else besides Joseph go missing?"

"We lost a fair few of our own," Morgana said.

"Who?" Fear made Natalie's voice hoarse.

"Bill, Drew, Russell, and Jezebel," Misty said.

"We found this place because we were looking for an outbuilding that had a view of the lighthouse but not the ocean and had hills in the background."

Morgana looked at Misty and raised her eyebrows, widening her eyes. Misty curled her lip and shrugged. She had no idea what Morgana was trying to tell her. Morgana mimed pulling her fingertips, then thrust her hands dramatically forward, looking more than a little like a very well-dressed zombie on the hunt for brains. It was at that moment Natalie turned around. "What are you doing?"

Misty sighed. Morgana was usually smoother than that. Wait a minute...she looked back at Morgana in time to see her wink before she tripped and pushed Natalie towards Misty. Misty reached out and caught her, grabbing her upper arms with her bare hands. She closed her eyes and shed the psychic gloves, then concentrated on Drew.

None of the images that shot forward had anything to do with recent events, so she changed her focus to Joseph. Her thoughts there were a lot less innocent but unrequited and not recent. She opened her eyes. "Are you okay?" she asked.

"What did you do to me?"

"I tripped," Morgana said. "I was play acting a zombie because I thought it would be amusing in your abattoir and did not account for the slipperiness of the floors. Please forgive me."

"I'm not talking about you. I know what you did." Natalie offered Morgana a hard stare before turning her attention back to Misty. "What did you do to me when you touched me? I felt the buzzing."

"I was looking into you, seeing if you had any knowledge of the disappearance of Joseph or the others."

"Why?"

Misty pulled out her phone and played the voicemail she'd gotten from Drew. Natalie's brown skin turned several shades paler at the end.

"I didn't have anything to do with this."

"I know. Unless you have fantastic mental shields, you couldn't possibly be hiding something that big."

"So now what? You're here because clues led you to this place and Drew yelled my name. What do we do next?"

"I only wish I knew," Misty said.

MISTY TRUDGED BACK INTO THE HOUSE, FOLLOWED BY PASKA AND MORGANA. Andy left to go take care of his business, and Misty suddenly wondered who was taking care of Bill's.

When she voiced the question, Paska shrugged, and Morgana didn't answer. Sandy handed over a mug of cocoa and answered, "I called Bill's part-time assistant. She's taking care of it."

"Thank you. You are magnificent."

Sandy blushed and ducked her head. "I'm only doing what anyone else would do. Bill really took care of me when I needed help, and I want to be able to do the same for him."

"What about Russell?" she asked, kicking herself for not thinking of her friend's jobs until now.

"I called his employer and let them know he wouldn't be in for a couple days. After his initial annoyance at having to find another bartender to cover his shifts on such short notice, Mr. Archer professed to being more than a little pleased that Russell was finally taking some time off."

"I also put notes on Jezebel's and Drew's shop doors letting people know they were out for an emergency and that if there was a prescheduled appointment, to call and reschedule."

"You really did think of everything! I almost hate to ask, but..."

"I called back everyone who called you yesterday regarding the bazaar, met with the school superintendent, confirmed all the vendors, and started to set up the bake-off area—although I had a lot of help for that last bit." She smiled fondly at Vincent, and Misty's heart lurched with the fear that she'd never experience that feeling again.

"I have an idea," John said, standing up and interrupting all the conversations that were taking place. "Misty, Morgana, will you ladies come with me? It's time to ask Billie."

"Why not me?" Paska asked, and Misty was certain she could detect a hint of whine in his voice.

"Billie will know what you did with Goatzilla," John said. "I don't want her to be nervous."

Paska shook his head but didn't argue further, and stood aside to let Misty, Morgana, and John out of the house.

John led the way to the main barn, opened the door, then turned and said, "Wait here. She's still a bit skittish after her adventure, and it'll take a bit of convincing to get her to leave the kids and come with me."

Misty shrugged, looked at Morgana, and did as she was told. After a couple attempts at conversation with Morgana, she gave up and resigned herself to a damp and silent wait.

About ten minutes later, John walked out with Billie trailing behind him.

"You don't have her on a lead?" Morgana asked.

"Of course not." John sounded offended. "She's not a dog or a pony."

Misty bit back a half-formed comment about dog and pony shows and glanced at Morgana who wasn't looking at her at all. She'd always thought that once she hit thirty, she'd feel in control and be confident that she knew what she was doing. She thought thirty was that magic number that would allow her to feel comfortable in her power and no longer young and untried.

And then she found out she was the youngest psychic in town—not by years or even decades. In some cases, centuries. She had no idea how old Morgana and Paska were really—but they weren't as careful about letting things slip that sounded like total anachronisms in the twenty-first century. Drew and Ceri were always cagey about their ages. Sandy was her age—maybe a little younger—but she was also brand new to everything and Misty hadn't had a chance to do a formal "I'm older than you" taunting ceremony. As for Jezebel...she was even cagier than Drew and Ceri. One moment, she seemed as young as Misty, and the next as old as Morgana.

It didn't help that the local bartender was obviously also an ancient, her faux-Aunt Sybil was at least a couple of centuries old, and even the damn goat was older and probably wiser. It was enough to give a woman a complex.

"What troubles you, child?" Morgana asked, pushing the knife further into the wound.

Misty shrugged and smiled. "What doesn't? It's been a troublesome week."

"You have nothing to prove. There is no one who doesn't have faith in you, your abilities, and your capabilities."

Misty's lips thinned to a harsh line, and she turned up the corners in an approximation of a smile.

John and Billie stopped in front of a nondescript building Misty didn't remember seeing before. John opened the door, and Billie trotted in ahead of him. John followed her in, pausing and stretching up to reach the long string that hung from a precariously mounted fluorescent bulb.

The cold white light flooded the enclosure, and Misty looked around at the whitewashed walls. Something felt different here. It looked familiar in that maddening way things do, floating on the tip of your brain, but you can't quite put your finger on it. Then John pulled another string, and the naked incandescent bulb attached lit up a circle near the far wall.

"Ohhh," she said. "This is where the pictures were taken."

"What pictures?" Morgana asked when John merely nodded.

"Joseph was being blackmailed for a million dollars to be dropped in an unspecified location at a similarly unspecified time. The leverage was photos taken here, allegedly of Joseph. There were some of him and Billie looking at the Wall Street Journal—"

"Someone was blackmailing him with pictures of him reading the paper to his goat?" Morgana asked. "That is not the tactic I would've taken."

Misty flashed her a tight grin before continuing. "The other pictures—the ones where you never saw Joseph's face—were of what looked like satanic rituals involving animal sacrifice."

"Oh. Well. That is a lot more blackmail worthy. Are you sure they weren't legitimate photos?"

"Yes. Have you ever seen Joseph with his goats? He loves them. There is no way he'd sacrifice one in some weird ritual."

"Not only that, but none of the goats are missing," John said. "We keep meticulous records."

Misty glanced over at Billie. The goat nodded, then head-butted John hard enough to get his attention but not so hard that he lost his footing.

"What next?" she asked.

"I've never had an audience before, so I think it'll be best if you wait near the door."

Billie shook her head in John's face, grabbed Misty's jacket hem with her teeth, and pulled her forward, pawing the ground in front of her.

"Do you want me to stand here?" Misty asked.

Billie nodded, pawed the ground again, and went to fetch Morgana. Morgana took a step back before Billie could get teeth on her. "I'll follow you, goat. But do not slobber on my clothes." Billie led Morgana to a place opposite Misty, watched her for a minute to make sure she'd stay still, and then trotted back to John who was staring at her in open-mouthed amazement. She butted him again to get his attention.

He shook himself, then walked over to the west wall, and opened a cleverly hidden panel. He pulled out a large roll of paper which he spread on the floor between the two women—it was a detailed map of the area. "We have to hide the map in a cupboard a goat can't open because there's something about this paper that is apparently delicious. We use this one to pick the grazing land that will give us the best milk," Joseph explained. Billie pulled another roll of paper out of the cupboard and drug it over to lay at his feet. "What's this one, then?" He unrolled it and gave Billie a sidelong glance. "A map of...Italy? Why? And where'd this come from?"

Billie gave what sounded like an audible sigh. She knocked the Italy map out of John's hands and unrolled it with her head, standing on one side until John weighted it down. Then she stepped off the maps and looked up expectantly.

John shook his head. "I know you know what I want, so I'm not sure why you're making me go through this, but I'll play ball. Billie, close your eyes and think about Joseph. Concentrate on where he is right now. Once you find him in your mind, reach out your front right foot and show us on the map."

Misty watched in wide-eyed fascination as Billie did just that—

eyes closed and everything. Her hoof tapped a spot three times, and John rushed forward with a piece of dark chalk to mark the spot. Before he finished, Billie walked across the map and repeated the action. John marked that spot, too, and looked at Billie. "How can he be at the lighthouse and in Castiglioncello, Tuscany? That doesn't make any sense.

Billie snorted then tapped each map again, this time harder. Her third tap on Italy tore the paper.

John stared at her. "We've never needed to have actual conversations. Mostly it's picking pasture land or dates on a calendar. Guess it's time to find the old letter board we used to teach the kids the alphabet."

Billie tapped the ground in front of John with her front hoof and bobbed her head.

"I have an idea," Morgana said. He shrugged and stepped out of the way. Morgana knelt before Billie and laid a hand on the side of her neck. "You are able to understand our speech, is that correct?"

Billie nodded and tapped the ground with a front hoof.

"Fantastic. Nod and tap for yes, glare at me with impatience and recrimination for no. Does that work?"

Billie nodded and tapped again. Morgana grinned.

"The one who has Joseph and the others is an Etruscan goddess name Menrva?"

Yes.

"And she is obsessed with haruspicy for the purpose of finding something that has long been lost to her?"

Yes.

"And you believe she is in Tuscany and Washington simultaneously?"

The look Billie shot Morgana was pure contempt.

Realization dawned on Misty. Years of RPG gaming were coming in handy. "The lighthouse is a portal to a place in Tuscany, and that's where she's holding the others!"

Tap, nod.

"That's impossible," John said.

"Mr. McEwen," Morgana said softly and gently. "We are talking to a goat right now. Who's to say what's possible and what isn't?"

He stared at the goat and shoved his hands deep in his pockets. "There's no arguing with that."

Morgana looked back at Billie. "Don't you think this has gone on long enough? People are in danger. Someone who's cared for you for years is in danger. I don't know who you are and why you're a goat right now, but I know that this is not your original form. How long will you hide?"

Billie bleated, lowered her head, and pawed at the ground like a tiny bull ready to take on a matador.

"It's up to you, of course," Morgana said coolly. She stood and dusted off her knees. "I can find the lighthouse, and maybe, with Andy's help, find my way to Tuscany. But do you think that we can stand against a goddess and win?"

Billie took a step back, looked Morgana in the eye, and bleated once.

The room filled with white light. Misty closed her eyes against the brightness and brought an arm up to further protect herself. When the light faded and spots stopped flashing behind her eyelids, she opened her eyes again, cracking them open slowly and peeking through protective fingers.

There was a tall woman with a long, straight nose and dark, curly hair standing against the side of the building, hands over her eyes. She was naked, which better served to show off a figure that looked as though it'd been carved in marble then lightly bronzed.

Misty looked around. John's expression mirrored hers, but Morgana had a sly smirk on her face.

The woman slowly uncovered her face and Misty gasped before she took three steps forward, intent on delivering what would likely be a weak right hook.

Before her arm was more than half-cocked, Morgana grabbed it. "It's not her. It's not Menrva. Look closely."

Misty dropped her arm but not her guard. She peered more closely at the naked woman in front of her. She hadn't spent much time in Menrva's presence, but it was enough to recognize the differences. This woman's eyes were a little rounder and the brown a little softer. Her expression didn't hint at madness, but rather of compassion.

Misty stepped back and inclined her head in apology. She couldn't yet bring herself to speak.

Morgana stepped forward and took Misty's place. "This is your mess, Your Grace. We can help, but it's up to you."

The woman straightened to her full height, her head brushing the ceiling where it slanted down to meet the wall. "Mortal, you dare question me?"

"I am not questioning, just stating the obvious. I don't know what she wants, but I'm guessing you do. After all, you're her mother, aren't you, Uni?"

seventeen

Misty paced in front of Joseph's house. The last few days had been an information overload. Between oracular goats and missing boyfriends and goddesses—times two!—and family secrets, she was done. She wanted to go back to coordinating the bazaar, cultivating her reputation as being hard to work with but ultimately fair, and ignoring romance and the suggestion that there was anything more in the world than a few psychics who liked to hang out on the western edge of the world.

She tipped her face up to catch the mist and cool the heat that came with being overwhelmed. She stood like that for long enough that she lost track of time and only came back to herself when someone touched her arm. She started and opened her eyes. Morgana stood before her.

"I'm sorry to interrupt your introspection, but it is time. Uni has agreed to take three of us through the portal in the lighthouse. It is to be you, for your ties to the missing folk are the strongest, Andy, for his magic is the most practiced and offensive, and me, for my knowledge of the arcane is surpassed by few."

"Surpassed by at least one," Paska muttered, coming up behind them. "I don't know why I can't go. I'm missing all the good stuff lately."

Morgana smiled at him, a sweet smile laced with strychnine. "You make the goddess nervous. You smell of goat blood and darkness."

"Andy's darkness is much smellier than mine," he grumbled.

"I heard that, old man." Andy clapped Paska on the shoulder with enough force to cause him to stagger and passed by him to open the door to his BMW M5. "Get in, the rest of you. Clearly, the goddess gets shotgun."

Uni glided towards them, the rest of the group trailing in her wake. Those who were more mortal than not looked star struck and awed. The psychics seemed less impressed—for the most part. Sandy's adoration matched her boyfriend's. Misty tried not to think about riding in a car with a goddess, spending time with a goddess, believing in a goddess.

Uni reached out her hand and caressed Misty's face. "Do not be afraid. I will not hurt you. You are the beloved of my disciple."

Misty couldn't hold back her bark of laughter at the thought of Joseph being a disciple of anyone.

"Are you laughing at me?" Uni tucked her chin and jutted her forehead forward. It was so goat like that Misty lost what little composure she'd been managing to hold onto and erupted into laughter with a tinge of hysteria.

Uni looked at Morgana. "Why does the young one laugh at me?"

Morgana glared at Misty. "Nerves. Her paramour has been missing for several days, and she watched you transform from a goat. It's a lot for a young mind."

Uni gave Misty a considering look. "Indeed."

Misty reined in her laughter, wiped the tears from her eyes, and got into the back seat of Andy's ridiculous car. Morgana climbed in beside her, and they both watched as Uni struggled with the seatbelt, doing rather better than Misty would've expected considering she hadn't had hands for well over a thousand years. When the belt snicked into place, Andy shook his head, started the car, revved the engine, and peeled out of the driveway, leaving a spray of gravel in his wake.

· · · · ★ ★ ★ ★ ★ · · ·

By the time Andy pulled into the parking lot of the lighthouse, after careening around the chained off entryway, Misty was positive her complexion was a mottled white and green. Andy drove like a man possessed. Morgana looked almost as nauseated as Misty felt, but Uni was whooping and laughing. Her hair was disheveled from hanging her head out the window during the drive, and only the insistence of the others had kept her from climbing out of the car in an attempt to ride on top.

"Thank you," she said to Andy. "That was a truly magnificent trip. It is a lot more fun as a human than as a goat in a trailer."

Misty shook her head and got out of the car, hoping that she wasn't shaking too much.

Morgana led the way to the lighthouse and turned the doorknob. It didn't turn. "Your turn," she said to Misty.

Misty rifled through her purse and pulled out an enormous keychain. She flipped through the meticulously labeled keys until she found the one she was looking for. She inserted the key into the lock and opened the door.

"Why do you have a key to the lighthouse?" Andy said.

"I own most of the town now," Misty said. "And before that, I managed the properties that are mine now. Most people only think about Main Street, but this was one of the properties included."

The quartet walked into the lighthouse. "It's smaller than I thought it'd be," Morgana said. "Where's the portal?"

Andy and Uni exchanged a glance, and he bowed slightly to allow her to take the lead. Uni didn't hesitate. She walked to the spiral staircase and went up.

At the top of the staircase, Misty was more out of breath than she liked and was secretly pleased to see Morgana and Andy were breathing heavily, too.

"It is here."

"Just...here? In the—" Misty realized she didn't know what the top of a lighthouse was called. A cupola? Tower? Belfry? "—top?"

Uni walked out onto the balcony overlooking the Pacific Ocean. "Here." She pointed towards the far end of the balcony. A section of railing was cut away. It wasn't a big enough gap for an adult to accidentally fall through, although a small child could slip through with little trouble, and an adult could shimmy through if they wanted.

"No."

"What do you mean no?" Uni asked.

"The portal is one step off of the balcony, isn't it?"

"It will likely lead straight through to solid ground," Uni said. "There is very little likelihood my daughter constructed a portal that opens sixty feet above the ground in Italy. Even if she has enough divine power to ensure she doesn't fall to her death, she has been moving enough people around that she would need the portal to open somewhere more conducive to preserving human life."

"Your vocabulary and speech patterns are remarkable for someone who hasn't spoken in centuries," Andy said.

"I listen whenever I can, and Joseph would read to me when I was kidding."

Misty was confused for a moment until she realized that Billie—Uni—was talking about the birthing process.

"It matters not, though. The portal is here. We must go through to confront my daughter and rescue the others. I will go first. That way, if there is an unexpected drop, I will find it and can be there to arrest the fall of anyone else."

She didn't wait for agreement or even acknowledgment. As soon as the words were out of her mouth, she turned sideways and took a side step into thin air. For a moment, she appeared to hover in mid-air, and then she disappeared.

"Who's next?" Morgana asked.

"I'll go," Misty said. She knew if she didn't go now, she'd never be able to take that step. She walked to the rail, took a deep breath, and squeezed herself through the hole. Her body scraped against the metal edges of the railing that clutched at the loose edges of her clothes. She closed her eyes, half-turned her body, and jumped.

Note to self. Never jump through a portal that likely leads straight through to solid ground. Misty stumbled forward a few steps then caught her balance and glanced around. She was surrounded by hills that didn't look too different than anything near Washington but had an aura of foreignness about them.

Morgana and Andy stepped out of nowhere, and everyone's attention turned to Uni.

"Now where?"

"Nowhere," Menrva answered. The group whipped around and came face to face with Menrva. Now that she was no longer trying to hide her true self, she was well over six feet tall, bore a striking resemblance to her mother, and exuded static electricity so intensely Misty could feel the hair on her arms standing up.

Behind her was a field greener than anything else in the valley. In the field were five tall, white posts. There was one person tied to each post, and Misty recognized the person in front as Joseph. She started towards him and was rewarded with a lightning zap to the chest. She flew backwards and landed on her back, gasping for air.

Uni strode forward, pausing by Misty to place a hand on her cheek. Breathing came easier now, and the coolness that came with Uni's touch spread over her body dispelling the heat from the lightning bolt Menrva had aimed at her.

She stood up with an assist from the goddess.

"You should stay behind me," Uni said. "I will deal with my daughter."

"What do you need us for, then?" Morgana asked.

"Backup." She walked forward, Andy a half step behind her. Morgana and Misty fell into step after them. Uni led the way into the center of the valley. The sun peeked over the horizon shining through the mist and fields of sunflowers and casting a golden glow over the valley.

"Menrva!" Uni called, her voice ringing out impossibly loud. Misty covered her ears, but it did nothing to dampen the echoes.

There was no answer, but the figures hanging from the polls woke up and looked around. Joseph's dazed glance fell on Misty first, and his expression was a mixture of terror and surprise. Their gazes caught and held, and everything else fell away.

"Misty," Morgana hissed, bringing her back to herself. "Pay attention. It's almost our turn."

"Our turn for what?" Misty asked. "I thought we were just backup."

"Things are changing. Take off your psychic gloves and get ready to kick ass."

* * * ★ ★ ★ ★ ★ * * *

MISTY STOOD NEXT TO UNI AND LOOKED UP AT HER, APPRECIATING FOR THE first time how tall the goddess was. Menrva was about five feet in front of them brandishing what looked like a...liver. It appeared fresh, and Misty tried not to think about where it might've come from—who it might've come from.

"When I give the signal, I want you to run forward and grab her hand. Concentrate on Menrva and why she's doing all this now. You'll know when it's time to let go."

"What's the signal? How will I know?" Misty's questions were lost in the sound of a gale whipping up around her. The sun which had just begun to spill out over the entire landscape all but disappeared as dark clouds tinged with green rolled in. The air temperature dropped several degrees raising goosebumps on Misty's arms and causing her to shiver. She kept her eyes on Uni, squinting to see through the dust and dirt swirling around.

Uni walked up to her daughter and slammed down the spear that appeared in her grip. Her clothing shimmered and changed—

instead of the modern garments borrowed from Joseph's mother, she was dressed in flowing robes of sky blue draped and tied in a fashion reminiscent of the toga.

"What are you doing with my spear, mother?"

"What are you doing with my grandson's liver in your hands?" Uni asked.

"You lower yourself to be a beast for eons, and consider your spawn to be children? Should I have called him brother before I slit his throat?"

"I am a god, not a mortal. Nothing I do lowers myself more than what you've done."

"What do you want? Why are you doing this?"

"I am lost. I needed succor. There is no one left but us."

"You did all this because you're lonely?" Misty blurted.

Uni turned and glared at her, but it was too late. Menrva's attention was drawn past her mother. "Oh, it's you. The little girl with power she doesn't know how to use. Last time I saw you, I pushed you into a grave. This time, I'll make sure you can't get back out."

Uni sighed. "The signal is now." She used the spear as a baseball bat, swinging at Menrva's hands and sending the liver flying.

Misty darted in and grabbed one of Menrva's now-free hands and held on with all her might, concentrating on the goddess and the motivations that drove her fractured mind.

Images rushed past, faster and faster, as her gift searched for the answers she sought. Menrva tried to pull away, but Misty gripped harder and focused.

The scene changed a little. Instead of late autumn, the valley was in mid-spring. The sunflowers were gone—instead there were rolling green hills and trees gathered in bunches like clumps of cliquish teenagers. Walking away was an old woman and a goat. A tsunami of grief washed over her, tightening her chest and forcing tears into her eyes. She was alone. Her family was all gone—dead or faded into obscurity. Her mother had been the only one she'd had left, and now she was gone, too.

She couldn't let this happen. She had to stop them! Menrva ran forward, hitching her skirts to aid her passage, and then she tripped. She hit the ground hard enough to knock the breath out of her, and when she was able to climb to her hands and knees, the first thing she saw was the sandaled feet in front of her face. She rocked back onto her heels and looked up. A man, naked but for a loin cloth and his sandals, stood in her path. His great golden wings framed his body, the tips almost brushing the ground and the tops rising well above his head. His skin and hair were a dark mahogany, and his brown eyes burned with blue fire. She rose to her feet and saw a second figure—another man, this one had alabaster skin and russet hair, but the same golden wings and blue fire eyes—standing behind the first.

She rose to her feet and took two slow, deliberate steps back. "Who are you? What do you want?"

"Our names are not important," the first one said. "We are messengers."

"Messengers from who?"

"From our god. The god who even now gains more and more footholds in the lands that were yours. No one worships you anymore, but soon, no one will even remember you. We can change that."

"How?"

"We will have the ancient depictions of your image discovered and will ensure that your name is the name associated with the sacred relics. You will not be mislabeled Minerva or Athena; you will be Menrva, daughter of Uni. Your worshippers might be gone, but your memory can live on."

"What is the price I pay for this shallow immortality?"

"It is a small price, and one easily agreed to."

"Be that as it may, I will not agree to any bargain until I know the extent of what I'm agreeing to."

"That is wise," the second man said.

"The price?" Menrva asked.

"You will leave the goat alone. Sometime in the future, we will contact you, and you will find the goat and take her back. We are setting cosmic events in motion, starting the first breeze that will turn into the storm. This goat will follow fate and be present when it's finally time to bring balance back to heaven and hell."

"You want me to abandon my mother to the shape of a goat for an indeterminate amount of time so I can help you start a war that will benefit the god who is precipitating my disappearance so I won't disappear?"

"Exactly." The first being sounded smugly pleased that she'd grasped everything so quickly.

"I will live a life of solitude—the very thing I was trying to prevent today—on the off chance I'll get a message in the future?"

"You'll achieve true immortality—your memory will live on forever. And when the time comes, you'll no longer be alone. If you follow the goat now, she will rebuff you. But if you wait—and the years are but drops in the bucket for beings like us—you will have a true family forever."

Menrva thought about it. She could still find her mother and try to talk her into changing her mind. It didn't have to be like this.

"I know where there are hundreds of places where your relics are buried," being number two said. "You will never be forgotten."

"It is an acceptable bargain." She held out her hands to the men. They each grabbed one, and the goddess's mind splintered. Menrva lost track of who she was and lost herself to the passage of time, searching for something she couldn't recall. A bright flash of light pushed Misty out of Menrva's head and back to the present

"Do you know what she wants?" Uni asked. Her voice was tight, and she was breathing hard. The reason became clear a moment later when a bolt of lightning came out of the sky aimed at Misty's head. Uni jumped up, wrapped the goatskin around herself, and shielded Misty.

"She wants you. She wants family. And she wants her name to live on forever. She lost her mind when you left her and has been trying to find you ever since. She had only the vaguest sense of who she was and what she wanted. It was all about family, but she couldn't remember in more than flashes how to find you. It took her more than a millennium to track you down, and right now, her mind is so splintered it's a wonder she recognized you at all."

"Run," Uni said.

Misty let go and ran away just as Uni sprang forward and grabbed Menrva, wrapping her arms around her and rocking her back and forth. "Baby, baby. Mama's here."

· · ★ ★ ★ ★ ★ ★ · ·

MISTY RAN BACK TO THE OTHERS. ANDY WAS WAITING WITH A LARGE KNIFE. "Let's get everyone down," he said. "Joseph first because he's likely been up the longest, but Misty, you can't stay with him. You need to come with us to help lower people down as I cut their bindings."

"Of course," she said.

Morgana and Misty supported Joseph while Andy cut the ties. Once he was safely on the ground and portal-adjacent, they headed to the next pole to cut Bill down. In less than fifteen minutes, the rest were free and sitting on the ground near the portal. Andy went to the valley where Uni and Menrva were still locked in an embrace that more resembled war than affection.

Misty couldn't hear what he said to the women—the wind whipped up and a funnel cloud formed in the distance. He ran back towards the group. "Uni wants us to leave. She'll handle Menrva. We just need to handle getting home safely."

Andy lined everyone up in a single file line. "I'll go last this time. Morgana, will you do the honors of leading us off?" After she nodded, he said. "Go through quickly. Once you're on the other side, move out of the way into the lighthouse. Do not think about what you're about to do. Just do it."

Morgana walked forward through the natural gate made by two

trees growing close together. Drew followed, then Bill, Russell, and Jezebel. "Ready?" Andy asked Misty.

She nodded and walked forward. Just before she stepped through, the earth shook, and she stumbled backwards. A small cyclone roared by in front of her, and only Andy's grip on her shoulders kept her from being sucked forward. Dirt and dust filled the air, and when she was able to see again, the trees framing the portal were gone.

"Andy? Is the portal still there?"

He looked around to ensure no more surprise tornadoes were on their way, and then walked forward, hand out in front of his face. He dropped his hand. "It's gone. She destroyed the anchors, and the entire gate fell."

"We're stuck in Tuscany? Ordinarily this would sound like a romantic wine drinker's dream come true, but after all the trouble we went through to rescue my boyfriend and friends, I'd like to not be the one in need of rescuing now."

"Patience. We're not stuck. I can get us back. I'll just need to call in a favor."

He closed his eyes and folded his hands. Less than a minute later, he raised his head and smiled. "They come."

Another burst of wind caused Misty to close her eyes against the onslaught of dirt and debris. When she opened her eyes again, two more men stood in front of her. Her jaw dropped. They were the men from her vision, the ones from Menrva's past. "Where are your wings?" she blurted.

"You didn't say the mortal would know of our kind," the fair-skinned man said as his wings appeared behind him in a shimmer of golden light.

"She's only mostly mortal," Andy replied. "She has the sight."

The darker skinned man said nothing, but he, too, pushed his wings out, spreading them wide in a manner that reminded her of a frilled-neck lizard under threat. She all but expected him to hiss at her.

"Where do you want to go?" he asked, his eyes on Misty.

"Here," Andy said, reaching forward to touch the man's temples with his fingertips. The man mirrored the gesture. A moment later, they each dropped their hands.

"We can do that," they said in unison.

Before Misty could register what was happening, the darker skinned man picked her up, held her close, and lifted himself off the ground with slow, sure strokes of his wings. "This will be uncomfortable and bumpy. Please do not vomit on me. You'll be back soon." He leaned forward, making himself more aerodynamic, and started flying. About ten minutes into the flight, the world around them disappeared and the speed increased. Ten minutes later, an audible pop and the feeling of raindrops announced a change in venue. Misty opened her eyes and tried to ascertain her whereabouts. Before she could figure out where they were, her carrier stopped abruptly, set his feet down with a jerk, and dropped her. "I look forward to our next meeting, Mystic." He disappeared.

A couple minutes later, Andy appeared. His bearer didn't do him the courtesy of landing before dropping him, and Andy landed on the lighthouse balcony hard enough to shake the whole structure.

"We're here," she said stupidly.

"Let's go find the others."

Misty ran down the stairs in record time. The whole group was waiting. "You're really here," she said, eyes on Joseph.

"Andy has the keys," Morgana deadpanned.

Misty was already walking towards Joseph. They didn't say anything, he opened his arms for her, and she walked in. It was good to be home.

eighteen

An hour later, everyone was back in Joseph's kitchen sitting around the table having pie. Bill and Drew were carefully keeping the entire room between them, Russell kept giving Misty and Sybil enough side-eye to last for the rest of the year, and Jezebel hadn't said a word about their kidnapping and captivity. There was only one thing Misty wanted, and that was ten minutes—okay, who was she kidding?—ten hours alone with Joseph. She squeezed his hand and tried to give him a look that conveyed her desire for everyone else to go away now.

He seemed to catch her drift. He stood up, stretched, and said, "It's been a long few days. I'm sure I'll have another long day tomorrow answering questions at the police station. I know many of you have unanswered questions—as do I—but I'd love a raincheck on answering."

"Of course," Sybil said, winking at Misty. "You should definitely get to bed."

Misty looked at her feet and willed herself not to blush.

People finished their cocoa, carried their empty plates to the kitchen, and trickled out, arranging rides and planning to meet up tomorrow after the bazaar.

"The bazaar!" Misty shouted. "It's tomorrow! Oh, no!"

"It's okay," Sandy said. "It's taken care of. Everything will be great."

"It won't," Bill groaned. "There's no way I can pull together anything for the bake sale, at least not anything worthy of first place."

"I can help," Ann said. "What time do you need to get started?"

He shook his head. "Yesterday. Joe, do you have any cream?"

"I don't know," he replied. "I've been out of town the last few days."

"Right. Sorry. And Billie...I'm sorry about her, too."

"It's not like she died. She just because a little less goaty."

Misty smiled, trying not to let her impatience show on her face. She was exhausted. Her stress levels the last few weeks had been through the roof, and she needed a glass of wine and several smooches to get through the rest of the night.

"There's cream in the dairy fridge," John said. "I'll walk you out and help you get everything you need."

After they disappeared, Ann busied herself with the dishes, and that's when Misty remembered that Ann and John were staying at the house, and even if they retreated the bedroom and pretended they weren't there, Misty and Joseph wouldn't be alone. Maybe ten minutes was the more realistic target for the night. John came back a few minutes later and helped Ann finish cleaning up the kitchen. Misty and Joseph looked at each other, and he shrugged. She didn't want to deprive his parents of time with him. They'd been worried about him, too, and deserved the whole story at least as much as Misty did, but she felt selfish. He was hers, and she'd been so scared.

John brought Misty a glass of wine and Joseph a bottle of beer. "Sit down, kids. Relax. It's over."

"Is it, though?" Misty asked. "Uni was still fighting with Menrva when we fled, and if she doesn't win, what steps will Menrva take next?"

A blinding flash of light lit up every dark corner of the room, and Misty threw up her free arm to shield her eyes. She braced for the rumble of thunder sure to follow such a close strike, but there was nothing but silence. The brightness faded and the spots stopped dancing behind Misty's eyelids. She opened her eyes cautiously. Uni stood in the middle of the living room facing her and Joseph.

"I didn't get a chance to thank you," she said. "You took such good care of me; you and your family."

"No, thank you. You..." his voice broke, and he dashed the tears from the corner of his eyes.

She reached out a hand, and he took it. "You gave me a place to hide when I desperately needed a respite from the world. Immortality is exhausting, and I'm not the first to take a thousand-year break. The newest kids will serve you almost as well as I could. Keep them both, and they will be blessed with long life, sweet milk, and twins. They won't live as long as I did, but a great deal longer than the rest of your goats. You'll know when their successors have been born. They will be marked with my symbol—a spear along their spines. I must go. Menrva needs me now. Her mind was fractured by the beings who promised her true immortality, and she is only just beginning to understand the true scope of her illogical actions. I hope my healing powers can truly repair her mind, but it will take every bit of my skill to do so. If you ever have need of me again, call my name—my true name and the name I was given. I will come to your aid one time, and once to the aid of your heir, and so on, for all time. I'll see you, though, even sooner than you expect."

Another flash of light and she was gone. Misty took a gulp of wine and looked at Joseph. His eyes were still damp with tears, and he drained the rest of his beer in one drink. John was much the same —tears streaked down his cheeks, and Ann went to him and put her arms around him. "Let's go to bed," she said. "We can give the young ones a chance to say goodnight without being in the way. She led the way to the back of the house, and the door to the guest room clicked shut.

"I guess I should go?" Misty asked.

"I wish you wouldn't," Joseph replied. He put an arm around her and pulled her closer to him. She rested her head on his shoulder.

"Tomorrow's another long day. I have to be at the school by six to start setting everything up..."

He sighed and rubbed his hand through his hair. "It's my house, and we're adults. If I want to have my girlfriend stay overnight, I can."

The petulance in his voice made her grin, and she twisted her body towards his and stretched up for a kiss. He met her lips with an unbridled passion that surpassed any heat they'd generated before. She threaded her fingers through his hair and pulled him closer, trying to get more of him. His right hand reached over and grabbed her left hip. He pulled her over until she was sitting astride him, arms wrapped around her neck. He tugged her shirt up and slid his hands under the hem and up against her skin.

"Joseph?" John called. "Did you lock the front door yet? Want me to get it?"

Joseph groaned, and Misty slid off his lap. "I'll get it, dad. Go to bed."

"I'd better go," she said. "I'll see you tomorrow?"

"Don't be daft. I am coming home with you. It is definitely not time to say goodnight."

Misty grinned, kissed him again, pressing her body closer to his. "Race you to the car."

· · · · · ★ ★ ★ ★ ★ · · · ·

Joseph bought a dozen raffle tickets to appease the next person who stood in his way, then side-stepped the third person who appeared in front of him so he could finally get into the bazaar. His eyes darted around the room, looking for Misty. She'd crawled out of the bed they'd shared at five o'clock, which was his usual wake-up time. It was nice to be in a bed and not responsible for the welfare of his flock. He'd grabbed her waist, pulled her back into bed, and made her only a few minutes late.

On the left half of the gymnasium, dozens of tables covered in local arts, crafts, and baked goods were set up. Everything from children's toys to knitted sweaters to hand-forged iron jewelry was on display. The right half of the gymnasium was dedicated to food. About two-thirds were food vendors, selling a variety of hot and cold items for breakfast and lunch as well as more baked goods than anyone could ever need—they sold out every year. The other third was for the Great Oracle Bay Bake-off.

This year's contestants were prepping their items for the judges. Each contestant had one item for display (and later sale) and one for taste testing. Although the majority of the points were awarded for flavor and texture, there were points for appearance, as well. Joseph caught Bill's wild-looking eye. Ann was standing behind him, patting his arm. Joseph wasn't the only one who noticed Bill's nervous pacing. Matilda Ryan, the postmistress and eternal first runner-up was eyeing Bill with a look that could only be described as avaricious glee.

He waved at his friend and his mother and barely got a nod of acknowledgment in response. His dad was at a table in the food vendor area doing a brisk business with cheese and crackers accompanied by jam and a variety of charcuterie offerings he must have scammed from Natalie who had her own table selling sausage, bacon, and prosciutto. "What are you doing, Dad?"

"Helping out! Selling McEwen cheeses, getting our name out there more, and helping the town! Isn't this what you do every year?"

"I, uh, usually just hand the cheese off to whoever shows up to collect it. I don't know what they've done in the past."

Misty breezed up behind him, smiled up at him, and subtly

pinched his butt. He grinned down at her. "Hey. I was looking for you."

"You found me. At least for a minute. The bake-off is about to begin."

"My son tells me he didn't do any of the work to sell the cheese and get his name out in the past."

"I usually gave Natalie the cheeses to deal with and saved one out whole to be a raffle prize. She did much the same as you're doing now—selling mini meat and cheese trays. Joseph has never been much for socializing with the town."

"I think that might be about to change," he said.

She slid an arm around his waist and squeezed. "I hope so."

· · * ★ ★ ★ ★ * · ·

Misty paused in the doorway of the back room at The Pour House. The room was packed with psychics and the assorted people they'd gathered up over the last few weeks. Russell was tucked into a back corner, sipping a dark beer, and looking distinctly uncomfortable. Joseph's parents were next to him; Ann had spent all day at the bazaar and looked dead on her feet. Sandy and Vincent were holding hands and sharing a taster tray of Andy's best seasonal beers. Even Bill was present, sitting as far away from Drew as it was possible to sit.

Misty'd thought things looked to be thawing out between Drew and Bill before they'd been kidnapped by Menrva, but whatever had happened between the Pacific Northwest coast and the Tuscan countryside had dialed the tension up to eleven.

The only people missing were Sybil and Joseph. She'd had a voicemail from Sybil when she woke that morning.

"I've topped up enough for now, Mystic. Take care of yourself, your cousin, and your man. I'll be back before the storm breaks." When she'd run into Russell earlier, he'd confirmed he received a similar message. She tried to call Sybil back, but the number she had was disconnected. Why did everyone have to be so mysterious all the time?

That left Joseph as the sole absent but expected person. Even Andy had foregone working the floor to sit with them and have a beer. Misty walked the rest of the way into the room, and a spontaneous cheer rose up! "Here's to another great Bazaar!" Drew called out.

Misty shook her head. "Morgana and Sandy did most of the work this year."

"Nonsense," Morgana said. "You've been working on this thing since last year at this time and all Sandy and I had to do was step in and follow the detailed path you'd already paved. There was nothing you hadn't thought of, and your notes were so detailed and precise that neither of us had a single moment of wondering what to do and how."

"I was the Bazaar chair this year, anyway," Sandy said. "It couldn't have gone smoother. You made it all possible."

"Like you do every year," Joseph said.

Misty whirled around. He was looking down at her and the guarded expression he usually kept in public was gone. Instead, all she saw was everything she felt, too. She took a step closer to him and reached out her hands. He took them and dropped a kiss on her upturned lips.

"Guess explanation time is gonna have to wait," Paska grumbled. "I want to know what happened."

Misty slid her arms around his neck. "I missed you," she whispered, heedless of the large audience behind her.

"I missed you more." This kiss wasn't a gentle greeting. It was ferocious and heated. His hand slid down her side and landed on her hip.

"Get a room!" Bill yelled.

"Good idea," Joseph murmured. "Mom, dad, I booked you a room at the Sleeping Inn for the night and took the liberty of dropping off your bags there. Call before you come over tomorrow. Misty and I are going home."

He looked at her. "If that's what you want, of course."

She kissed him hard and briefly pressed her body against his. "Definitely. Let's go home."

Misty stretched and yawned. She knew light was streaming through the curtains, but she wasn't quite ready to open her eyes. She breathed in deeply, enjoying the feeling of warm sunlight on her face accompanied by the knowledge that she had almost nothing to do today. Her inhalation carried the scent of coffee, and that was enough to pop her eyes open.

A cup of coffee, still steaming, was on the dresser—just far enough away that she'd have to get out of bed to reach it. She scowled at the window, hoping Joseph was feeling the full effect of her wrath. When he didn't reappear to hand her the cup in bed, she sighed heavily and slipped out of bed. After putting on her robe, she grabbed her cup of coffee and padded to the kitchen. On the high kitchen counter next to the coffee maker was a note.

"Last night was perfect. Every night for the last two weeks has been perfect. There's French toast staying warm for you in the oven and mimosa fixings in the fridge. Pour a couple drinks, eat your breakfast, and I'll be back in no time to toast the morning in. Love, Joseph."

Misty smiled and tucked the note into her robe pocket. After going home with Joseph the night of the Bazaar, she'd spent every night in his bed, and her clothing was slowly migrating out to the farm. It made sense—he had to be here to take care of the goats, and now that Goathilda and Goatzer were orphans, he was spending a little extra time with them to make sure they stayed healthy.

She pulled her breakfast out of the oven and dug in between sips of coffee. Spending time with a man who got up at the crack of dawn —or earlier—had its benefits.

When she'd finished her French toast and estimated that Joseph would likely be back soon, she poured two mimosas and took them to the big kitchen table next to the window with the ocean view where they'd shared that first doomed beer so many weeks ago. She didn't hear him come in, she was so wrapped up in her own thoughts, and she started when his hands found her shoulders.

"Whatcha thinking about that has you looking so serious?" he asked, abandoning her shoulders for his mimosa and taking a seat beside her.

"The coming storm," she answered. "As always."

"Anything new since last time we saw Andy?"

"Nope. He still refuses to talk about his winged friends and denies any knowledge as to what they might be, even though it seems pretty obvious. How many winged humanoids are there?"

"I don't know. How many?" Joseph asked.

"Very funny. You know what I meant."

"I do, and I'm concerned, too. It'd be so much easier to know what to expect and how to save the town if he would be a little more trusting."

"At least your situation is sorted, now," Misty said. "The cops are back to normal now that Menrva isn't messing with them anymore. The only mystery left is who's been trying to blackmail you all these years? It can't be Menrva...she didn't even know who you or Billie were until a few weeks ago. So convenient that the cops 'lost' all the blackmail material they received."

"It wasn't that big of a deal before. I'm sure it'll be fine."

"You were considering leaving town over it!"

"I'm not anymore. It's Oracle Bay. We'll make it work, no matter what. I'm putting it behind me. It's nice to only have one thing to worry about at a time."

The doorbell rang, and Misty and Joseph both froze.

"You said it, not me. This is your fault."

"It might not be trouble," Misty said. "It could be Bill, dropping by to say hello."

"At nine o'clock in the morning on a Saturday? Pretty sure he's at Caffiend Dreams."

"I guess we should answer it."

"I'll get it. I'm a little more dressed than you."

"You get the door. I'll get clothes."

Misty headed to the bedroom and hastily dressed. When she returned to the kitchen, Drew and Ceri were sitting at the kitchen table.

"What's up, guys?" Misty said, grabbing her mimosa. "Want one?"

"No thank you," Drew said. "I know I should've called, but something weird happened, and I needed to tell someone."

"Why me?" Misty asked. "Not that I don't appreciate being the go-to for weird, but Morgana and Paska are better equipped if it's the kind of weird we've been having lately."

"I couldn't reach them," Drew admitted. "Ceri showed up as I was leaving to find you, and can verify that it's weird."

"I don't care that you didn't call me first. But I do care that you're talking about a weird you haven't defined. What's weird?"

"My ball is missing."

Misty bit her lip to keep from grinning and heard Joseph snort. Even Ceri looked like she was about to giggle.

"My crystal ball. My focus stone. It's missing."

"That's terrible," Misty said. "I know how much it meant to you and how hard it was to find such a perfect stone that worked with you so well. Do you think it was a standard breaking and entering situation? Or something else."

"Definitely something else," Ceri said. "There was nothing standard about this."

"Why? What was weird?"

"When I walked into my shop this morning to get set up for any drop-in clients, the first thing I noticed was that my front door was unlocked. The second thing was that my sign was on, but instead of the regular neon, it was a painting. And the third thing was that there was a Styrofoam ball the same size and shape as my focus stone and a skeleton in a Halloween wizard's robes and pointy hat was sitting in my chair gazing at the ball."

"Oh," Misty said. "That is weird."

CLICK TO BUY WING AND A PRAYER, BOOK THREE IN THE ORACLE Bay series. Keep reading for a brief excerpt.

want more amy cissell?

And why wouldn't you?

Love it, hate it, somewhere in between? Please leave a review for **First Hand Knowledge** at Goodreads, Bookbub, or your favorite online retailer.

Links to all retails sites are at:
https://books2read.com/FirstHandKnowledge

Reviews are always appreciated & allow me to keep writing what you love!

Sign up for Cissell's Epistles at https://amycissell.com for new release updates, exclusive content, and a bevy of book recommendations! (You'll also get to choose a free book as a thank you for hanging out!)

Come hang out in my Facebook Reader Group - the Amyzonians can always use another shenaniganator. (It's a word. Promise.)

https://www.facebook.com/groups/amycissellauthor/

Join my patreon - https://www.patreon.com/ACissellWrites - for early access to books, free copies of my digital books, free paperbacks, and access to my entire back catalog!

* * * * ★ ★ ★ ★ ★ * * *

wing and a prayer

PYSCHICS OF ORACLE BAY #3

ndras Sterling stood in the back of The Pour House, crossed his arms, and surveyed his bar. Brandy had gone all out for Halloween—flickering red lights lined the walls and wound around cutouts of demons and monsters, giving an uncomfortably familiar impression of flickering flames and hellfire.

The post-Halloween party crowd packed the bar, and everyone was in costume. He looked down at his jeans and orange shirt and grimaced. It was orange. It counted.

A glass shattered near the bar and interrupted the buzz of conversation. He moved towards the commotion, weaving in and out of the rubber-necking crowd. Brandy was standing behind the bar, arms crossed and an unyielding icy expression on her face.

"What you mean, I'm cut off?" the man in front of her shouted. He strode forward, and a crunching sound pulled Andy's eyes downward. The ground under the belligerent drunk was littered with broken glass. "My money's just as good as anyone else's here."

All conversation in the immediate vicinity stopped, and waves of silence rolled outwards until an unnatural hush lay heavy on the bar.

"You broke several glasses, and you're swaying," Brandy said. "Let me call you a cab."

"Like hell! I'm an angel, and I can drink where I want."

Andy shifted position to get a better look at the man's face. He didn't look like he was in an angel costume, but the alternative made his stomach churn, and Andy wasn't ready to accept that possibility. The drunk was about six feet tall and was wearing black jeans, a white t-shirt, and a black leather jacket. There wasn't an ironic halo or fake pair of wings in sight. His face was familiar—he'd been in before and hadn't been much better then—but it wasn't ringing any specific alarm bells.

Damnit. This was not what he needed.

"Sir, you need to leave," Brandy repeated. "You can come back and settle your tab tomorrow."

"Who's gonna make me?" he taunted.

"I will," she responded, drawing up to her full height, which was a good three inches taller than his. She stood, arms akimbo, and flexed her biceps. Andy couldn't help but grin. He'd lucked out when he'd hired her.

Three more guys, all dressed identically to the first, strode up to stand behind the drunk. They looked equally sauced, and Andy took a few more steps forward. Brandy was charismatic, efficient, and stronger than most of the people who frequented his pub, but she wasn't a match for four drunks—especially if they were what they claimed to be.

"You and what army?" the first drunk asked, roaring with laughter.

"She doesn't need an army. She has me." Andy walked up to the man and inserted himself between him and the bar. The minute he was within arms' reach of the man, he knew the truth. He and his companions were angels of the Lord. He gritted his teeth and said, "You will leave, and you will leave now. This is the last time you'll cause trouble in my bar. I've watched you, and you are not the kind of customers I care to have. This is your last warning."

"What are you going to do?"

"This," Andy said. He reached out and cuffed the first guy on the neck, causing him to crumple to the floor. Three more quick movements and three more bodies hit the ground.

"Brandy, call the cops if you haven't already," he said.

"On it. They'll be here in five minutes."

"Just enough time to get these idiots out of here." Andy drug them out one at a time. He tossed them, none too gently, in a heap far enough away from the door that they wouldn't bother anyone, but close enough that the cops would be able to find them when they arrived. "Damn halos," he ground out as he tossed the third to the ground. The instigator was coming to by the time he grabbed him.

The man blinked groggily. "You shouldn't have done that, Andras. Now I know you and soon, everyone else will, too."

Andy cursed under his breath. He shouldn't have used demonic power on the angels, but he'd wanted to get rid of them quickly. "Grow up. If you run fast enough, maybe you'll outrun the cops. Otherwise, you and your friends will end up spending the night in jail for a drunk and disorderly."

"And if I press assault charges against you?"

"Then you bring attention to yourself, too. Let me know how you want to play it."

The guy stumbled to his feet and out the door.

Andy turned and faced the too-quiet bar. Everyone was staring at him, and he forced himself to play the part of affable pub owner. "My apologies, folks!" Andy boomed. "I know that group of jackasses has made trouble here before, but they won't be back. They've earned themselves a permanent ban. To make up for the disturbance, Brandy and I are gonna come around with a pint of Broken Halo Bitter for each of you, on the house."

A cheer spread through the pub as Brandy started pouring pints. Andy loaded them up on trays as fast as she could pour them and started handing them out, but quickly handed over his duties to the new guy, Zeke, with the excuse that he needed to check something in his upstairs office.

· · · ★ ★ ★ ★ ★ ★ · · ·

Andras closed the door to his office and locked it behind him. The Halloween festivities were still going strong, and the dull roar of his crowded bar provided a background for his racing thoughts. He slumped in the large, leather chair behind the desk and rested his head in his hands. There was no way around it—those halos needed to be kicked out—but his actions would leave him well and truly screwed. The only question was how long he had left.

The itching started between his shoulder blades; he tried to ignore it. It was neither the time nor the place. He needed to be back in the bar keeping an eye on things. The halos wouldn't be back tonight, but it was Halloween, and a lot of people were celebrating. It was not the time to leave the crowd control, not to mention the bartending and table service, to Brandy and Zeke. They were great employees and more than capable of managing the entire brewpub on most nights, but there was something in the air tonight. It wasn't just the halos, there was the inexplicable smell of ozone even though there was no storm on the horizon, and it hadn't rained in a week.

The odor deepened and blended with the smell of sulphur. He spun around the room looking for the demon, but he was alone. He thrust his arms outward and repeated his spin, sure he'd run into someone cloaked in shadows, but he touched nothing.

The itching between his shoulder blades intensified, and drops of sweat broke out on his brow. With sudden surety, he lifted one arm and took a deep sniff. The ozone and sulphur smells were emanating from him. Rage overtook him, and heat rippled across his skin, sparks jumping free and flying through the air. He grabbed his desk—a solid slab of wood more than six feet long and half again as wide—and tipped it over.

Someone knocked at the door, and Andras looked around the

office in a panic. Besides the tipped desk and the papers scattered about, singe marks polka-dotted the ceiling and walls, and the distinct odor of rotten eggs permeated the room.

"Andy?" Zeke called. "Everything okay in there?"

He pulled back a growl, took a breath, and answered, "It will be in a minute. I'll be down in five, okay?"

"Okay. Need anything?"

Andy grinned in spite of himself. He didn't know where Zeke had come from or how he'd wandered into his bar, but he'd shown up a couple months ago and was the second-best bartender he'd ever had. He and Brandy complimented each other perfectly, and if it wasn't for the rougher crowd—and the presence of the psychics— he'd leave them to it. The sound of shuffling feet on the other side of the door stirred him, and he remembered that Zeke was waiting for an answer. "Could you bring me a couple pints of the Brimstone Porter?"

"I think the Storm Cloud Cream Ale would be a better choice, sir."

Andras stared at the door, willing himself to see through it so he could read Zeke's expression. He'd never been called "sir" before— well, not since he was much younger and less prone to displays of temper, and the choice of beer, not one of his favorites nor anywhere near the top of the best-seller list, seemed significant.

"Why that one, lad?" he asked. He could feel his speech patterns regressing and needed to get a hold of himself before he stumbled into a dead language.

"Easier to survive a storm than a brimstone bath if you're feeling a bit grim."

"Aye, you're right. I'll have the Storm Cloud, then."

Zeke's footsteps faded down the stairs, and Andras looked around his office again. There was nothing he could do about the scorch marks, but once he righted the desk and picked up the papers, it wouldn't look too bad.

By the time Zeke walked through the now-open door with two

pints, things looked almost normal. An open window and a box fan got rid of most of the smoke and lingering stench, and the cool, coastal air dampened what was remaining.

"Here you go, boss," Zeke said, handing over the pints.

"Thanks. Go help Brandy. I'll be down in a few minutes to jump back in. Any more trouble?"

"Nothing we haven't been able to handle. Take your time. Change your shirt. See you in a few." He left, pulling the door closed behind him.

Andras downed one pint in a long drink then looked down at his shirt. The burnt orange button down he wore every Halloween was flecked with black, sooty holes. Most were the size of pinpricks, but a few were closer to silver-dollar size. He unbuttoned his shirt, shrugged it off, and grabbed a t-shirt from the bottom desk drawer that housed the extra bar shirts. The largest one he had was a bit too small for him, and it stretched uncomfortably across his chest and upper arms. He shrugged, and a few threads popped. He drained the second beer, grabbed the empty glasses, and headed back down to his bar.

Andy walked into the bar, dropped off his empty glasses, and surveyed the room. He'd been gone less than fifteen minutes by the clock over the bar, but he felt like he'd aged another lifetime. A couple regulars at the bar pulled him aside to chat for a moment, and he offered up perfunctory answers. The trouble should be over for the night, but something still felt off.

The front door opened, and Andy tensed before he could stop himself. The man who walked through was human-enough that he allowed himself to relax—until he saw his face. He was the ex-husband of the new psychic. What was her name again? Sandy. It was Sandy the tarot card reader.

The ex looked around the room, and the expression on his face made Andy pause. He'd seen men looking for a fight. Hell, he'd been that guy. This jerk was definitely looking to punch someone, and Andy wasn't sure if it was Sandy's new boyfriend, Sandy herself, or anyone who got in his way. He murmured an excuse to the women at the bar, grabbed the tray of beers Zeke had poured for the psychics and went to hand out their drinks. "Heads up to the new girl," he said. "Your ex-husband just walked in, and he looks like he's spoiling for a fight. If he even tries to start anything, I'll give him the same treatment I gave those punks, but he won't shake it off as quickly as they did."

"Thanks for the warning," Sandy said. She took a large gulp of beer, nearly spilling when her hands began to shake.

"We've got your back," Paska reassured her. "He still thinks I'm a cop, right? He'll be too scared to start anything but an insult match." Andy shook his head and picked up the tray. He didn't even want to know why anyone would think Paska was a cop. He walked over to the bar as Misty pulled off her gloves and positioned himself in a prime location to keep an eye on the psychics *and* the ex.

Sandy's ex ordered a beer from Zeke, took a drink, and slunk closer to the psychics. He stood too long, obviously trying to eavesdrop, and was getting tenser and more agitated by the minute. It was time for Andy to wander back over.

He sidled up to the table and heard Sandy say, "No one wants you here, and you can't hurt my feelings by insulting my clothes, my makeup, or my nerd cred. Unless you have good news for me and our divorce is final, there is no reason for you to be here."

Aaron opened his mouth to protest, but Andy'd had enough. "I believe my best customers just asked you to stop bothering them. Finish your drink and get out, or I will kick you out."

"You can't do that. I have a right to be here."

"I have a right to refuse service to anyone, and since douchebag isn't a protected class, the law is on my side. I've changed my mind about letting you finish your beer. Leave now." Andy grabbed the beer from Aaron and stared him down. He kept an eye on Aaron's fists and smirked as they clenched and released before he turned and silently walked out.

"Thank you," Sandy said to Andy.

"No problem. I like kicking people out." He meant it, too. The heat of anger swelled, and he took a deep breath to tamp it down. No one needed to smell sulphur on him today. "If you guys want to work Misty up about our sad lack of Long Island Ice Teas, I could probably find a reason to kick her out, too."

Misty stuck her tongue out at him, then froze, tongue extended. Drew had also gone still. Andy turned around in time to watch Joseph and Bill walk into the pub. He relaxed. They might get insufferable after a couple of drinks, but they wouldn't cause trouble.

They made their way to the bar, sat down, and said something to Brandy. Neither Drew nor Misty moved, but Andy didn't have enough interest to wonder why. He took a step back but didn't leave.

Sandy picked up her beer and raised it in the air. "To us! The best-dressed group of nerds in Oracle Bay."

Everyone clinked glasses and drank deeply. "Can we have another round?" Vincent, Sandy's boyfriend, asked.

Andy shook his head but returned to the bar to put in the order.

· · · ★ ★ ★ ★ ★ · · ·

STAY IN ORACLE BAY AND LITTLE LONGER AND GRAB YOUR COPY OF WING and a Prayer now!

THE
POURHOUSE
Wing and a
Prayer
USA TODAY BESTSELLING AUTHOR
AMY CISSELL

raising a demon

MIDLIFE MAGIC IN EDEN VALLEY #1

Raising a Demon is the first book in Midlife Magic in Eden Valley, a magical new paranormal women's fiction series. Eden Valley & Oracle Bay are in the same universe, and there are some crossover characters and cameos!

Being a single mother has its challenges, but Evie never imagined that "the talk" would involve Ouija boards and pentagrams.

Evelyn Addams is forty-three and fabulous. She has a great kid, fantastic friends, and doesn't need a man to complete her. But when she catches ten-year-old Lily summoning a demon to ask for birthday wishes—and the demon who turns up is Evie's summer fling from eleven years ago—her comfortable life is shattered.

Reuniting with an old flame is tricky enough but finding out he grows horns and a tail makes a romantic reconnection downright complicated. And when Lily is kidnapped by her newfound grandfather, the last shred of her old life is destroyed, and everything goes to hell.

Will Evie and her friends rescue Lily from hell before the lights go out and the lost souls come out to play? And can she ignore past and Luc's family complications to take a second chance on love and learn how to raise a demon's daughter? Get your copy of Raising a Demon today!

http://www.books2read.com/raisingademon

acknowledgments

Thank you, Jessy. Joseph McEwen exists on page because of you. I hope you enjoy his story.

My child, my heart, Liana—you are so brave and so resilient. You inspire me to be a better mother and a better person. Sorry I only have magic goats and no magic beaver in this book.

Last, but not least, thank you to my partner in all things, Chris. You're my first reader and my final proofreader, not to mention my wine and water fetcher, ledge talker downer, main encourager, and number one pun bouncer-offer. I am so lucky to have someone so supportive of and enthusiastic about my work. Thank you. (PS - thanks for the bathtub joke in chapter 11.)

amy cissell - i spell trouble

Amy can be found on most social media channels @acissellwrites. Come visit her website at amycissell.com for blogs & books! (autographed copies, if you want!)

Amy Cissell is a USA Today Bestselling Author of urban fantasy and paranormal romance novels. She lives in Portland, OR with her husband, her haunted house-obsessed daughter, their three cats, and the murder of crows she's conspiring to turn into her vengeful army.

When she's not working or writing, she's sleeping because that's all she has time to do! There are few things Amy loves more than a well-timed pun, a good book, a glass of wine, and time at the Oregon Coast.

Although she reads anything and everything, her first love is fantasy. Eleven-year-old Amy discovered fantasy when she 'borrowed' her father's copy of The Hobbit and an enduring love affair (mostly with dragons) was born.

facebook.com/acissellwrites

instagram.com/acissellwrites

bookbub.com/authors/amy-cissell

goodreads.com/acissellwrites

tiktok.com/@acissellwrites

patreon.com/ACissellWrites

also by amy cissell

Paranormal Romance

Psychics of Oracle Bay

Not in the Cards (October 2018)

First Hand Knowledge (November 2018)

Wing and a Prayer (January 2019)

Belle of the Ball (December 2019)

Hell and High Water (June 2022)

Tempest in a Teapot (April 2023)

Elements of Surprise (April 2023)

Dead Giveaway (2024)

Bad to the Bones

Shoot for the Stars

Fun and Prophet

Box Sets (ebook only)

Seeing is Believing in Oracle Bay (Books 1-4)

Paranormal Women's Fiction

Midlife Magic in Eden Valley

(complete series)

Raising a Demon (June 2021)

Devil and the Deep, Blue Lake (September 2021)

Valley of Angels (November 2021)

Guardian of Eden (February 2022)

Eden Valley World Novellas

Match Made in Hell (June 2021)

Hell's Bells (December 2021)

Fall From Grace (January 2022)

Devil May Care (February 2022)

Box Sets

Welcome to Eden Valley (Novellas 1-4)

Vamps in the Vineyard

Here to Slay (September 2022)

Vamps in the Vineyard Novellas

(newsletter subscribers only)

Stakes and Stems (September 2023)

Slay Bells Ring (January 2023)

Contemporary/Urban Fantasy

An Eleanor Morgan Fantasy Adventure

(complete series)

The Cardinal Gate (February 2017)

The Waning Moon (June 2017)

The Ruby Blade (October 2017)

The Broken World (March 2018)

The Lost Child (June 2019)

The Iron River (May 2020)

The Dark Throne (February 2021)

Box Sets (ebook only)

Eleanor Morgan Books 1-4

Eleanor Morgan Books 5-7

Ghosts of Valhalla

As Yet Untitled (late 2023)

www.ingramcontent.com/pod-product-compliance
Lightning Source LLC
Chambersburg PA
CBHW060911210726
48293CB00006B/2048